Putting Your Daughters on the Stage

Lesbian Theatre from the 1970s to the 1990s

Sandra Freeman

CASSELL

London and Washington

Cassell
Wellington House
125 Strand
London WC2R 0BB

PO Box 605
Herndon, VA 20172

First published 1997

British Library Cataloguing-in-Publication Data
A catalogue record for this book is available from the British Library.

ISBN 0-304-33310-7 (hardback)
      0-304-33309-3 (paperback)

The author and publisher wish to thank Nick Hern Books for permission to quote
from Phyllis Nagy, *Butterfly Kiss* (1994) and *The Strip* (1995); Reed Books for
permission to quote from Jill Davis (ed.), *Lesbian Plays* (Methuen, 1987) and
Lesbian Plays: Two (Methuen, 1989), Annie Castledine (selector), *Plays by Women:
Ten* (Methuen, 1994) and Philip Osment (ed.), *Gay Sweatshop: Four Plays and a
Company* (Methuen, 1989); and Routledge for granting permission for quotations
from Lizbeth Goodman, *Contemporary Feminist Theatres* (1993).

Typeset by Action Typesetting Ltd, Gloucester
Printed and bound in Great Britain by Biddles Ltd, Guildford and King's Lynn

Putting Your Daughters on the Stage

This book
is dedicated with thanks
on behalf of myself
and many others to
Kate Crutchley

Contents

Introduction

During the sabbatical term I was granted in order to produce most of this book, my neighbours, suspicious as ever of university lecturers having long holidays, asked me what I was writing about. I always fashioned my response according to what I thought the questioner was prepared to hear. I was living in a small village in the Languedoc, far from the comforting, liberal sophistication of Brighton; my neighbours were a miscellaneous selection of French country people, Parisians with second homes, ex-patriot Brits and various other European vagrants. So, to some I said, 'fringe theatre in London', to others, 'the equivalent of café-théâtre in England', to the more enlightened, 'certain aspects of British feminist theatre', and to the chosen few, 'the history of British lesbian theatre'. Now, despite appearances to the contrary, my reticence was not due to a desire to remain in the closet, but to a fear of being drawn into fruitless discussions. The term 'feminist theatre' is already provocative, 'lesbian theatre' is to most an incomprehensible juxtaposition. 'What do you mean?' 'Is there such a thing?' I certainly had no ready answers to such questions; I still don't. There is no one answer to what lesbian means, nor is the definition of theatre, usually taken for granted, by any means self-evident. In Chapter 1 I shall deal with what 'lesbian' means and has meant in different cultural contexts; in Chapter 2 I talk about the development of 'fringe' or 'alternative' theatre in Britain. I then proceed to a detailed analysis of specific work.

Lizbeth Goodman in *Contemporary Feminist Theatres* says:

> The term 'contemporary lesbian theatre' refers primarily to the work of a very small network of women and primarily to the few individuals who have founded lesbian performance groups or management collectives.[1]

My observations are based on extensive interviews with some of these women as well as the study of published and unpublished play scripts.

I could also perhaps be regarded as one of them, since I have worked with Character Ladies, one of the groups that Lizbeth Goodman mentions. Three of my performed plays could be described as lesbian plays, though not everyone would describe them as lesbian theatre, but more of that anon. It was my practical involvement which led to the conviction that there was a book to be written, indeed that a book *must* be written, to prevent important work disappearing totally. This is not to say that studies of contemporary British theatre, including Lizbeth Goodman's book, have not devoted chapters to lesbian theatre; there have been interesting and illuminating articles also, but these chapters and articles appear generally within the larger context of feminist theatre. It is feminism which attracts attention, with lesbianism appearing as a minor variant thereof.

It was clear to me that there was enough specifically lesbian work to warrant a separate study. Lesbians have frequently complained about society's tendency to render them invisible, to deny their existence except as a part of some other phenomenon. Indeed, they have themselves at one and the same time claimed and rejected the label, for various complicated reasons. When I asked one of the women who had been centrally involved in 'lesbian theatre' if she would talk to me about her experiences, she replied 'Lesbian theatre? Is there any?' She had moved on, as others had moved on, tired of lack of money, lack of recognition, of a theatrical half-life on the fringe. She had acted in, devised and written several important shows which now existed only as a kind of folklore.[2] Looking back, they seemed to her to lack real seriousness, so perhaps it would not matter too much if they were forgotten.

It matters very much to me that they should *not* be forgotten. On the contrary, I believe that they should be brought to the attention of a much wider public. This book will perhaps be the beginning of more extensive studies. There will no doubt be omissions; I hope that lesbian playmakers who have been ignored will write to me so that I can give them due credit. I would be very happy to continue my interviews, which were a rich source of information. Conducting them and playing them back was by far the most enjoyable part of my research. Women who began with, 'What shall I say? You'll have to ask me lots of questions', proceeded to talk at length about their work and ideas. My selection of interviewees was based partly on personal contact, so there is an element of arbitrariness in my account. But then that is true of all histories.

I have tried to keep this account comprehensible to a wide range of readers by avoiding, wherever possible, language which would be understood only by those immersed in a particular field of study. Much of the general work that I have found helpful in the formation of my conclusions is, in fact, discipline-specific and makes reference to theorists whose work has been particularly influential, especially in the field of critical theory – Lacan, Foucault, Irigaray, Kristeva, Derrida and, above all, big daddy Freud. I shall try to avoid engaging with any of these, although by so doing I may well be seen as guilty of extreme over-simplification. I shall also use personal anecdotes, mine and other people's, in the hope of capturing the attention of that figment of an author's imagination – the general reader.

Notes

1. Lizbeth Goodman, *Contemporary Feminist Theatres: To Each Her Own* (London: Routledge, 1993), p. 115.
2. Scripts of all shows professionally produced should be lodged in the British Library; sometimes this fails to happen because a legible, comprehensible script does not exist. Putting a working script in order takes time; presenting it in an acceptable form takes money. Besides which, a written script may be a totally inadequate record of performance. The incentive of publication may make a difference, but that option is rarely available.

Acknowledgements

I would like to thank all those who gave their time to be interviewed – Jane Boston, Penny Casdagli, Lois Charlton, Jackie Clune, Kate Crutchley, Winnie Elliott, Sue Frumin, Fleur Howard, Charlie Hughes-D'Aeth, Sarah McNair, Phyllis Nagy, Julie Parker, Nina Rapi, Joelle Taylor and Lois Weaver.

I would also like to thank the following who lent me their unpublished scripts, from which I have liberally quoted: Gay Sweatshop, Sue Frumin, Susan Hayes, Nina Rapi, Red Rag Theatre Company, Siren Theatre Company, Joelle Taylor, Spin/Stir Theatre Company.

My thanks also go to Jill Davis, Rose Sharpe and Mel Steel for much helpful advice, to David Ward in the Founders Library of RMBNC for giving me access to Gay Sweatshop archives, to Alan Sinfield for encouragement and support in the whole venture, to Faith O'Reilly for patience and lots of hot dinners and finally to Valerie Blamey for all her hard work and her almost psychic ability to read my dreadful handwriting.

Chapter 1

The Meaning of the Word 'Lesbian'

In 1960, a vindictive letter was received by the mother of a friend of mine, accusing her daughter of being a lesbian, as well as having an affair with a divorced, older man. There was an emotional confrontation: 'I don't care if you do like women more than men, just tell me. I want to know. Is it true you are one of those?' (In 1960 the word 'lesbian' was often uttered in a shocked whisper, if it was spoken at all!) 'I don't know what you mean,' my friend insisted. In spite of the tears and entreaties, she stood by this reply. In 1995 this seems a reasonable, honest response; in 1960 it was a desperate strategy for self-preservation. She knew very well what was meant. To be accused of being lesbian was to be accused of unacceptable deviance, tantamount to criminality (although to have sexual relations with a woman has never been a criminal offence in Britain), of having some terrible malformation which meant you preyed like a vampire on those of your own sex. You would be condemned to a miserable life, rejected by normal society, confined to the shadows with those few jealous, rapacious individuals who resembled you. Thank goodness for the affair with the married man – the two apparently contradictory assertions cast a doubt for the mother over the trustworthiness of the letter, and it was not discussed again.

Before feminism, particularly radical feminism, being lesbian was considered to be an affliction rather than a revolutionary act. It was not a choice – who would choose an identity which separated one from the security of friends and family? The desire of a woman for another woman inspired a range of negative feelings in 'normal' heterosexuals, chief among them being fear and disgust. Desire itself implies a wish to possess, a wish to touch, to stimulate the most intimate parts of another's body in order to achieve one's own sexual satisfaction. This is what *men* do with women, women do *not* do it with each other, for this would be 'unnatural' and what is unnatural is a threat to social order; therefore it is stigmatized. To admit to lesbianism was to make an irrevocable statement about one's total being, usually after having denied this being, before finally saying, with some defiance, 'This is what I am. This is the way I am made. This is natural for me, I can't help it.'

This image of the woman born different from other women stems largely from the work of nineteenth-century sexologists, such as Havelock Ellis and Krafft-Ebing, who categorized a type of masculine woman with entirely different physical characteristics from the 'normal' female. This was the female 'invert' whose nature drove her to seek sexual satisfaction with other women. Her 'partner' was more problematic, since she would look like other women, her identity as lesbian being therefore less stable than the invert. What drew this latter type to her own sex was more difficult to ascertain.

The idea of two distinct and natural types of lesbians persisted until the 1970s among lesbians themselves. The 'masculine invert' was transformed into the 'butch' and her partner into the 'femme'. Since 'femmes' could 'pass' as 'normal' women, there was an assumption that the 'butch' was the *true* lesbian. Within the lesbian community in lesbian bars, the butch, who would be immediately recognized, stigmatized, and perhaps even victimized by heterosexual society, was the powerful strong one of a couple, the 'hero'. This was partly seen as role-play, partly as a result of biological difference. Butches did not identify with 'women' because they did not 'feel like women'. This was the way they were, rather than the deliberate assumption of a power position. Without recognizing the possibility that all gender may be constructed, they wanted to be to their femmes what men might represent to women. Men and women were essentially different and lesbians were different from either while having to fit into a system which only admitted that two categories exist.

The question of essential difference is now hotly debated. Diana Fuss writes:

> The lack of consensus and the continued disputes amongst feminists over the definition of 'lesbian' pivot centrally around the question of essentialism. Exactly who is a lesbian? Is there such a thing as a lesbian essence? Does 'woman' include lesbian? Can we speak of a 'lesbian mind' as distinct from what Wittig calls 'the straight mind'? ... My own position is that 'lesbian' is a historical construction of comparatively recent date, and that there is no eternal lesbian essence outside the frame of cultural change and historical determinism.[1]

This view is known as constructionist – men, women, lesbians, gays are made, not born. It is not sexuality but society expressed through language, which creates gender. A woman who desires a woman is just that; it is society which has invented the name lesbian and invented a set of characteristics to go with it. In the essay referred to, 'The Straight Mind', Monique Wittig suggests that the definition of a lesbian is a person of female sex who stands in a totally different position from men. She is therefore not a woman, because she exists outside the 'heterosexual system of thought' which can conceive only of a market-place relationship – man/subject woman/object of an exchange.

> What is a woman? Panic, general alarm for an active defence. Frankly, it is a problem that the lesbians do not have because of a change of perspective, and it would be incorrect to say that lesbians associate, make love, live with women, for 'woman' has meaning only in heterosexual systems of thought and heterosexual economic systems. Lesbians are not women.[2]

As a 'materialist feminist' Wittig is less concerned with the origins of lesbian behaviour (biological or psychological) than with the significance of this behaviour for dominant heteropatriarchal society. Lesbians as a category are different, are outside the norm because they are not economically dependent on men, and this independence is clearly not a deformation they were born with. The 'lesbian mind' is a result of social existence, not genetics.

The feminist attitude to sexuality, which predominated in the 1970s, was that it was a choice. Lesbian feminism declared itself proud, not ashamed. Sheila Jeffreys writes:

> The political theory of lesbian feminism transformed lesbianism from a stigmatised sexual practice into an idea and a political practice that posed a challenge to male supremacy and its basic institution of heterosexuality.
>
> ...
>
> Any woman could be a lesbian. It was a revolutionary political choice which, if adopted by millions of women, would lead to the destabilization of male supremacy as men lost the foundation of their power in women's selfless and unpaid, domestic, sexual and reproductive, economic and emotional servicing.[3]

The idea of lesbians being divided into two types, one which seemed to emulate men in appearance and dominant attitudes, the other seeming to imitate the 'femininity' of women through make-up, frivolous clothes and passivity, was quite unacceptable. Lesbian feminists rejected any resemblance to men or heterosexual role-play.

If society is capable of conceiving only the men/women binary then lesbians would be associated with women, while refusing to look like heterosexual women out to attract a man. A lesbian was woman-identified, not man-identified. The pre-1970s butches and their femmes were persuaded to see the error of their ways. It is in this context that the history of lesbian theatre will start – when it becomes important to be out and proud.

However, the problem of defining a lesbian was not resolved – far from it. Any woman could be a lesbian, but most did not want to. 'Straight' feminists and lesbian feminists often co-existed rather uneasily. There was also the problem of how to relate to gay men. Women's liberation and gay liberation had separate agendas – lesbians were identified as 'gay women' until they insisted on the constant use of the word 'lesbian' as well as 'gay'. Heterosexual society certainly identified them in this way. When the battles were different, which band of soldiers should one join? Trying to march with both may well be an ideological contradiction: gay men were men after all; they were part of the dominant patriarchy, although not of the hetero-patriarchy.

Jeffreys states:

> The conservatism of the '80s in the malestream world had a particularly damaging effect on the lives of lesbians and gay men.... These pressures led to changes in the lesbian community, more acceptance of gay male politics and priorities, and, interestingly, a return to the sexological model by some lesbian theorists. There was a new politics of outlawry, of sexual deviance which depended on the construction of sexology, a politics which was already well developed by some gay men which was in direct contradiction to the lesbian feminist philosophy.[4]

Once again, the notion that perhaps lesbians and gays are *born* re-emerged, but this time because it might be politically more expedient than the claim that sexuality was a total choice. Sexuality and gender could be talked about more openly than it ever had been, could be theorized more extensively and could be brought into the academy. Sheila Jeffreys sees the entrance of literary criticism or critical theory on the scene as somewhat unfortunate.

> There is no reason why a literary critic should not make a valuable contribution to the development of political theory, but when all that is seen as 'theory' by a whole new generation of lesbian and gay students and teachers emanates from the arts rather than the social sciences, then there may be reason for alarm.[5]

One of the reasons for Jeffreys' frustration is that the lesbian feminist, who saw herself as making a political choice which had nothing to do with her 'essential' sexual orientation, was now accused by some new theorists of being 'essentialist' for offering a definition of the lesbian as radically different.

> What is now called essentialism is the belief that a lesbian can eschew gender, or the belief that it is possible to practise a sexuality not organised around the penis or the power imbalance. Such beliefs are said to be essentialist by the post-modernists because they rely on the existence of an unknowable essence of lesbianism.[6]

The dangerous literary critics are now identified as post-modernists. Post-modern theory has prioritized language as the dominant political force, so that 'the cultural critic becomes a political activist by wielding a pen'. Jeffreys sees the dominance of language and of binary oppositions as lying at the root of the gender problem in the new lesbian and gay theory. Binary oppositions for lesbians means a revival of butch/femme, this time round as self-conscious manipulative role-play or masquerade. Enter the lipstick lesbian who will confound the expectations of straight society by looking like an ultra-feminine woman, a sought-after consumer, who will spend money on fashionable clothes, perfume and glossy magazines. She will also spend money on 'sex toys'. Dildos, once unmentionable because they were copies of the male penis, now come in a choice of colours and shapes and they are definitely *not* seen as a penis substitute, but as a source of specifically lesbian pleasure. This is gender-bending, contesting fixed heterosexual norms, confusing categories. This is the new sexual revolution which Jeffreys sees as not one at all.

> There was a time when lesbian feminists saw it as consciousness raising to appear in public or on television in a guise which deliberately eschewed femininity. We believed that this would show women that an alternative to femininity was available. Now we are told by the parodists, mimics, performance artists that for a lesbian to appear dressed up in the way that might be expected of an extremely feminine heterosexual woman is more unsettling to male supremacy. It's hard to see why. Those most likely to be unsettled are surely the feminists and lesbians who feel completely undermined and even humiliated by having a lesbian show and tell the world she wants to be feminine.[7]

This is a complex problem. The word 'pass' has often been used in lesbian circles to suggest that one can get away with pretending to be a heterosexual. Mainly it was femmes who passed as women; occasionally butches passed as men. To 'pass' means that to all intents and purposes you are absorbed into the man/woman binary of the heterosexual world. You disappear. Which is in fact what lesbians often did when they emerged from the twilight zones of the bars – they still do sometimes. This was a strategy for protection. The contemporary young lesbian who looks like Madonna does not want to pass, to disappear; on the contrary she wants to be noticed, to proclaim, 'Look at me, I'm not what I seem, not what you thought.' She also wants to be listened to, which may be more likely to happen if she does not place herself by her dress in a kind of sexual no-man's-land. However, the average straight viewer, less aware than she that all gender is masquerade, will see the lipstick and think 'woman'.[8] The reaction when she asserts that she is not a woman but a lesbian may be one of surprise, or one of disbelief, because, whatever she says, 'lesbians do not look like that'. In order to persuade heterosexual society that lesbians do not look like anything, that there is really no such thing as 'a lesbian' or 'a heterosexual', requires a clearing away of years of prejudice. If you do succeed in clearing away the prejudice, you must surely be careful what image you establish in its place. As Judith Butler writes:

> To argue that there might be a 'specificity' to lesbian sexuality has seemed a necessary counterpoint to the claim that lesbian sexuality is just heterosexuality once removed, or that it is derived, or that it does not exist.
>
> . . .
>
> There is no question that gays and lesbians are threatened by the violence of public erasure, but the decision to counter that violence must be careful not to reinstate another in its place. Which version of lesbian or gay ought to be rendered visible, and which internal exclusion will that rendering visible institute?[9]

The above dilemma presupposes that lesbian identity, like any other identity, is invented and performed. It is the result of acting out a role partly dictated by existing expectations, partly the result of individual creativity confounding these expectations. A lesbian takes account of what the world says she is, decides what she wants to be and performs a part which will establish the desired image in place of the existing one. The role is subject to continual renegotiation between both parties, there is no fixed essence, identity itself is unstable, needing constant reaffirmation. However, if each lesbian plays a different part, then the category 'lesbian' is meaningless. As a group, lesbians disappear. Ultimately this may be desirable, just as the transcendence of gender may be desirable; meanwhile, as Butler suggests, the sense of community, of something which provides a common identity, is necessary to fight the oppression of heterosexual society, which still has a firm sense of 'the lesbian'. Judgements are made against gays and lesbians; laws are passed on the assumption that 'they' are all the same and all different from heterosexuals. Thus, while being aware that no two lesbians are alike, every lesbian also recognizes that there is something, whatever it is, that she is perceived to have in common with every other lesbian.

Celia Kitzinger, in her detailed sociological study *The Social Construction of Lesbianism*, talks about the way that individuals giving an account of their lesbianism can all too easily reinforce, rather than contest, established norms. Based on identity accounts given by forty-one self-defined lesbians aged between seventeen and fifty-eight, who were asked to reply to sixty-one questions, her research revealed seven different accounts of lesbianism, most of which allowed the respondents to fit into ideals set for them by the dominant order.

The accounts which place personal fulfilment as central, the discovery of one's 'true self', 'getting in touch with real feelings', Kitzinger sees as unthreatening to the establishment.

> To conclude, then, an explanation of lesbianism in terms of personal happiness and self-fulfilment serves to remove lesbians from the political arena and to reduce it to a private and personal solution. This, then, is an account clearly acceptable in terms of the dominant patriarchal order.[10]

Equally, the dominant order can happily accept an identity based on 'falling in love'. This again is represented as based on a fundamentally personal experience, which is morally acceptable.

> The lesbian in invoking the culturally approved rhetoric of romantic love is accredited with a fundamental humanity and similarity to heterosexuals, and the morality of the dominant order is articulated, vindicated and reinforced.[11]

The only account of lesbianism which provided a real challenge to the dominant (heteropatriarchal) order is the radical feminist one.

> The great achievement of the radical feminist lesbian account of lesbian identity is to alienate and disturb proponents of all other lesbian identities. This hostility is derived from the fact that this account of lesbian identity fails to explain and justify lesbianism in terms familiar and acceptable to the dominant order: instead it attacks that order, presenting lesbianism as an explicit threat to society.[12]

The women who give this account of themselves describe their lesbianism as an active choice: they were not born lesbian, nor made lesbian by early environmental factors. They reject heterosexuality because it is constructed in a patriarchal society for the benefit of men. They are 'women-identified women'; they do not identify themselves as 'gay women', nor feel solidarity with gay men.

Kitzinger's study with its social scientific methodological foundations – interviews, careful selection of samples, questionnaires, statistics – is presumably the kind of work which Sheila Jeffreys can approve of, as opposed to the more abstract arguments of literary theorists, whose undermining of certainties makes political activism difficult.

We now have at our disposal a variety of approaches to the question of lesbian identity, from personal accounts to philosophical discussion. It is clear that there can be no easily describable phenomenon called 'lesbian' theatre. If I were to state that lesbian theatre basically reflects a lesbian point of view, could I really define what I meant by that? If I were to say it is theatre made by lesbians, it is also obvious from this chapter that I could give no satisfactory explanation for that choice either. So is there any such thing? The base-line should perhaps be that those who are involved in a major way in the decision-making of any production should identify as lesbian. This would mean ignoring certain plays which I think are important because they deal centrally with lesbian concerns. In the end plays were selected for a variety of reasons. In many of them the exploration of lesbian identity is a major concern. Some are discussed because their authors identify as lesbian, and this informs their approach to whatever they write.

Notes

1. Diana Fuss, *Essentially Speaking* (London: Routledge, 1989), p. 44.
2. Monique Wittig, 'The straight mind', in *The Straight Mind and Other Essays* (Hemel Hempstead: Harvester Wheatsheaf, 1992), p. 32.
3. Sheila Jeffreys, The *Lesbian HERESY: A Feminist Perspective on the Lesbian Sexual Revolution* (London: Women's Press, 1994), p. viii.
4. *Ibid.*, p. x.
5. *Ibid.*, p. 98.
6. *Ibid.*, p. 102.
7. *Ibid.*, p. 98.

8. Julia Penelope also has interesting comments to make on the subject of lesbians who look like 'women'.

   Whatever one chooses to call them, 'lipstick lesbians', 'dykes for spikes', or 'femmes', they have appeared in our communities and our movement in a variety of guises, demanding our support and approval for their appearance and behaviour, asserting their 'right' to wear make-up, high heels, and garter belts, to allow men to fuck them and to exploit, use, and abuse Lesbians at will. When Lesbians like me object to their assertions, they insult us, belittle our lives, and call us their 'oppressors'. In short, their agenda is to destroy the Lesbian political movement by alternately playing the 'victim' and then bullying, by lying, by coquetry, by manipulation, and by just plain stupidity. (Julia Penelope, *Call Me Lesbian*, Freedom, CA: The Crossing Press, 1992, p. 78)

9. Judith Butler, 'Imitation and gender insubordination', in Diana Fuss (ed.) *Inside Out: Lesbian Theories, Gay Theories* (London: Routledge, 1991), p. 17.

10. Celia Kitzinger, *The Social Construction of Lesbianism* (London: Sage, 1987), p. 102.

11. *Ibid.*, p. 100.

12. *Ibid.*, p. 119.

Chapter 2

The Development of Alternative Theatre in Britain

The West End. For almost any British person, even those who never go to the theatre, these words represent the same glamour as 'Broadway' does to an American. The West End of London is where commercial theatres are to be found, places where you can have 'a good night out', at considerable cost maybe, but for a real night out the price adds to the excitement. They provide the kind of experience which is exhilarating but never truly, deeply, disturbing. This is theatre as 'entertainment' – a good laugh, a good cry, breathtaking spectacle, even intellectual titillation. Commercial theatre is not mindless: for many spectators, being made to think is part of the enjoyment. These spectators will pay to see good performances and clever, well-made plays which stretch the boundaries of that imagination a little. Only a little, since too much stretching makes the brain hurt and one goes to the theatre seeking pleasure not pain. There is an immense capital outlay involved in theatrical production: the investors, the 'angels' who fund the West End, need to know that they are going not only to get their money back but also to accrue some profit. A show which looks as though it is making a loss will close very quickly. In order to make a profit you 'give the public what it wants', thereby guaranteeing 'bums on seats'. What does the British public want? What will spectators flock to see? A difficult question, with many possible answers. What it is assumed the public *won't* like is revolution, subversion and deviance. Which is not to say that plays about revolution, subversion and deviance do not find their way on to the commercial stage, if in the end the norms and values of bourgeois society are upheld. These are what we call *mainstream* values. The West End theatre and the mainstream are virtually synonymous. This was all there was in Britain until the 1950s, as regional repertory theatres inevitably used the same material as the West End.

In 1956 George Devine founded the English Stage Company at the

Royal Court Theatre in Sloane Square, London, thus providing a space in which alternative voices could be heard. The establishment could be attacked, and a new kind of defiant hero emerged in John Osborne's *Look Back in Anger*. The angry young man hit the stage. In the East End of London, much further from the commercial heartland than Sloane Square, Joan Littlewood set up in the Theatre Royal, Stratford, a 'working-class' theatre in a working-class area. Opposition to the mainstream had begun. Both these theatres found a ready audience, eager for a change from what a friend of mine refers to as 'vicar's tea-party type' plays, which portrayed middle-class life in middle-class drawing-rooms. Whether the comfortably off denizens of Chelsea who made the long journey to Stratford to see such productions as *Oh, What a Lovely War!* (1963) had changed their minds about anything whatsoever by the time they made the journey back, is impossible to say. The most important factor was the widening out of their ideas on theatre and theatrical space.

Meanwhile in Edinburgh, the definition of theatre and theatre space was annually reformulated by the numerous small companies, often students, who took their work to the Arts Festival in August–September. A 'theatre' could be any vacant space large enough to provide a minimal performance area and hold an audience. Apart from official festival events there were productions on the 'fringe' of main events. The Edinburgh Fringe has been known since the inception of the festival as a showcase for young talent. You can get noticed in Edinburgh, even if you have no sets, no costumes and no money. Through Edinburgh the word 'fringe' generally came to mean outside the establishment – poor theatre where real experiment could take place.

In the late 1960s the Fringe arrived in London, offering another sort of alternative to the West End. Venues began to sprout in empty buildings; later on, in the 1970s, in the upstairs rooms of pubs. Scenery and props were cut down to a minimum so that productions could be transported elsewhere, to other multipurpose spaces. This kind of theatre was non-commercial, usually created by young people who lived at subsistence level and were often registered as unemployed, and therefore it was not subject to the censorious gaze of investors. It could be provocative and difficult. Until 1968 an official theatrical censorship had existed in Britain in the form of the Lord Chamberlain, who had to approve all scripts. As well as putting a blue pencil through naughty sexual references, he also banned plays which dramatized political issues. It is interesting that the first reaction to the abolition of the Lord Chamberlain's Office was to people the stage with naked bodies. Kenneth Tynan's *Oh! Calcutta!* (1970) was a popular review which dealt with all manner of strange sexual practices. Politicization came a little later, as Clive Barker points out:

When the Alternative Theatre movement arose in Britain in the late 1960s, as in other parts of the developed world, it arose out of a particular set of circumstances. A succession of governments had failed to deliver their election promises, which peaked with the failure of the Wilson administration in 1964 and 1966 to deliver the anticipated socialist revolution. ... What was at first called fringe theatre arose out of a response to the failure of the Labour government to create positive cultural and political change and to the continued triviality and sterility of the establishment stage.[1]

There arose two sorts of alternative theatre in Britain: that which was motivated primarily by theatrical experiment and that which was inspired by the desire to make 'political' statements. This does not mean there were no politically motivated experimental plays; indeed one could maintain that experiment with form is a political act, in the sense that it challenges existing structures. When I make the distinction between concern with form and concern with politics, I am using the latter in a more specific sense. Graham Holderness has some useful comments to make on this point:

Politics is normally understood to be concerned with systems of government, the processes by means of which such systems are changed, and the nature of social participation in these changes, win relations between these systems of government, in co-operation and competition, peace and war, and with the individuals, parties and ideas which sustain, develop and overthrow government and the ideological formations by which their power is maintained. So to identify theatre as 'political' is to define a certain type of drama, but also to suggest a certain habitual relationship between theatre and politics; that they are *normally* very different areas of experience, which happen to become, in the activity of political theatre, interconnected.[2]

Thus 'political' theatre is generally seen to be challenging systems of government, encouraging social change and often, therefore, as Clive Barker maintained, is created in response to particular governmental situations such as 'the failure of the Wilson administration in 1964 and 1966 to deliver the anticipated socialist revolution'.[3] The creators of this type of theatre will choose forms perceived to be most effective in raising the consciousness of the spectator. Social change will be effected only if audiences are made to *think critically* about the status quo. The appeal is to the intellect. Much of the alternative political theatre in Britain was influenced by Bertolt Brecht's 'epic' theatre, which rejected the emotional involvement of the public with the play, encouraged by the established mode 'dramatic' theatre, since this led to a feeling of helplessness and an acceptance of the inevitability of the status quo.

> The dramatic theatre's spectator says: Yes I have felt like that too – Just like me – It's only natural – it'll never change – The sufferings of this man appal me, because they are inescapable – That's great art; it all seems the most obvious thing in the world – I weep when they weep, I laugh when they laugh. The epic theatre's spectator says: I'd never have thought it – That's not the way – That's extraordinary, hardly believable – it's got to stop The sufferings of this man appal me because they are unnecessary – That's great art: nothing obvious in it – I laugh when they weep, I weep when they laugh.[4]

To make an audience think critically rather than identify emotionally with a character is difficult, when the predominant mode has for so long encouraged identification of a play with 'real life'. The possibility of seeing the characters as 'real' people, of believing that 'real' life is happening on stage needs to be removed from the start, even before the beginning of the performance, by using scenery, costumes and a style of acting which are a constant reminder that it is all only a play, a story, with a meaning to be discovered on reflection. Theatre, for Brecht and his followers, should stimulate an awareness of the possibility of change. Revolution starts in the mind.

Or does it? Perhaps it starts in the organism. Brecht has affected, still affects, generations of alternative theatre practitioners in Britain, but his ideas are not the only ones which have proved to be profoundly important in changing concepts of what the theatre is and how it works. It is generally agreed among theatre historians that the theory and practices of Antonin Artaud were equally as influential as those of Brecht. Artaud also wanted theatre to change the audience, but not through consciousness-raising. He addressed the physical being, not the intellect. Like his fellow Surrealists, he was most concerned with the mysteries of the *unconscious*, and since this by definition was beyond rationality, it was to be reached through the *senses*. The spectator was to be transformed by direct physical, sensual participation in a mystery, performed by actors whose own bodies would have been refined into a highly skilled instrument. Artaud's Theatre of Cruelty produced physical shock; it showed us that the sky could still fall on our heads.[5]

This is theatre as magic, as mystery, what Peter Brook calls Holy

Theatre. The actor is no longer a real person pretending to be a different real person. By transcending everyday reality in performance, the actor compels the spectator to go beyond 'real life' to reach a more meaningful state of being. In order to change, in order to effect change, the bourgeois audience has to be battered out of its complacency. It is debatable whether, given Holderness's definition, Artaud's theatre could be called 'political'. It was certainly anti-bourgeois, as was the whole Surrealist movement. However, Artaud was perceived by his fellow 'Surrealist revolutionaries' as being too concerned with art and literature at the expense of the promotion of social change, so he was cast out of their midst. Which brings us to the notion of theatre as art, and back to those whose primary concern is with experiment with form.

In 1968 there was a rebellion in British art schools against the kind of 'education' that young artists had hitherto received. This was not an isolated phenomenon; it was part of a revolution which took place throughout Europe and the USA. Students everywhere in the Western world were dissatisfied with the state of higher education. By striking, by occupying, by manning the barricades they managed at least to make their voices heard and bring about some changes. As far as the art schools were concerned, the definition of art was opened up, which led to the creation of new forms such as 'conceptual art' and 'performance art'. Art students began to produce theatre which bemused, bedazzled, excited the onlooker, without the necessity for a detailed explanation of what was happening. The group called Welfare State, which was born in Bradford Art School, was one of the first to work in this sort of way. This kind of performance is more reminiscent of Artaud than of Brecht. The seeds of revolution are still present: they will grow through the challenge to art rather than through a clearly stated challenge to a governmental system. The visual aspects of the production are predominantly important; words are used often not for their sense, but for their sound value – there are no logical conversations leading to 'meaning'.

So we see that the challenge presented by alternative theatre in Britain is not always to the government but often to those who have made up their minds what theatre should be. With the spread of feminist ideas in the 1970s, women formed theatre groups which would criticize patriarchal society. The structures had been created, the 'fringe' existed, the idea of using different kinds of venues outside 'proper' theatres was accepted. In fact, left-wing groups such as David Hare and Howard Brenton's Portable Theatre had established theatre as a major way of disseminating political ideas, just as agitprop theatre had been used throughout Russia after the revolution to propagandize Communism. It is pointless here to write a shortened history of feminist theatre in Britain, since excellent detailed books have been written on this subject.[6] What is important is the fact that women began to use the theatre to draw attention to their unfair lot in patriarchal society, thereby opening up the possibility of lesbians making points about heteropatriarchal society. As we saw in Chapter 1, feminism and political lesbianism have always been closely intertwined. Lesbians often wanted to deal with the same issues as their heterosexual sisters. When I interviewed Kate Crutchley about the groups who had passed through the Oval House during her time there, several times she said, 'Of course, now I think of it they weren't lesbian, they were feminist'. 'Feminist' almost always meant socialist. Lesbians had been empowered by feminism to stand up and be counted. There was, of course, some confusion, as to whether they wanted to be counted as women or as gay.

None of this 'alternative' practice would have been possible without financial subsidy. This came from the Arts Council of Great Britain and regional arts councils, who decided how much of the taxpayer's money should be given to whom. Theatre panels sat in judgement, allocating modest sums on the strength of project proposals, scripts and panel members' reports. Even the most minimal of productions costs something. The Edinburgh Fringe is a mixture of amateurs and professionals who generally finance their own productions in the hopes of making a reputation. The London Fringe is made up of 'professional' groups (the Arts Council is not in the business of financing amateurs), of actors and technicians whose job is making theatre. In theory this activity pays them a living wage; in practice they may well settle for a share of the box-office takings. Even if the actors and technicians are paid very little, the venue, the set and the costumes will need a substantial budget. Most theatre in Britain is subsidized, including the Royal National Theatre and the Royal Shakespeare Company, which take very large slices of the cake indeed, and regional theatre throughout the UK. The West End still exists, commercial theatres outside London still exist, still subject to the notion that the public will pay good money only for a show which reassures and makes no demands. Without public funding there would be no real innovation. The Arts Council is no fairy godmother, however; it is subject to changes in governmental arts policy, so that subsidies may be withdrawn, in what might seem to be a somewhat arbitrary fashion. Explanations about a decline in the quality of the work may be a substitute for other more sinister reasons. In her introduction to *Lesbian Plays: Two* (1989), Jill Davis sees the lack of funding for gay and lesbian theatre companies as the most serious threat to their existence.

> Not since Gay Sweatshop lost its annual funding from the Arts Council has any gay or lesbian theatre company received sustained public subsidy. The effects of working without regular subsidy, increasingly the situation of most small scale theatres, are manifold. ... If the women who have been the creators of lesbian theatre will in future be working in other types of theatre, and in between jobs working in whatever position the DSS [Department of Social Security] has sent them to, then it seems likely that there will be less and less space in which lesbian theatre can be created. Sustained subsidy, whether from public or private sources, is the only remedy.[7]

Experience has shown that in Britain private sponsorship for lesbian theatre is virtually impossible to find; the only option is public subsidy. By 'sustained subsidy', Jill Davis means an annual grant as opposed to a grant allocated for a specific project. The security necessary to produce good work is absent if a company continually has to ask for funding for each production, never being sure whether it will be granted or not. Perhaps for this reason lesbians writing in the mid-1990s do not necessarily categorize themselves as inevitably 'alternative'. The West End might be a possibility; a play written by a lesbian could perhaps get 'bums on seats'. Whether such a play would have to appear to have something other than lesbian concerns as its subject is an obvious question. At the moment 'alternative' theatre in London is advertised as being either 'fringe' or 'Off West End'. Off West End venues include the Drill Hall Arts Centre (Chenies Street, London WC1) and the Royal Court Theatre (Sloane Square, London SW1); on the other hand the Oval House Arts Centre (Kennington Road, London SE11), the cradle of much lesbian theatre, is 'fringe'. A dramatist who starts on the fringe would naturally aspire to move into 'Off West End' and finally to the West End. Productions have frequently moved from the Royal Court to the West End, where they have proved their commercial worth. Caryl Churchill's *Serious Money* is a piece which played to full houses at the Royal Court and in the West End, although it attacks London's business heart, the City. I shall talk at some length later about the way that different audiences understand theatre – a West End audience's 'reading' of a play may be so different from that of an 'Off West End' audience that it might as well be a different play. It could be said that when the establishment enjoys what had seemed to be an attack on its values, then the original message has ceased to be heard. For playwrights wanting to make their mark, the risk of being misunderstood is one worth taking. Remaining on the fringe means poverty and obscurity; having work performed in a major subsidized or commercial theatre could mean relative fame, if not the acquisition of a fortune. The same holds true for actresses – there is no such thing as a 'career' in alternative theatre.

In this chapter I have simply touched on issues which will be explored at greater depth in my discussion of the work of individual companies. There is a final point I would like to make about the British theatrical context. All creation owes much to preceding models. There are traditions to be followed, or broken with. There is what is termed an 'intertextuality' operating in the theatre as it operates in literature. Our idea of what a play is comes in the first instance from the plays we have seen or read. Even though we react against 'drawing-room comedy' as being bourgeois and superficial, it remains as a model of what *not* to do. We may want to parody it, to deconstruct it, to make fun of its upper-middle-class values, but we cannot totally ignore it, any more than we can ignore the peculiarly British social structures which have provided theatrical characters for generations. The stock characters of English farce are the vicar, the colonel (or major or brigadier), the policeman, the spinster, the 'squire', the butler, the maid, the housekeeper, etc. And much English farce involves cross-dressing. There is a notional English village, a notional English country house. Even in the 1990s one of the most popular authors represented on the English stage is Agatha Christie.[8] Perhaps all this is what makes the distinction between British and American theatre. Julie Parker, administrator of the Drill Hall, suggested to me that there is a fundamental difference between American and British lesbian theatre.[9] She did not elaborate on what that difference was. Perhaps there was no need. Personally, before I discovered French theatre, my models were Noël Coward and Terence Rattigan – both gay men, both mainly describing upper-middle-class English society totally outside my experience – and Ben Travers, the king of English farce, about whose sexuality I knew nothing.

Notes

1. Clive Barker, 'Alternative theatre/political theatre', in Graham Holderness (ed.), *The Politics of Theatre and Drama* (London: Macmillan, 1992), p. 32.
2. Graham Holderness, Introduction, in *The Politics of Theatre and Drama*, p. 2.
3. Barker, 'Alternative theatre/political theatre', p. 32.

4. Bertolt Brecht, 'Theatre for pleasure or theatre for instruction', in John Willett (ed. and trans.), *Brecht on Theatre: The Development of an Aesthetic* (London: Methuen, 1982), p. 71.
5. Antonin Artaud, 'No more masterpieces', in *The Theatre and Its Double*, translated by Victor Corti (London: Calder Publications, 1993).
6. Lizbeth Goodman, *Contemporary Feminist Theatres: To Each Her Own* (London: Routledge, 1993); Trevor R. Griffiths and Margaret Llewellyn-Jones (eds), *British and Irish Women Dramatists since 1958: A Critical Handbook* (Buckingham: Open University Press, 1993); Helen Keyssar, *Feminist Theatre: An Introduction to the Plays of Contemporary British and American Women* (London: Macmillan, 1984).
7. Jill Davis (ed.) *Lesbian Plays: Two* (London: Methuen, 1989), Introduction.
8. Agatha Christie's *The Mousetrap* opened in November 1952 at the Ambassadors Theatre and has run at St Martin's Theatre since 1974.
9. Interview with Julie Parker, July 1995.

Chapter 3

Gay Sweatshop

(GINNY *enters and speaks to the audience. The other members of the cast are sitting amongst the audience.*)

GINNY: You are looking at a screaming lesbian,
A raving dyke,
A pervert, deviant,
Queer, fairy, fruitcake, freak,
Daughter, sister, niece, mother, cousin,
Mother-in-law,
Clippie, actress, bishop's wife, M.P.,
Machinist, typist, teacher, char,
I'm everywhere,
In your armies, in your schools,
Peering at you out of passing trains,
Sitting down next to you on the crowded bus,
in seat D22, yes sir, right next to you.
I'm here to stay
to infiltrate
to convert.[1]

Before Jill Posener's character Ginny (in *Any Woman Can*) confronted her audiences with this absolutely unequivocal statement about her sexuality, lesbians had been represented on the British stage, without the word itself being uttered. In 1927 the translation from the French of Edouard Bourdet's *The Captive* was performed at the Arts Theatre Club in London to members only, since the Lord Chamberlain had banned public performance. In 1965 the West End saw a production of Frank Marcus's *The Killing of Sister George,* followed shortly afterwards, also in the West End, by John Bowen's *Trevor,* half of a double bill called Little Boxes. Interesting though these may be, I choose not to discuss them here, since they were written by men and were not mainly concerned with lesbian issues. For me, the speech I have quoted marks the beginning of lesbian theatre in 1975.

Jill Posener herself quotes the main influence on her writing as being the American play *Kennedy's Children* by Robert Patrick, a gay writer. As stage manager for the London production, she had the opportunity to talk to Patrick, who encouraged her to make a statement about her sexuality using the same theatrical style he had himself used – a series of monologues addressed to the audience – a kind of stream of consciousness. It was clear from the success of *Kennedy's Children* that this method could be very effective, so the script was written. The actors, director and designer for the first public reading were found through professional contact with other lesbians, Kate Crutchley and Mary Moore, when Kate and Jill were both working at the Orange Tree, Richmond, on a production of *Lady or the Tiger*. Kate moved on to the West End, Jill to the Leicester Haymarket, having talked about the possibility of putting on *Any Woman Can* with Kate playing Ginny. Preferring to direct, when the opportunity arose to perform it at a Women's Theatre Festival in Leicester, in November 1975, Kate asked Miriam Margolyes to play the lead instead. The audience loved it. So did the members of the recently founded gay men's theatre group Gay Sweatshop. This had been set up by four drama students, Drew Griffiths, Gerald Chapman, Alan Pope and Gordon McDonald, as the first company to be dedicated to homosexual concerns. The opening production, *Mr X* (by Drew Griffiths), had been about a drag artist. Now they felt that they would like to do something about women and to ask women to join the company. *Any Woman Can* seemed the ideal play.

> Early in 1976 Drew Griffiths and Gerald Chapman, founder members of Gay Sweatshop, invited us to put on *Any Woman Can* during the Gay Sweatshop season at the I.C.A., in those days a radical Arts Centre. They also invited us to join the company – the first women to do so. That was my second 'coming out'. Gay Sweatshop was Britain's first professional gay company and to be involved with them was to devote your life, on and off stage, to being a professional lesbian. We learned a lot during that season. We realised that even radical and alternative theatre was providing few, if any, positive images of gay men and lesbians.[2]

The production moved from the ICA to the King's Head, Islington, was performed at the CHE Conference,[3] and subsequently went on tour administrated by Kate Crutchley, with a variety of different performers, including Julie Parker, now administrator of the Drill Hall, who had seen the play in its earlier version with the original cast, before it had undergone many changes and refinements. The first tour lasted for six months, had an all-lesbian cast, and was very exciting. Performances were in remote rural areas as well as big cities and were followed by consciousness-raising sessions with the mainly, though not entirely, lesbian audiences. These were often led by Nancy Diuguid, who frequently played the lead and who had been instrumental in introducing Julie Parker to radical theatre when they were both students at the Central School of Speech and Drama, London. It was all very 'agitprop', but in fact played mainly to a converted public starved of positive theatrical representation. (Most universities by now had Gay Societies (Gaysoc), many large towns had CHE groups and many arts centres were open to a production which had proved its worth in London. The show's outspokenness and the consciousness-raising sessions provided an opportunity to come out and make contact.) There was an element of danger, though: the show was banned in some towns and threatened with bombs and closure in Dublin. Heady days!

The structure of *Any Woman Can* was initially inspired by an American play but the references are to British institutions. Kate Crutchley indicated that the opening address, some of which I have already quoted, was based to some extent on the speeches of the lesbian activist Jackie Forster, who used similarly provocative expressions when she appeared on Sundays at Speakers' Corner in Hyde Park.[4] Ginny, the central character, is the focus of the crowd's attention. She is alone on the stage. Her words indicate that she feels quite isolated since she assumes her listeners to be, if not heterosexual, subject to all the usual prejudices about lesbians. The other characters, eight of them including a 'voice', enter from and return to the audience, leaving Ginny always on her own. They are all part of her narrative, conjured up as she recounts her life, remembered with pain, constructed as part of an oppressive society. Even her fellow gays are perceived as 'other'.

> I'd like to tell you about me. Me, jolly Ginny,
> compassionate Ginny, who used to fight to help a fellow
> gay find the strength to 'come out', but who went home
> alone. Ginny who spent her days in the company of
> others, laughing, joking, camping it up. I was the loudest
> mouth, and the loneliest.[5]

This last statement is followed immediately by the entrance of the headmistress of Ginny's boarding-school. This would appear to be where the loneliness started, with the appearance of kindness on her arrival masking the intense pressure to conform to stifling rules:

> This is your first day at our boarding school, nestled in the
> Titsey Hills, and we love you. ... From here on in we'll
> punish you for being here. We'll do our best to reform
> you and those who won't conform to our kingdom's rules
> we'll simply do away with.[6]

There is no escape, day or night, from the imprisoning institution.
Ginny describes her desperation to get out, her half-hearted attempts
at suicide, which led to one of the few expressions of tenderness she
had received from a fellow pupil, an older girl Ann, who subsequently
for one blissful night became her lover:

> This was the night we'd both been longing for. For – well
> for what? – for the release of all our hatred, all our misery
> at that place.[7]

The euphoria is short-lived. Ann sends Ginny a letter asking her to
forget the whole thing, to leave her alone to get on with her A-level
exams. Boarding-school experience has thus confirmed the loneliness
while offering a glimpse of possible happiness. After school this
promise of a more satisfying relationship is offered by an old friend,
Jean, who declares her love at the end of a letter describing an inci-
dent with her boyfriend. The reading of the letter is followed
immediately by Ginny's comment that the whole affair was catastrophic. Jean married the man she said she could not be more than
friends with, whose jealousy then prevented them from meeting. The
first actual interchange in the play is between Jean and Ginny, when
Jean starts to see Ginny again without telling her husband. Marriage
is not enough – she needs Ginny as well in a secret liaison which will
not interfere with her heterosexual image. She exits back to the audience. Ginny's line immediately following her departure is:

> My greatest fear is that I was the only one.[8]

Her next encounter is again with a married woman, Mrs Allan, who
is very willing to have 'a bit on the side' when her husband is away.
This experience proves to Ginny that sex is not actually what it's all
about.

> Sex didn't seem to be what I wanted. I needed to know
> that women could love each other, because they had
> chosen to do so, not as a furtive fuck when hubby was out
> of town.[9]

Eventually she makes contact with other lesbians, goes to a club,
meets someone. The next dialogue is with Julie. This time, instead of

sex without love, she is offered love without sex. After first denying that she is a lesbian, Julie says she is a lesbian after all, but cannot have sex with another woman. There is a discussion about this which concludes with Julie's departure to look for a suitable man.

Until this point in the play the auditorium has been the focus of heterosexuality, of normality. After Julie's exit a Voice speaks up, suggesting that Ginny try the Gateways, a well-known lesbian club in Chelsea. Ginny's reply to this presumed 'friend' is a description of sordid scenes in the meat markets of gay clubs. An 'Older Woman' climbs on to the stage, the first real lesbian character, an old-fashioned butch with a femme wife at home. Ginny takes her home, then is repelled by her.

> Suddenly you realise you've spent your life getting away from that. That wasn't a woman, that was a male impersonator and that's not what I want. I want a woman who wants to be a woman.[10]

This is the voice of 1970s lesbian feminism. Ginny becomes an active feminist. She finds her woman-identified partner, Debbie, but 'neglects' her in order to go to meetings. 'Couplism' is difficult, subject to another renegotiation. There is a brief discussion of the changes in fashion as far as monogamy is concerned – why and when it is considered permissible or not to remain faithful to one partner. It would seem that 'rules' are being imposed on lesbian behaviour by lesbians themselves, and actions that are not considered politically correct are condemned by the sisterhood.

The last section of the play is concerned with 'coming out'. Three women stand up, presumably remaining in the audience, to explain why they are not openly gay. The first describes herself as more like a man than a woman, she has a 'wife', she enjoys a drink with the boys at the club – she is happy with heterosexual role-play. In fact she is 'not really gay'. The second is ambitious, sees no point in jeopardizing her career by alienating male interviewers when she is up for promotion. The third does not want to attract attention, to be victimized for something she cannot help. She just wants to be 'allowed' to get on with her life; she does not want to cause trouble.

The final word is, of course, Ginny's. Coming out, revealing your sexuality, is supportive to others who may have been suffering the same isolation we have witnessed throughout the play. The audience is no longer treated as the heterosexual other; an appeal is made also to lesbians.

> I realised that I had in fact made my sexuality public
> property. By wearing a badge I had invited this woman's
> approach, made it possible for her to talk with me. What
> these women have just said seems to make perfect sense –
> but how long can you keep up the pretence? And why
> should you? You are still looking at a screaming lesbian
> and I'm looking right back at you![11]

The message, then, to straight members of the audience is 'I'm here to stay – I'm out and proud', to the lesbian members 'I understand your fear but there's more to gain by showing yourself'. In her afterword to the play Jill Posener emphasizes the importance of this all-lesbian cast playing to lesbian audiences.

> After seeing our show, women would literally come up to us and say 'I've
> never met another one …'. And it is for these women *Any Woman Can*
> was written. And for them it was vital that we didn't turn round and say
> 'Sorry love, I'm just playing a part'.[12]

Writing in 1987, while admitting the play's flaws, such as lack of dramatic cohesion and lack of political analysis, she still sees it as relevant in that it provides the affirmation that lesbians constantly need.

The Gay Sweatshop Women's members had already started to think about their next show before the tour of *Any Woman Can* ended. They had talked among themselves and with their audience members about suitable and popular topics. The two favourites being harassment at work and lesbian custody cases, it was decided to concentrate on the latter. Since a collective way of working had already been successful, it was decided that the basis of the new piece would be interviews, articles, etc. gathered by the group. Audiences were interviewed during the tour, after the show. More and more material having been accumulated, the Arts Council was persuaded that the project was worth funding. Back in London the expanded company set about improvising scenes around the material. There were new members already experienced in writing or improvisation, for example Helen Barnaby, Kate Phelps and Tash Fairbanks, who had written a play called *Son of a Gun* with a similar autobiographical theme to *Any Woman Can*, performed by Sidewalk at the Round House, Camden, London.[13] The improvisations were written down and pinned up around the walls of the Oval House, where the company was rehearsing. They were 'shuffled around',[14] until it was concluded that the only way to arrive at a proper structure was to bring in an outside author. Michelene Wandor was thus invited to produce a coherent script from what had already been written. The resultant play, *Care and Control*, is still performed, still popular, its appeal perhaps largely because it is based on accounts of actual events. It was also the first production of a new separate women's company. Michelene Wandor explains that there are two reasons for this.

> The first was similar to the split that had occurred within the Gay Liberation Front itself, in that lesbians felt that many features of their oppression were shared more with other women than with gay men. One of the consequences of this was to be seen in a conflict between theatrical styles, in that the men drew on an already familiar camp and drag tradition which they both celebrated and tried to stand on its head, whereas the women leaned more towards the newer agitprop, documentary based styles, as a means of sharing hitherto suppressed lesbian experience.[15]

I think that it is worth quoting Kate Crutchley at some length on the subject of the different priorities of the gay men and lesbian theatre practitioners:

'They got very interested in music. The women always wanted to do "things with music and bands in" not structured plays. It tended to be like a bit of song, then sketchy bits and a bit of through-line and some of the people were not like trained actresses, they were more like activists who wanted to have a go, and there was a certain point where you thought members of the audience could have got up and done it just as well. And I think they liked that, I think the audience liked it. It was not threatening. ... It's this whole thing about how you present yourself and how you look, you know, you go through phases when you want to look very much the image of the audience. ... We had to be so right on and we had to be seen to be non-sexist, non-racist, non-ageist, non-everything. The rows with some people whether they should wear a bra or not! The Plays had to be everything for everybody. You couldn't have a single (bad) remark or character in it unless it were a villain.'[16]

She went on to say in answer to my question about who the villain might be – a straight white middle-class man for example? –

'No, not necessarily. No, we'd given them a bit of a trouncing in *Care and Control* but on the other hand I think lots of people felt personally that straight white men, if they were really nice new men sort of thing, were closer in sentiments to gay women than gay men might be. That's my theory, because there's a bit of a conflict of interests. ... *We* were always the hard-liners – for some of the men, it was a bit of a dichotomy. For instance drag. Drew Griffiths was marvellous at drag, but at the same time he was doing anti-drag, anti-stereotype work. He, at the same time, liked to dress up in a frock, but he liked to do political theatre that said "I don't want to do anti-queen jokes". He trod a really delicate line. ... He was looking at why people did this but at the same time not wanting them to be made figures of fun. It was so cleverly done.'[17]

This last point may seem a little obscure, but it illustrates the different concerns reflected in gay men's theatre. Also, in order to reverse stereotypes, women, who were supposed traditionally to be tender and supportive, had to present a more abrasive, more aggressive image.

'You're always supposed to be tender and loving and caring and all that. You'd see men playing a lovely love scene where they're all tender and loving and caring and everybody went "Aah". And it seemed like women could only get harder, more tough and more positive, with more solidarity, and we didn't have anywhere to go in the tenderness stakes. So we tended to be more militant. ... It was what was needed at the time.'[18]

What was needed at the time that *Care and Control* was devised was a play about child custody cases which had resonances for both heterosexual and lesbian women. The bond was between mothers, the issue was the control that patriarchal society exercised over them and their children. In her chapter on lesbian theatre, Lizbeth Goodman describes the care and control issue as being 'clearly infused with a dynamic of gender and power, associated with paternalistic ideas about women's roles and biased by economic circumstances weighing in favour of men.'[19]

What the Hell Is She Doing Here? (1978), the next show devised by the Gay Sweatshop, was even more loosely structured than *Care and Control*, being more like a revue with music, songs and sketches. I have been unable to find out further information about their next piece, *I Like Me Like This* by Sharon Wassaner and Angela Stewart Park (1979).

In 1980 Gay Sweatshop lost its Arts Council revenue funding, which had guaranteed an annual subsidy whatever the play. From now on they were to rely on project funding, i.e. an application had to be made for each production, including a detailed budget proposal. This meant there was always a possibility of receiving too little, or no funding at all, after a great deal of preparation work had already been done.

Nevertheless, in 1984 the women's company reintegrated into the mixed Sweatshop company. In 1985 there was the first all-female cast since 1979, for Sue Frumin's *Raising the Wreck*, described by Rose Collis as:

A truly significant landmark in lesbian Theatre, it contained a multi-racial cast, a celebratory historical content, and a reaffirmation of Women's, particularly lesbian women's, strength and determination in overcoming socio-political obstacles and disadvantages.[20]

When asked to write a play for the company, Sue Frumin chose the subject of women pirates, researched thoroughly at the Piracy Museum in Greenwich, London, where she found details about the lives of women such as Mary Read, Grace O'Malley and Ann Bonney. The wreck in the title is a boat on the seabed in which four pirate women have taken refuge through the centuries; whether they are ghosts or figments of the imagination is irrelevant. They represent the historical reality of women driven to piracy through oppression and adversity.

The loose structure of the play provides an opportunity for each of the pirates to tell her story. In the opening scene we are in the present, on board a pirate radio ship, run by Jenny and Maggie. Jenny is trying to work on a new programme about Women Whizz Kids, while her partner goes off duty, forgetting to take with her a book about pirates, borrowed from the library by her son. It would seem to be this book which triggers off a strange experience in which Jenny appears to be hurled to the bottom of the sea and caught in the net spread by the pirate women to catch the thief who has taken some of their most precious objects. After initial misunderstandings on both sides, Jenny learns the histories of a black, a Chinese, an English and an Irish pirate. What she hears is how the objectification of women can at length lead to violent rebellion. Zoa was a slave, shipped from Africa to the West Indies for a Dutch master. Posing as a boy, she escapes, and is carried to the sea in a stolen boat. Picked up by pirates, she works as a 'powder monkey' lighting their guns, becoming a slave again when they land on a desert island, until the slaves revolt and she escapes once more, taking to sea in a frail craft. Smashed in a storm, her boat sinks and she finds herself on the seabed with Grace. The two of them make a home in the wreck.

Aku's story is longer and more complicated. Her mother, Tan Chin, passed her off as a boy to avoid the wrath of her father P'ing, who, like all Chinese men, was desperate for a son. When it was discovered, by accident, that the child was a girl, her mother placed her on a piece of wood to float down the river. The current carried her into the middle of a battle between American sailors and the Pirate Queen, Ching Pang Tun, who fished the baby out of the water and brought her up her daughter, giving her the shoes of her lover, Brave Orchid, assassinated by soldiers. These shoes, like the drum which was given to Zoa by her own mother, were her most precious possessions and, like the drum, had disappeared. Aku's story has a truly epic quality.

> Aku Ching Pang Tun and her band of pirates were very busy, and very rich. Everyone on the river was chasing them, apart from the fisherfolk who only chased small fry. The British chased them inland and in the South China Seas, and the Americans chased them around the Yellow Sea and the Eastern Sea. Ching Pang Tun was so busy she had not time to pray to her Goddess. She had been chased into the mouth of the Yangtze River with two platoons of pirate junks. She was pacing the decks angrily. None of the crew dared speak to her. For dinner that night she had eaten 2 chickens, 3 lbs. of water chestnuts, 2 lbs. of bean sprouts and 42 mushrooms. She had drunk 4 bottles of Sake and smoked enough opium to put three platoons of river pirates unconscious at the bottom of the river. She was ready to do battle.[21]

Grace was a pirate in Ireland at the time of Elizabeth I. She was also a chief as well as a sea-captain. At war with England she wrote directly to the Queen, receiving in return not only a pardon and settlements, but also a silk handkerchief on which to blow her nose. This too has been 'stolen'.

Mary Read was brought up as Mark Read, taking the place of her dead brother. She stayed Mark until she was dragooned into the navy. At fifteen she deserted to join the army. Several adventures later, still as Mark Read, she was aboard a ship which was attacked by pirates and acquired a taste for the life. She finally met the love of her life, Ann Bonney, when the latter was enlisting a crew to sail to Cuba. Their first night of love, in Ann's cabin, is reminiscent of the Arabian Nights:

MARY: Her cabin was beautiful, full of the spoils of piracy. Silks and satins draped the walls, there were statues and carvings from many lands, birds in gilded cages sang to her and a monkey sat on her shoulder all during dinner, and ate almost as heartily as she did herself. There was a smell of incense in the air and a hint of opium.[22]

Grace, Mary, Aku and Zoa are the stuff that legends are made of. They are heroes, whose courage shows itself both in love and war. They were violent in violent times, for survival. Their contemporary equivalent is the Greenham Common women, whose struggle is equally courageous although it is anti-war and non-violent. In the final scene Jenny, back in the present, tries to persuade her partner that they could make programmes about women's history which would be an inspiration to their listeners. She turns on her tape recorder to play her recordings of the pirates' stories; instead she hears the news that the American ship which had been trying to raise the wreck of the *Lady Intrepid* has been hit by such bad weather that they have had to abandon the attempt. They have also lost certain items that they had recovered from the wreck and were taking to a museum – Zoa's drum, Grace's handkerchief, Aku's shoes and Mary's sword. The pirates live on triumphant.

Also in 1985, a festival of gay and lesbian plays was organized, known as Gay Sweatshop Times Ten Festival. Ten plays were selected for rehearsed public readings and four more were given full production. The two women's plays chosen for production were *Julie* by Catherine Kilcoyne and *More* by Maro Green and Caroline Griffin.

Julie is a monologue, although it is an amalgamation of several women's stories. The central character who, like Ginny in *Any Woman Can,* conjures up other characters (although unlike Ginny she performs them all) is described by the author as 'an independent ex-punk', of about twenty-five or twenty-six.[23] She is in fact the Julie in *Any Woman Can,* who was unable to have a sexual relationship with Ginny. Catherine Kilcoyne intended her to be recognized by as many women as possible, heterosexual and bisexual as well as lesbian; the experiences she describes are mainly with men. The play was originally called *Crossing Over,* a passage from heterosexuality to lesbianism. It was changed because there is no definite conclusion – the journey might be made again in reverse – 'journeys such as this take a life-time and go through many stages'.[24]

The setting is Julie's sitting-room. When the action begins she is slightly drunk, having just returned from 'a night out'. Her first words are spoken into the telephone, to complain about the behaviour of the taxi-driver who has just brought her home, at two o'clock in the morning. He took her the long way round, overcharged her by a pound, made 'filthy remarks' all the way and touched her up. We realize that her complaints will be disregarded, since the person she was talking to asked if she sat in the front, a move obviously regarded as an encouragement to sexual advances. The opening situation, then, is one which will be familiar to many women in any audience, one of the more frequent sorts of harassment.

When Julie addresses us directly, it is to confuse us somewhat. She describes her clothes as intended to catch men. Stiletto heels to spike them with. She finds giving up heterosexual sex as difficult as giving up smoking. Early in the evening she had seen a stranger in a bar. She wanted him. She came home, made the bed, dressed up and went out to get him. His name was Dave. Then follows the first version of the story: they are both sexually aroused but Julie is prevented from taking it further by a realization that this is just a boring repetition of the same old scene. Dave walks her to her cab, kisses her goodnight. Later she gives a second version – the truthful one. She goes home with Dave. They begin to fuck immediately. She freezes, feels sick. He calls a cab and pushes her out, muttering 'Silly slag'. Sex with men is 'the wrong sex' but it is addictive. It gives relief from the isolation which she is afraid of if she 'crosses over' once and for all. She relives a scene with two straight women flatmates who taunt her about her presumed lesbianism until she goes to bed with one of them, while the other looks on. The straight woman has an orgasm, and Julie feels 'used'. After that she lost her trust in women, in herself. The world is less hurtful if you deny yourself, hide behind some man's cock.

Towards the end we begin to get an indication that, in spite of the apparently persistent heterosexual addiction, Julie has changed. Remembering her life with Ginny (using an actual scene from *Any Woman Can*) she relives the dilemma of loving without being able to give this love physical expression, loving women, sleeping with men. However, while remembering, she removes her make-up, which is the mask of 'the man's woman'. Looking at her naked face, she realizes who she really is. The break with heterosexuality finally came when someone proposed marriage:

> Babies.
> Love.
> Security.
> Chains.
> Lies.
> Deceit.[25]

Julie admits love and desire for her lesbian friend Jane. This is what she wants, she is sure, though sleeping with men might prove a hard habit to break. Jane had taught her to realize women:

> Jane, I went shopping today. I saw women
> for the first time.
> Looking in their faces, their eyes,
> Little smiles.
> I was connecting, communicating.[26]

In the final section of the play Julie takes off her clothes, faces herself, her true self in the mirror. Gazing at herself, she addresses the absent Jane.

> Jane, you turn me on.
> Up here (*head*)
> Down here (*çunt*)
> In here (*heart*)
> And Everywhere.
> Turn me inside out.
> She gave my body back to me.
> I've got it back
>
> . . .
>
> My body does not belong in male hands
> any more.
> The man's woman meets the woman's woman.[27]

Any Woman Can in 1975 had marked the first lesbian 'coming out' in British theatre. Ten years later it inspired a play concerned with 'finding out'. Ginny was never in doubt about her lesbian inclinations; Julie, who has been much more thoroughly socialized by the heterosexual world (perhaps she never went to a girls' boarding-school!) is forever vacillating between cock and cunt. Her final statement could be seen as the affirmation of a choice, not a genetic predisposition. A brave choice which makes her vulnerable, to friends and lovers as well as enemies.

The other full production arising out of the Times Ten Festival, *More* by Maro Green and Caroline Griffin, had a very different focus – the 'hidden' disabilities of anorexia, bulimia and agoraphobia. The lesbianism of the two characters is taken for granted. It is a passionate love story written in a humorous way, using pantomime techniques. Coquino, a 'failed escapist', who is agoraphobic, has affinities with one of the authors, while Mavro is a lapsed bulimic like the other, Maro Green, who in fact played the part. Coquino has a rope tied to her at the beginning of the play, symbolizing a kind of umbilical cord, both tying her to safety and representing her fear of the world. It is a connection between the two characters themselves:

COQUINO: One way or another, whoever holds the rope is in charge.
MAVRO: You can never say you haven't heard this. From now on
         you're responsible too, or culpably naïve.[28]

The action is set in a timeless, unidentified space, suggesting that the performance is a ritual which could take place anywhere. The audience is challenged to take part in this ritual or remain outside. The conditions of the lives of the disabled people are presented not as an entertainment, in spite of the humour, but as a revelation.

Another production which in part owed its impetus to the Times Ten Festival was Jackie Kay's *Chiaroscuro*, first performed as a finished piece at the Soho Poly in London in 1996 by the Theatre of Black Women. Jackie Kay had been commissioned by Theatre of Black Women in the spring of 1985 to write a half-hour play. After reading the draft she sent them, they encouraged her to extend it to an hour, which she did. This draft, called *The Meeting Place*, was read at the Times Ten Festival to an appreciative audience. It was subsequently worked on by the company for four weeks until a more polished version, *Chiaroscuro*, had been finalized. The author acknowledged her debt to the company.

> The workshops delivered a plot, which the original draft did not have, and added flesh to my rather thin-boned characters. ... Through improvisation, games and background work, the four women in the play began to form with more solidity. It was this version of the play which was produced and toured for three months.[29]

It is not the published version, however. The play went through a good many more stages, with the author retrieving ideas which had got lost in the workshops. What is common to all drafts is an obsession with naming and an interest in communication. Jackie Kay wants to show how difficult communication is in a racist homophobic society. As with *More*, painful real-life situations are presented in a more abstract, poetic form (both Jackie Kay and Caroline Griffin were established poets), a symbolic reconstruction of the lived-through experience of black lesbians. All four characters have 'invented themselves'; what they perform for the audience is the story of this invention, arrived at through a recognition, an acceptance of their racial, sexual heritage. In a neutral (mainly grey) set, wearing neutral costumes they take accessories from an old wooden chest, whenever they need to demonstrate a particular moment. They dance, they sing, they speak poems, they replay their conflicts. This is the kind of storytelling we have seen already in *Any Woman Can* and in *Julie*, where the character in her enlightened present state takes us back through the journey she has made. One of the main differences between this play and the other two is that we witness the making of relationships. These four women are in continual interaction with each other. They begin by singing and dancing together, before recounting their separate selves.

ALL (*singing*):
> Time changes light
> light changes time
> here we are with the dawn in the dark
> the dark in the dawn
> trying to find the words
> trying to find the words.[30]

When they do tell their individual stories they begin beyond the beginning, beyond their birth, with their namesakes: Aisha was named after her mother's mother, who was born in the Himalayas at dawn, causing *her* mother to shriek with pain. Beth's namesake is even more distant – her great-great-great-great-grandmother on her father's side, taken into slavery. It was Beth's black daddy from St Vincent who named her, after the strong, brave woman whose African name had been whipped out of her. The history that her name recalls is a history of survival in oppression. Opal is an orphan and of mixed race, since her skin is almost white. She thinks she may have been named by an old nurse who wore opal earrings. Opal is a rock and a jewel, constantly changing in the light. Yomi's name has to do with her own birth (although we are not told what it means exactly). She was born at midnight, by Caesarean section, after her mother despaired that she would ever leave the womb of her own volition. Her mother called her Abayomi. Later in the play there is reference to an 'old Yomi' she is named after, but not at this point.

For all four, origins, racial origins, are an essential part of their identity. The colour which marks them out as different from the white majority causes them to seek a community beyond British shores. When they first meet, Yomi asks Beth where she is from. She replies that her father is from St Vincent, her mother is white. Yomi herself is from Nigeria. They are alike in that they are 'black' but their blackness is not the same. None of them is 'white', none is 'black' in the way the others are black. Their darkness comes from different sources, from their origins. So the identity which knits them with each other is opposed by the identity which they feel with a larger community elsewhere.

AISHA (*sings*):
>My dreams are in another language
>My heart is overseas
>a need is stretching like the water
>to meet and meet and meet
>I want to put it all together
>these different bits of me
>show them to my mother and
>all my family, my family.[31]

There *is* another sort of 'family' to which Beth and Opal belong: they are lesbians. Beth picks Opal up in a café; it is love at first sight for both of them. Beth already knows what she is; as with Ginny, her realization goes back to her schooldays. Opal is taken by surprise. Her feelings are deep and passionate, yet she is confused by having no knowledge of what loving another woman might mean. Never having been part of a nuclear family, she has dreamed of being wanted, now she has found Beth she is afraid of loving her, afraid of the outside world which seems to be so hostile.

Hostility is present on stage in the person of Yomi, who has all the usual homophobic prejudices.

YOMI:
>And I pictured it ugly
>like the ugliness of something
>you don't want to look at
>imagining one might accost me
>in the Ladies' restroom
>as soon as I heard lesbian
>I saw ugly and blue
>and lonely and not being able to get
>THE REAL THING
>and a tall angular looking woman
>white with men's things on,
>too much hair around the mouth
>and always on the prowl
>she was so lonely
>would die lonely
>never knowing any kind of love
>because lesbian and love
>could not come together
>like man and woman.[32]

Yomi says she would never have guessed about Opal: unlike Beth, she does not fit the stereotype. Indeed Opal herself, who has always disliked her own image, would appear to be hovering on a bisexual borderline.

OPAL: My face is up like a big baboon
My eyes are swimming pools. My nose
is an ape's nose. My lips are rubber.
My face is dark and smooth. My cheeks
are high and mellow. My eyes are deep
and knowing. My nose sniffs new
scents. My lips are soft and gentle.
Which is me?

BETH: Both.

OPAL: I'm afraid I'll lose face.

BETH: With who?

OPAL: You, Yomi, lose face with myself.
I have a string of boyfriends. I liked the
feeling of a penis inside me!

BETH: So?

OPAL: So does that mean I'm not a real
lesbian?

BETH: No of course it doesn't mean that.[33]

Opal *is* a 'real lesbian' if the phrase has any meaning. Women have loved women in every country, therefore she would like to know what they are called, these women. She would like to know about this other community, to join them to discover her natural mother in order to tell her about this new self she recognizes.

Being faced with Beth and Opal 'looking good together', Yomi is forced to think again, to remember that her mother had talked to her of African women who had loved each other but lived with their husbands. Yomi's mother had been surprised, not condemning. She had thought it a pity that they had to hide their love.

Beth has come to terms with her own lesbianism; the problem for her is to recognize her mixed racial status. Opal never knew her mother; Beth finds it difficult to own hers since she has become black identified, although in her childhood all her friends were white. So in a sense, both lesbians are motherless, in contrast to the other two who refer back to what their mothers said or did, as the source of wisdom, as an inspiration. Continuity through generations of women is shown to be important, part of living mythology. When Yomi's mother called her after 'old Yomi' she handed on a gift not only to her daughter, but also to her daughter's daughter.

Old Yomi was born with her tongue missing; she became a gifted artist. Young Yomi seemed to have no tongue at birth – she did not cry until spanked. Her own daughter, Fubayo, also did not cry until spanked. She did not talk until she was three, but she showed signs of real artistic gift.

Aisha's mother, her whole family, have a strong hold on her still. She is struggling with her attraction to women, not daring to give way to it because it would be 'too risky'. She is disturbed by Beth and Opal's delight in each other; she longs to find similar happiness with a woman. She may make a conventional marriage but she suspects she will always regret it.

Sexuality is thus finally a question of choice, unlike the colour of one's skin. Aisha could choose, wants to choose women, but lacks the courage; Opal could have chosen men but falls in love with Beth. Beth chooses to confirm what she has always felt is most 'natural' to her; Yomi chooses to conform to the heterosexual norm.

Jackie Kay's next play, *Twice Over*, was first performed as a rehearsal reading in the Gay Sweatshop Times Twelve Festival in 1987. It was subsequently performed at the Drill Hall in 1988. Race is not an issue in this play, although three of the six female characters are black and three white. 'Black' can mean racially mixed, which for Tash, one of the teenagers in the play, presents problems in that she never has any contact with the family of her white father, because they disowned him when he married her black mother. She describes her parents as truly hating each other. Tash and Evaki are described as black in the cast list; their close friend, Sharon, is white. The other three characters are all of an older generation; one of them is Evaki's grandmother, Cora, and the other two are Cora's lover Maeve, in her late fifties, and Jean, a younger black woman and a workmate.

Cora and Evaki are the central characters, although all have important roles. Cora is dead when the play opens, sitting on her coffin watching her own funeral. Throughout the action she addresses the audience and the other characters with a commentary on what is happening. Maeve stands apart, isolated, bereaved without being able to admit it. She and Cora had been lovers for years, in secret. We are reminded of Opal's speech in *Chiaroscuro*:

> and she is suddenly dead.
> I am at her funeral
> and no-one there knows what we meant
> to each other
> and all her remaining relatives wonder –

> who is the sobbing woman in the dark
> coat
> at the back with a pew to herself?[34]

Cora tells us that being dead gives her a different perspective on things, that if she could live her life twice over she would never have pretended. In fact she is so disturbed by the false impression of her life that she has left behind that she resolves to reveal her 'true' self, the self who loved Maeve, to her granddaughter.

> I can't bear to go through my death the same way as I went through my life. That's expecting too much of a person.[35]

She compels Evaki to 'find' a letter and diaries. After struggling with her conscience over reading 'private' papers, Evaki succumbs. She is shocked, disgusted by the thought of a sexual relationship between two old women. It is a terrible thought that her own flesh and blood, the person in her family with whom she identified most closely, should have been a lezzie. As she thinks back she remembers scenes, moments between Cora and Maeve, which ought to have given her a clue – but after all Cora was a grandmother and Maeve a respectable married woman. And they did not look like the conventional image of the lesbian.

> I would never have guessed. They both wore skirts.
>
> . . .
>
> And they don't look like men or walk like men. They just don't look like lezzies, know what I mean?[36]

The knowledge of Cora's deviance is a burden which young Evaki finds difficult to bear alone. She is tempted to tell her schoolgirl chums, in spite of their prejudices. A strong theme throughout is that secrets are bad as much for the young as for the old. Tash is worn out by keeping to herself her father's abuse of her. It is not clear whether he actually rapes her, but there is certainly sexual abuse which she was on the point of describing to the most sympathetic person she knew, Cora, before she died. Sharon's secret is that she is pregnant, by Jean's son Stephen. Fear, guilt, concealment, all are demonstrated to be wrong. When Evaki tells Tash about Cora and Maeve, Tash is supportive, just as she is to Sharon when she confesses her pregnancy.

Being open requires courage in a disapproving world. When Evaki confronts Maeve with the diaries Maeve's immediate reaction is denial, not of her love, but of sexual involvement. She trusts no one, since more than once close friends have let her down:

MAEVE: I mean, it's all very well for you to come here and wreck
my life and Cora's out of it, isn't she, she's safe in her
grave? Have you thought of what it would mean for me if
everyone knew. Look at someone like Jean. She would
ostracise me.[37]

We, the audience, know that this would not be Jean's reaction. She
already guesses about the relationship and would like to show sympathy.

JEAN: ... What a shame really. I mean they weren't doing
anybody any harm. It must be terrible for Maeve now. Not
a soul to talk to about it. I don't suppose she's ever told
anybody, she's so secretive. Maybe I should broach the
subject with her. No she's so private, she'd resent it. I'm
sure. So I'd better just mind my own.[38]

Jean is what could be generally called a 'nice woman', a representative of heterosexual tolerance. Her understanding attitude is
contrasted with that of Sharon who uses the word 'lezzie' as an insult:

(EVAKI *puts her arm around* SHARON *drunkenly.*)
SHARON: Geroff. Lezzie Cow.
EVAKI: What did you call me?
SHARON: I said you're a lezzie cow.
EVAKI: Piss off. Go on get out.
SHARON: Aw come off it. I was pulling your leg. Mind you it must
be true for you to act like that. Evaki! Darling. Why
didn't you tell me?
EVAKI: Shut your fucking face. I'm warning you.
SHARON: You don't think I'd hang around with you if I really
thought that, do you?[39]

This is the second time Sharon has accused Evaki of being a
'lezzie'. The first was when Evaki talked about the lifelong friendship
which was likely to exist between her and Tash, who does not have a
boyfriend and has a jaundiced view of marriage. In the unpublished
script she later regrets what she has said:

I reckon Evaki's still mad at me for calling her a lezzie.
Silly cow. Still what if she really is? I shouldn't have
taken the piss. She must feel terrible man.[40]

This speech immediately follows a scene in which Evaki expresses doubts about her own sexuality:

EVAKI: I just hope it isn't hereditary, that's all. Cos people say
it's the hormones and it's catching. Nah. I would know,
wouldn't I? I've got boyfriends. Not right now, but still.
Mind you, Nan was married to Granddad.[41]

Interestingly, in the published version Sharon's attitude is harder. In
her last scene of the play she expresses common, homophobic prejudices:

SHARON: Most of them walk like men and do men's jobs, you know
building sites, shit like that.
EVAKI: That's crap Sharon.
SHARON: Even the clothes they wear. I'm telling you they're all
fucked up. They all think they're men, so they wear men's
stuff, do their jobs, it's sick man.
EVAKI: That's crap too.
SHARON: I'm not talking crap, I'm talking common knowledge.
Where've you been? I've even seen some. Yuck, it's
horrible. Can you imagine doing it with another woman?
It's so dirty it's not true. You have to watch lezzies
though, it's catching.[42]

More than anything else, the anxiety that the girls feel demonstrates
an adolescent ignorance about sex. Tash is the most mature of the
girls, but she has cut herself off from sexual contact. Sharon has
'done it' once, without emotion, without even meaning to have full
penetration. This youthful ignorance is contrasted with the passionate
tender relationship between Cora and Maeve, who were taken by
surprise after years of 'normal' marriage.

At the end of the play, from her coffin, Cora has her way. Maeve
agrees to come out, Evaki offers her friendship. We are back at the
beginning with a funeral scene. This time instead of remaining on the
sidelines, Maeve comes centre-stage to receive everyone's condol-
ences. Cora can rest in peace, Evaki has learnt to be proud of her
grandmother. The message is a more general one than to come out of
the closet, it is that we must trust each other, be open and truthful
especially about what is most important in our lives. Living a lie is
bad.

In his introduction to the published version of the play, Philip
Osment makes some illuminating comments:

In researching the play Jackie talked to young women and girls about their perceptions of lesbians – many of which are expressed in the play by Sharon and Evaki. One thing that struck her most forcefully is that lesbians were seen as being young. When asked if a granny could be gay, the young women expressed shock and even disgust. So she decided to examine this response. Gay Sweatshop had never done a play which successfully explained a relationship between two older women. The tenderness and love that Cora and Maeve have for each other made the play moving and poignant.[43]

Jackie Kay's *Twice Over* was a significant production for Gay Sweatshop for a number of reasons. It was the company's first play by a black writer, and the mixed-race cast of characters flowed naturally from the writing. This means that the policies which inspired the Gay Sweatshop Times Ten Festival had to some degree paid off. The play also strengthened the company's profile with regard to women's work. It was as popular and highly regarded as previous men's and mixed shows had been. Lastly it went out on tour just after Section 28 had been introduced on to the statute book,[44] and drew an audience that needed to be heartened and encouraged. Lesbians and gay men were under attack. We were being told that the rights that had been so slowly gained over the past years were privileges that could be withdrawn and that our relationships had no validity and were based on pretence. During the tour people travelled miles to packed-out performances in Sheffield, Bradford and Bristol and the play took on a significance that made the atmosphere in the theatre both emotionally charged and celebratory. At the beginning of the play we see Maeve excluded from Cora's family and unable to share her grief. At the end she is given her rightful place among the mourners and Evaki has learnt that the ties of blood and marriage are not always the strongest or most important.[45]

It is interesting that, when Jill Posener directed the play at the Theatre Rhinoceros in San Francisco, Justin Bond, theatre critic of the *Bay Area Reporter* (a gay newspaper in the city), found exactly the same merits as had Philip Osment. Even without the threat of Section 28, even in San Francisco, the celebration of gay relations in the theatre was still needed by the community. Justin Bond describes *Twice Over* as a 'feel-good' play:

Not to diminish the power of what 'feel-good' means. In this day and age where our art, theatre and the very right to exist are being attacked by the right-wing and moderate conservatives in this country, life affirming plays are very important.

With so many cosmetic-images of lesbian sexuality out there, it's lovely to see a relationship between two mature women. The dance and romance between Cora and Maeve is the high point of the show because it isn't something we see every day. Two middle-aged women kissing! It's always nice to learn about love. *Twice Over* contains quite a few lessons. Besides who *wouldn't* want a queer granny?[46]

In 1990 Sweatshop commissioned Bryony Lavery to write *Kitchen Matters*, which she described as 'an epic comedy'. This is a piece which is 'epic' in the Brechtian sense; it never lets the audience forget that they are watching actors playing out invented scenes which are not 'real'. The audience is reminded that this is Gay Sweatshop, that there is not enough money to put on a good show if one simply has project funding, that professional actors have to work side by side with volunteer amateurs in the chorus – all this is worked into the script of the play. There are references to Brecht and references to Noël Coward; there is talk about 'fringe' as opposed to mainstream theatre. In the end, we are left in no doubt that this is theatre about theatre, among other things, a condemnation of the lack of funding which prevents really good work being done. As well as being topical it is packed with in-jokes fully comprehensible only to London lesbians and gays. Although the styles are those of different theatrical genres, the overall impression is of an English pantomime with the good goddess, the absolutely wicked villain (Penny the Poison, a Thatcherite, anti-feminist, homophobic, meat-eating *Sun* reader) and a pantomime horse. The writer makes an occasional appearance; scenes are imagined, then abandoned for lack of money; a Bacchanalian blood-letting orgy is transformed into punishment by forgiveness. This is Sweatshop meditating on its fate in a suitably high-camp style.

The divine heroine of kitchen matters, Trixia, born of a god and of theatre, is American. With the help or hindrance of Angel (and 'angel' is one who invests in theatre) she condemns the baddies in the cast to go out into mainstream theatre and spread the gay message. In fact Lois Weaver, one half of the American company Split Britches, became co-director of Gay Sweatshop in the early 1990s, bringing with her years of experience at the WOW Café in New York and as part of Spiderwoman.[47] Split Britches were familiar to London theatregoers as they had brought over *Dress Suits to Hire* by Holly Hughes and other shows and had created *Patience and Sarah* in London under the direction of Kate Crutchley. Together with Blootips, a gay English group, they invented *Belle Reprieve*, a deconstruction of femininity and masculinity in Tennessee Williams's *A Streetcar Named Desire*.

Lois Weaver studied drama at a small single-sex college in the Blue Ridge Mountains of Virginia. She considers that it was a good training because the women played all the parts, men's and women's. Gender was an illusion to be created just as they had to create the illusion of theatrical space in areas which were not designed for performance. At the beginning of the 1970s she and her teachers were caught up in the excitement of the experimental work based in New York, which sent echoes throughout the USA. When she left college she decided to work in the inner city in Baltimore, rather than work in theatre, but after a while she was seduced back to study experimental theatre in the Open Theatre, where she learnt about the ideas and methods of Grotowski.[48] Realizing the possibilities of combining political action with performance, she eventually met up with the women who were to become Spiderwoman. This was her first experience of 'feminist' theatre although the members of the group did not necessarily use that label, regarding their work simply as growing from their experience as women. Lois worked with Spiderwoman for some years before she and Peggy Shaw (previously with a similar group, Hot Peaches) split off to explore lesbian themes in their work. As *Split Britches* was the name of a show Peggy and Lois created within the context of Spiderwoman, they gave the name to their new company formed in 1985. It was during the tour of *Belle Reprieve* in 1991 that the post of Gay Sweatshop artistic director was advertised. Two posts, in fact, a man and a woman. Revenue funding was at last to be given to the company, which meant a guaranteed amount of money each year, as long as they had a male and a female director. As a result of a campaign which mobilized important gay activists, the imminent collapse which inspired the writing of *Kitchen Matters* had been averted.

Asked in an interview 'What do you think Sweatshop was looking for in appointing an artistic director?', Lois Weaver gave the following reply:

'I don't know if they knew exactly what they were looking for. When I interviewed I said what I'd be interested in doing because of my experience of where "queer" theatre is, in the United States (as opposed to "lesbian theatre" or "gay and lesbian theatre", "queer theatre" is very politically based, it's very urgent, it comes out of a necessity around issues of the AIDS crisis for one, and censorship for another, much more agit-prop, not in style but in content, experimentation with form and space) that I'd like to (and I saw that as harking back to the beginning of Sweatshop, which came from the street) what I'd like to do is bring it back to the street and shake these foundations which had been built over the sixteen or seventeen years and make it much more grass roots and community oriented and community based. As a revenue funded company we'd be a resource to lots of lesbian and gay artists, queer artists, push the queer aesthetic, do lots of performance events – queer school, create queer school which would be a place for people to study queer theatre with queers, even though they might work out in the world, in the straight theatre; do platform performance series, encourage artists to get out of their living rooms and on to the stage and not wait to be funded, not wait for someone to cast them in a play but create their own work. All that kind of stuff that I'd been doing at WOW and in the States, I'd want to do here but with that funding base.'[49]

James Neale-Kennerley was appointed as the other artistic director. This was conceived as a job-share, but the two had enough in common for the situation not to be six months of what one of them wanted followed by six months of something completely different. They shared an artistic vision. Working together during the first year they hosted a series of five Sunday evening one-night stands; each evening had a theme, crossing over from theatrical presentation to party/club atmosphere, which they thought was a particularly queer work aesthetic. These included butch/femme night, horror night, and so on. They invited well-known and unknown performers to do something they had never done before. There was music and movement as well as text. Performers who had their initiation during the one-night stands went on to tour. They set up a two-week queer school, held at the Holborn Centre for the Performing Arts, giving classes all week in performance, acting, clowning, dance and singing, the latter leading to the establishment of the 'queer choir'. The café became a meeting place, a magnet for queer artists all over London, providing an alternative to the isolation in which they usually worked. There were 'cocktail seminars' held at cocktail time, at which drinks were served and queer political issues were discussed.

The Sweatshop's funding was still primarily for tours. These were sometimes of already scripted commissioned work, sometimes of work devised by the company. In 1992 they toured *Drag Act*, a one-woman show by Claire Dowie, *Jack* by David Greenman and *Entering Queens* by Phyllis Nagy. In 1993–94 they toured *Stupid Cupid* by Phil Wilmot and *In Your Face* devised by the company, scripted by Jan Maloney. In 1994–95 there was *F***ing Martin* adapted by Malcolm Sutherland and *Lust and Comfort* devised by the company. I think it is worth noting what Lois had to say about *Lust and Comfort*,[50] a collaboration with Split Britches, directed by James Neale-Kennerley, since it gives us an insight into a collaborative, inventive way of working:

'The aesthetic reality was a very good marriage between my and James' approaches. We did divide the piece. The three of us wrote the piece together, James actually did writing on it and then James directed it and I performed it, so it was a real nice dove-tail. ... I had been having a conversation with someone about how we'd like to see *The Servant* again. We were talking about these queer references in lots of films, these older films and particularly around issues of dominance and submission and power and eroticism. We were having these conversations and I said "Oh, maybe we should do *The Servant*", just, you know, how you do, "Maybe we should do our version of *The Servant*". James is also very interested in these issues, so he said "Yes let's do that, let's do that". So we started looking at *The Servant*. We knew we wouldn't do the play *The Servant*, but we would do our particular treatment of it. So we began with this. And also Peggy and I thought that there's a lot of business going on in the community about trans-gender, and we'd worked for the middle part of our work together as butch/femme, so we thought, let's take this a lot further, let's play men, and see what that's about. Let's play men, play that relationship that dominance power, submission, sex relationship of men. So we started with that and as we began to research it, I found the play itself, once you sort of get the idea of the film, once you get the idea that Barrett is overtaking Tony and he sinks into this abyss of decadence, it doesn't really go anywhere. It leaves you at a certain point. So we decided we weren't going to leave it at a certain point. We just had been watching lots and lots of movies, which we always do when we're working on a piece, and we found images in *The Bitter Tears of Petra von Kant*, again around power and same-sex relationship. Sometimes they've just issued images like the orange carpet in the Petra von Kant movie and her telephone call, that pathetic telephone call, the rug with the 'phone. Peggy said "I want to do that". In the German accent, you know. We also wanted to play with class and expatriates, being outside your own country, as an example of being outside your own gender. And then we saw another film called *Amore*, which is a film version of Cocteau's *The Human Voice*, with Anna Magnani. And that film was just her on the 'phone with an ex-lover. We call that "the pathetic 'phone call". So we decided that Peggy wanted to do one of these as well. Then we also wanted to do a kind of Beckettian thing, you know, little scenes. These are the stylistic references that we had the desire to play with. And then, as with everything, we write from our own lives. We were in a long-term relationship, at the time we were in our fifteenth year, so there are lots of issues around power, around attraction, around loss of attraction, around monogamy, non-monogamy, our staying together for comfort, or leaving each other for lust. So we knew the theme of the play would be that long-term relationship, that working out of balance between lust and comfort. So we decided to do that as this couple who play this out through these elements, although that's not obvious in the beginning. What it is is Lois and Peggy play Tony and Barrett playing Karen and Petra playing Anna Magnani and playing themselves in the kind of Beckettian underground basement of their real day-to-day life and coming back together after nearly leaving each other.'[51]

Sweatshop's evolution from 1975 to 1995 is exemplified if one sets the 1995 production of Stella Duffy's *The Hand* beside *Any Woman Can*. *The Hand* is a piece of theatre which relies largely on performance for its effect, so the written script can give only an indication of what the total performance might be. The written play is violent, challenging the reader by confronting her with images of shocking physicality. The narrative is far from straightforward, the characters elusive: there is a voyeuristic old woman, twin sister lovers Beth and Amy, there are narrators Sarah and Lisa – the relationship between all of them is obscure. In one sense they are all each other, each other's bodies. This is a play about bodies, as violent and beautiful as those in Monique Wittig's *The Lesbian Body*. Birth and death are an inseparable part of life. Horror movie vignettes follow this sensual passage:

AMY: I had thought to have my life flash before me. Our
murderous birth, she and I playing, bathing together, the
first stirrings of sexual complicity so simple and direct. I
had thought to enjoy the panorama of my past. But as soon
as the beating sunshine dries out my veins, it dries out my
memories too. My pane of glass is now a mirror in which
I show them to themselves. My dry carcass hanging in the
window gives them the charming reflected smile of their
passion. My waning juices make her wax fatter. And I am
clear that death is not the end.

SARAH AND LISA:
You are malicious. I love you. You are vindictive. I love you. You terrorise me. I love you. You are nasty. I love you. You are cruel. I love you. You are like no other. I love you. You are poisonous. I love you.
You are you love I malicious I vicious are you I you vindictive you love poisonous I cruel are love other no you I like nasty you I terrorise you.[52]

In this piece poetry and performance have replaced more straight-forward 'political' messages. The politics of feminism is clearly the politics of the flesh.

Notes

1. Jill Posener, *Any Woman Can*, in Jill Davis (ed.), *Lesbian Plays* (London: Methuen, 1987), p. 15.
2. *Ibid.*, p. 24.
3. ICA = Institute of Contemporary Arts, London; CHE = Campaign for Homosexual Equality.
4. My source of information for this is an interview with Kate Crutchley, October 1994.
5. Posener, *Any Woman Can*, p. 15.
6. *Ibid.*
7. *Ibid.*, p. 16.
8. *Ibid.*, p. 18.
9. *Ibid.*
10. *Ibid.*, p. 21.
11. *Ibid.*, p. 25.
12. *Ibid.*, p. 27.
13. The Round House was an alternative theatre venue converted in the 1960s from an old railway turntable house in Camden.
14. This information is also based on my interview with Kate Crutchley in October 1994. The expression is hers!
15. Michelene Wandor, *Carry on Understudies* (London: Routledge & Kegan Paul, 1981), quoted in Lizbeth Goodman, *Contemporary Feminist Theatres: To Each Her Own* (London: Routledge, 1993), p. 76.
16. Interview with Kate Crutchley, October 1994.
17. *Ibid.*
18. *Ibid.*
19. Goodman, *Contemporary Feminist Theatres*, p. 126.
20. Rose Collis, 'Sister George is dead', in Trevor R. Griffiths and Margaret Llewellyn-Jones (eds), *British and Irish Dramatists since 1958: A Critical Handbook* (Buckingham: Open University Press, 1993), p. 81.
21. Sue Frumin, *Raising the Wreck*, unpublished script, p. 33.
22. *Ibid.*, p. 59.
23. Catherine Kilcoyne, *Julie*, in Jill Davis (ed.), *Lesbian Plays: Two* (London: Methuen, 1989), p. 36.
24. *Ibid.*

25. *Ibid.*, p. 43.
26. *Ibid.*
27. *Ibid.*, p. 45.
28. Quoted in Goodman, *Contemporary Feminist Theatres*, p. 110.
29. Jackie Kay, *Chiaroscuro*, in Davis (ed.), *Lesbian Plays*, p. 82.
30. *Ibid.*, p. 59.
31. *Ibid.*, p. 63.
32. *Ibid.*, p. 78.
33. *Ibid.*, p. 75.
34. *Ibid.*, p. 68.
35. Jackie Kay, *Twice Over*, in Philip Osment (ed.), *Gay Sweatshop: Four Plays and a Company* (London: Methuen, 1989), p. 123.
36. *Ibid.*, p. 139.
37. *Ibid.*, p. 144.
38. *Ibid.*, p. 141.
39. *Ibid.*, p. 132.
40. Unpublished script from Gay Sweatshop archives.
41. *Ibid.*
42. In Osment (ed.), *Gay Sweatshop: Four Plays and a Company*, pp. 139–40.
43. *Ibid.*, p. lxv.
44. Section 28 denied local councils the right to fund anything which promoted homosexuality as being 'normal'.
45. Osment (ed.), *Gay Sweatshop: Four Plays and a Company*, p. lxvi.
46. Justin Bond, *Bay Area Reporter*.
47. Spiderwoman was a group of mainly mature American women, formed from white and African–American women.
48. Jerzy Grotowski (b. 1933) is a Polish theatre director who influenced European performers through his notions of a 'Poor Theatre', relying on the actor's physical presence as a major means of communication of political ideas.
49. Interview with Lois Weaver, Brighton, May 1996.
50. Split Britches, *Lust and Comfort*, in Sue-Ellen Case (ed.), *Lesbian Practice/ Feminist Performance* (London: Routledge, 1996).
51. Interview with Lois Weaver.
52. Stella Duffy, *The Hand*, unpublished script with additional material by Cherry Smyth and Caroline Forbes. In this extract only Amy's words were written by Stella.

Chapter 4
Siren Theatre Company

Siren Theatre Company is the longest-running lesbian theatre collective in Britain today.[1]

Joyce Devlin wrote these words in 1989, shortly before Siren disbanded. Her article describing their work is the most detailed piece on them to date,[2] but it stops before the show for which they had the biggest funding and which was their biggest failure. For ten years the collective had produced radical work on a shoe-string with small grants from South East Regional Arts Drama Panel. A grant of £9,000 from the Arts Council of Great Britain led them into the kind of experiment they had not dared to make, a much more 'physical' theatre than they were used to. Tensions in the company were exacerbated, their audiences were bemused; they were refused funding for their next show on the basis of unsatisfactory reports. To quote one founder member, 'It was the end of the line.'[3]

It all began in Brighton in the late 1970s, with Tash Fairbanks and Jane Boston. Jane was a student at the University of Sussex while Tash was a trained actress, a writer and musician. Radical ideas were in the air, in the town as well as on the campus. Jane had 'come out' and joined women's groups whose main expression of political life seemed to be through dance and music and theatre. Jane's own background was mainly musical with some theatre at school. She and Tash formed a band, The Bright Girls, as well as devising shows on particular political issues such as abortion, with a mixed group of performers. There was a vigorous radical lesbian movement in Brighton, a town which has always had a very large gay and a considerable lesbian population. A small core of women from the larger group formed themselves into a separatist company, concerned only with women's issues. Jude Winter, Tash Fairbanks and Jane Boston became Siren Theatre Company and set about creating a show, collectively, with no one person playing a predominant role.

Collective writing is exciting but difficult. Conclusions are arrived at only after hours of argument. Looking back, Jane Boston recalled that the discussion and the clarification of political positions seemed to be more important than its theatrical expression. The group dynamic was interesting because of different class and cultural backgrounds and also because Jane and Tash were 'a couple'. Under these circumstances there is no collective mind which emerges, rather a reconciliation of individual differences. The basis for the debates was Mary Daly's *Gyn-Ecology*, a book which described instances of men's violence against women. The script was the subject of constant renegotiation. It was considered necessary to present their rage, their sense of injustice, in an entertaining form with music, songs and humour.

Siren's first show in 1980, *Mama's Gone A-Hunting*, was set in a courtroom at some time in the future. In the opening scene an androgynous, intergalactic judge listens to Woman arguing her case for leaving Man and the planet and establishing an all-female civilization elsewhere. For his part Man puts his case for Woman being vital to his life-support systems.

The 'play' continues with a series of loose-knit scenes demonstrating the violence that women had suffered throughout history. After calling a number of witnesses (the Virgin Mary, the Perfect Wife) the judge asks Woman if she would like to cross-examine a female witness. She replies, 'How can I? She's been silenced', like every other woman who said something he did not want to hear.[4]

Songs, readings, sketches, all combined to drive home the point. The show went on the road, all members of the company sharing the administrative work. Since there was very little money available they carried no set, had simple costumes made from dyed sheets, and used the most basic lighting. In spite of its hard-hitting attack on patriarchal society, it was generally well received and well reviewed. Siren was established.

The second show, *Curfew* (1981), is also set in the future; it is again about male violence against women, this time more specifically rape and men's control of women's sexuality. It was devised in a similar way to *Mama's Gone A-Hunting*, with Tash Fairbanks having more responsibility for the writing and Jude Winter and Jane Boston composing the music. The title refers to the danger that women feel if they go out at night, a curfew imposed by a society unwilling to admit that rape is totally unacceptable under any circumstances, that a woman never 'asks for it'. The show coincided with a campaign throughout the UK for women to 'reclaim the night'. When it played in Leeds, the city in which the 'Yorkshire Ripper', who had murdered several prostitutes, was still at large, it was particularly relevant.

There were three main characters struggling to survive in a world controlled by a mysterious 'Menace'. Charlene is a lifetime lesbian, who has no time for sexual politics, whose life centres round a lesbian bar. She refuses to become involved in direct action until her lover Tracey, who is involved in an underground resistance movement, is captured by one of the Menace's guards. Women who are with men are described as 'manned'. The third character, Fi, is such a woman, and the conflict between resistance to the oppressive regime and loyalty to her male lover bring about her breakdown.

Lesbianism is a more obvious issue in *Curfew*. The homophobic response of many feminists to the radical, separatist feminism represented by Siren is symbolized by Fi, who reacts to Tracey and Charlene exchanging a kiss with these words.

> Oh, I never realised you were weirdo, twisted, queer, maladjusted, neurotic, manhating, inadequate, lonely, lesser beings.[5]

This is reminiscent of the adjectives that Ginny appropriates at the beginning of Jill Posener's *Any Woman Can*, and similar to Yomi's revulsion in Jackie Kay's *Chiaroscuro*. However, the context is humorous and surrealistic. The production had the benefit of a little more money in the form of a guarantee against loss, which meant a set, albeit minimal, and a new member, Debra Trethewy, technician and percussionist. The radical lesbian message, presented as it was in an entertaining, non-caustic form, seemed to find favour with a surprisingly large audience. On the occasion I saw the show in Brighton, I was surprised to see as many men as women in the audience, apparently applauding the sentiments. It played to good houses and had good reviews. Like Gay Sweatshop, Siren was concerned with consciousness-raising and to this end engaged in discussion after the show. Their approach was more total, perhaps, in that they wanted to make their audience think but they also wanted to get through on an unconscious level.

In 1982 Britain went to war with Argentina over the Falkland Islands and in 1983 Siren produced a show, *From the Divine*, based on this somewhat unexpected event. In an article about drama and the Falklands, Derek Paget calls this war 'a post-modern war',[6] the features of the latter being (1) that it takes place in countries 'remote' from home, (2) it lasts a very short time, (3) it ends in 'victory', (4) it involves opposition to political systems readily constructed as unacceptable by home public opinion, (5) it is unlikely to provoke much opposition from the rest of the world, (6) it depends on intelligence techniques which give one side a massive advantage and it provides an opportunity to test new weapons, (7) the loss of life is small. These characteristics are common to all post-modern wars, but Paget identifies the most important characteristic of all as 'intertextuality'. 'Cultural mediation' of the Falklands situation resulted in it being perceived as being related to the kind of 'Britishness' displayed in films, especially those about the Second World War.

> The images mobilised for the post-modern war are constructed mainly from the collective cultural memory of an apparently unproblematic and heroically 'successful' conflict (The Second World War) but they must be seen ultimately in relation to 'unsuccessful' conflicts.[7]

Without, at this point, going into any detailed discussion about more general definitions of post-modernism, these kinds of 'intertextual' references and the use of popular images which are part of our cultural memory were basic to Siren's way of working, in their case for subversive, deconstructive purposes. They chose to make their comment on a recent military conflict by setting the action in 1940 in an army camp in Europe. The characters are entertainers, providing a cabaret for the troops. We see them on stage, playing a variety of other characters and in their dressing-room being 'themselves'. They are Lily, the ingenue, Ruby, the old trooper who plays the more 'tarty' roles, Effie, the down-trodden mistress of the troupe's manager, Harry. Harry is represented in person and as a ventriloquist's dummy manipulated by Effie. The only character outside the troupe is a working-class angel, a figure from beyond who wears a white plastic mac, white wellies, handbag and knitted hat to match. Her cockney accent and her particular attire when she appears at the very beginning of the play cut across popular notions of long flowing robes, wings and haloes. She is *not* an agent of God, who appears as a blustering father figure later in the play; she represents 'the Divine', the angels who have their own pacifist message to deliver to the world. To quote from her opening song:

> Beyond the sky
> Beyond Paradise
> Beyond beyond
> Are the Angels.

> Such Divine Interference
>   not God given
>   not King driven
> Beyond the sky
> Beyond even Paradise
>
> Past moonbeams
> And the like
> Are the rebel rays
> Chanting
> Resistance pays
> the rebel rays[8]

So she signifies a powerful resistance from a heavenly underclass, whose bold intervention in the ENSA cabaret will completely undermine the morale-boosting intentions, demonstrating instead the anarchic chaos of war.[9]

The first movement of interference is during a scene in which the dummy Harry allows himself to be hypnotized by Ruby as Madame Rubella in order to take a journey into the unknown, into the world of waiting spirits. He comes under the real influence of 'angel noise' inaudible to the others, audible to the audience. Instead of sticking to the agreed script he describes what he sees in the crystal ball as the face of a horrible big man who is going to kill him.

This scene is followed immediately by one in the dressing-room in which the Angel announces to Ruby that she is chosen to carry the message 'from the divine' because she is really on the same side. There are elements this time of more conventional angelic signs – a bright light, a heavenly sound and biblical language – 'fear not, Ruby, For you have been chosen'.[10] In fact it would seem that both Ruby and Lily have been chosen, since they both succumb to angel influence in a long song-and-dance routine, the dance being a number performed by Lily and Harry while Ruby sits at the piano playing a pastiche of a Noël Coward song. The song tells the story of a working-class woman, a cleaner who becomes a rumba dancer and marries her dance partner. He goes off to war, is described as missing presumed dead, and she becomes a national hero as bereaved widow. However, he returns, hoping for domestic bliss, which should be a happy ending. Instead, Lily rejects him, declares she has had enough of marriage and leaves him flat.

Disturbances come thick and fast thereafter, with the action becoming increasingly surrealistic. The character in the original script intended to represent a sympathetic British Army Officer, Colonel

Yobbo, is accused of sinking his new ship. He becomes a caricature of a brainless, sexist dictator, who meets a proper end when he slips on the stairs deliberately highly polished by his despised cleaning lady. There are scenes played out between a young pilot and his sister, originally intended to praise the lads of Bomber Command but which makes them look like mindless sadists, whose 'masculine' values lead to massacre and mayhem. It is patriarchal values which lead to war, which denigrate all the qualities considered to be 'feminine'. In his very language man has excluded woman, thereby creating a violent world.

In the beginning	Son of MAN
Was the WORD	MAN in the street
And the WORD	MAN-MADE, MANKIND
Has always been ME	Doesn't mean me
He says HE includes ME	At a loss for words
It's only semantics	None of them are mine
But I'm not fooled	Your words fail me
By the royal WE	Every time[11]

This song marks the introduction of a more obvious feminist theme, the contrast between masculine and feminine values, expressed through language. It is followed in the next scene by a call to resist patriarchal attempts to name and therefore define women. A woman mechanic in overalls, called Mary, is transformed into the essence of femininity in a flower costume when Harry addresses her as Flora. She appeals to Ruby, who was looking for a powerful female role-model, to join her as a flower, since flowers have power. Ruby refuses, thereby inspiring Harry's wrath.

LILY: (*desperately*) Come into the garden Jill. Before it's too late.

HARRY: Shut up, you.

RUBY: Leave her alone.

HARRY: Sun-hater! You refuse to be floral in any shape or form?

RUBY: Yes.

HARRY: (*treading on her*) Right. Anything you say will be totally disbelieved.

LILY: (*squealing in pain under his foot*) Don't let her hurt me. Keep her away

RUBY: Don't you see? You are an oppressed flower. And what is more you are a plastic op-pressed flower.[12]

Lily throws Harry off her – a final rejection of patriarchal power.

In one way this is the end of Harry. His women have turned against him, leaving him to carry on the show alone. For the audience there is an additional insight into the male mind when the Angel decides to show us what is inside the dummy Harry's head. His brain is clogged with stereotypes of masculinity and femininity, mainly the latter. The scene has powerful visual imagery – Shirley Temple taking a skull from her muff, pin-ups on an erotic calendar who substitute beer bottles for pictures of themselves, a photograph of a wife cradling a skull, woman and death identified with each other. Mainly Harry is imagining, or perhaps dreaming, of two sailors, Porky and Gus, exchanging reminiscences and anecdotes when they are assigned to the same cabin. Their initial macho posturings give way to the affection of buddies who confess their confusion about war. Porky's father beat and bullied him into being a 'man', demanding gratitude for brutality. It was to show that he was 'as big a man as my pa' that Porky joined up.

GUS: He must be a fine man. You must really love him.
        (*Pause. Porky's face crumples.*)
PORKY: I hate him. When I was a kid, he beat me till I couldn't
        move, then he'd lock me in my room without food for a
        week, then he'd hold my head in the water butt till I
        nearly drowned.
GUS: That's bad.
PORKY: But he did it for love. He wanted to teach me. I'm grateful
        to him.[13]

Porky has a dream of himself as Jesus, his father as God. He is forced down to earth, arousing his father's jealousy when he becomes something of a celebrity, so that God gets his henchman Gabriel to fix up an exterminator.

GOD: The Lord giveth and the Lord taketh away.[14]

Harry's head is thus full of received notions of heroism. The 'intertextual' references in this sequence are numerous – to war films, to 'buddy' films, even to a scene in Joan Littlewood's *Oh, What a Lovely War!* The fact that all these 'butch' characters are played by women gives them an extra artificiality. They are caricatures of caricatures.

There are a lot of men portrayed in *From the Divine*. It was jingoistic patriarchal values which were reanimated for the Falklands War, therefore any play about the war had to take on these values. On the surface it would seem that lesbianism has disappeared from the agenda, yet the angel's insistence on a total rejection of male values reflects a basically radical feminist position. There is an indication that after the end of the play Lily and Ruby will form a double act, will enter into a partnership that will be more than professional. Effie has shut Harry up in his box; she has taken over control.

Although devised by the company after the usual lengthy discussions, the show was scripted by Tash Fairbanks. An outside director was brought in for the first time, not a member of the company, and a very successful tour was organized during 1983. There was a general feeling that formal theatrical considerations were becoming increasingly important. There was still an extensive use of music and song, some of these being based on popular songs of the 1940s. Taped music was also used to add complexity. Material used by well-known entertainers – Noël Coward, Joyce Grenfell – was imitated or parodied. Tash Fairbanks used her ventriloquist's skills as Effie, displayed incredible virtuosity by also playing the Angel and Harry.

Tash was now firmly established as the group's writer and most versatile performer. There were tensions within the group which made it advisable for Jane Boston to play a mainly administrative role, although she still appeared as a musician. A new member, Hilary Ramsden, was recruited. Class distinction had always been a theme in Siren's work; in *Now Wash Your Hands Please* (1984) it became of major issue. The enormous gap between the haves and have-nots, the privileged elite created by a divisive educational system, the North–South divide, the Tory government's hypocrisy in claiming to promote equal opportunity while actually increasing the power of the ruling class, Thatcher's anti-unionism, all were held up for criticism. The title refers both to the notice to be found in public lavatories in Britain and to the expression 'to wash one's hands' of something, meaning to give up all responsibility, to have nothing more to do with something. In this case the reference is to the dishonesty of scientists who make discoveries but deny any responsibility for the disastrous consequences.

PHYLLIS: ... Look this has all been a terrible mistake, it's got nothing at all to do with me....

POLLY: Course not. You just make the big discoveries, win the Nobel prizes, then wash your hands of it all.[15]

Phyllis is a nuclear physicist who thinks she is going to deliver a lecture but finds herself on a train full of nuclear waste, since she has been identified by the man in charge, P.R., as the scientist who will

keep an eye on the dangerous material. There is a total misunderstanding when he tells her that this is the first train to have a 'You
Know What' – 'a receptacle for waste'. Phyllis, who, despite her lofty
intellect, is not the brightest of women, takes this to mean a lavatory,
which leads to frequent references to body, as well as nuclear, waste.
P.R., a Thatcherite, describes the Labour Party's defeat in lavatorial
terms:

> You see, the Labour Party went into the election with the
> grime, and let's face it, the shit of old out-moded policies
> all over one hand and the turds of the Militant Tendencies
> on the other. They came out on to the hustings without
> having flushed their differences down the pan, with their
> trousers still round their ankles.[16]

P.R. belongs to the upper-middle classes. He is ruthless in his
suppression of working-class opposition. He cannot bear to hear the
words 'union' and 'strike'. When the railway track runs out through
a lack of sleepers he demands that unemployed people, who are, after
all, nothing but a drain on the taxpayer's resources, should be used
as sleepers. His job on the train is to keep out potential demonstra-
tors and introduce the press to the happy nuclear family willing to ride
beside the radioactive material. His second-in-command, Bert, is from
the working classes, trying to be upwardly socially mobile, failing
because he is not from the right background:

P.R.:   (*Uncorking a rare Mouton for himself*) Life is not fair,
          Bert. We do not live in a perniciously suffocating egalitar-
          ian society of commissariats. This is England. I did not
          learn to appreciate the finer things of life on a day-trip to
          a Dieppe Hypermarket. With me it is second nature,
          absorbed through the stitching of the old school tie, and
          the osmosis that comes with breeding, Bert, and having
          forelocks constantly tugged in front of your eyes.[17]

Bert puts up with P.R's condescension for the sake of keeping a job.
However, he is not the class traitor he seems. 'He' is a 'she', the
daughter of a Yorkshire miner. In a scene reminiscent of *Hamlet*, her
father's ghost appears demanding vengeance for the destruction of the
coal industry in favour of nuclear power. She forms an alliance with
Phyllis, in spite of the fact that Phyllis is from a different class and
an intellectual:

PHYLLIS: ... Now, Bert, I know you really are a good sort.

BERT: *(still half asleep)* You do?

PHYLLIS: Yes, and just to prove to you that I am. *(She pulls her to her feet, closes her eyes, puts one hand on her heart and holds a sleepy and confused Bert's hand high in the air with the other.)*

> 'By bully off and jolly dee
> And lob it up the pitch
> The Girls can always count on me
> I swear I'll never snitch.
> By midnight feast and dorm hi-jinks
> And lemon pud for lunch
> By secret pash and Head Girl's winks
> Forever I'm one of the bunch,'
> There, now you know you can trust me.[18]

Although this language of boarding-school bonding is meaningless to Bert, she recognizes Phyllis as a friend who will help her get her revenge.

The other major character, Polly, is Greenham Common Woman disguised as the dumb blonde daughter in what is supposed to be the typical nuclear family. Underneath her curly wig she has short hair; her high heels are swapped when the time comes for Doc Martens. She is a ventriloquist with a family of dummies – her 'mother', Mrs Persil, her 'brother' Uri, and their dog Pluto. They are a nuclear family in the sense that they come from Sellafield, the site of a big nuclear power station. This little band has been created by Polly as part of her resistance to nuclear power and in particular the carrying of nuclear waste on a passenger train, an event which has been given much publicity. P.R. needed an 'ordinary' family to meet the press on the train, to reassure them that there was no danger: Polly has provided this family. Needless to say the combined feminist force of the three women is able to subvert P.R's whole scheme.

In a general sense *Now Wash Your Hands Please* is anti-nuclear, as *From the Divine* was anti-war. In a specific sense it attacks the policies of Margaret Thatcher's Tory government in running down the coal industry, the lifeblood of the working class, to replace it with nuclear power, the brainchild of 'arse-licking Universitied Technocrats'. Nuclear power in itself is bad, radiation kills, nuclear power in the hands of the Tories is doubly bad as a weapon in the class struggle. It has to be said that everyone is caricatured – the ghost of the Yorkshire miner and his daughter are stereotypes of representatives of the uneducated, ungrammatical masses. The popular image of the public school product, who knows about good wines, is contrasted with the cockney who has her own culture:

BERT: ... Yon superior, stuck-up sodding son of a burgundy. I bet *you* don't know where to get the best jellied eels in London on a Saturday night after the pubs shut. Well *I* do and I'm not telling. I've got my roots too.[19]

It is not quite clear what these roots are – East End London or Yorkshire mining village? At any rate they are working class, so that for every middle-class reminiscence, Bert offers one of her own:

BERT: As I sip my tea I'm always reminded of the sound of wood and leather.
PHYLLIS: Ah, willow bat on leather ball. Cricket, you mean.
BERT: No, leather boot and wooden truncheon, pickets, I mean. Always a good supper in the coach after a punch-up.[20]

The dialogue throughout is extremely witty in a surreal, Marx Brothers way. Wisecracks and puns abound, so many of them meaningful only to a British audience. Political comment is combined with having fun with words, as in the following extract, in which a satire of British Rail and Tory policies is followed by a string of place-names, all of them English cheeses:

P.R.:   ... Stranded in the side-lines of one of the few branch lines that haven't thrown out their Parliamentary candidate, with only a Buffet car selling powdered tea at 21 pence a cup, they could only watch helplessly as the Thatcher 125 Inter-City Express hurtles by. A smiling Jimmy Saville waves and offers a Student Railcard to anyone who can get a place in Further Education. The Tory high-speed express is streamlined, comfy, and powdered tea at 30 pence a cup, and the fact that no-one can afford it makes it all the more appealing.
CHORUS: This is the Age of the Train.
BERT: The train now standing at Platform One will call at Gloucester, Double Gloucester, Cheshire, Cheddar, Wensleydale, Derby and Lymeswold.
PHYLLIS: But I don't want to go to any of these places.
BERT: Hard cheese.[21]

The show is playful, fast-running and hard-hitting. It was cited in *City Limits* as one of the most remarkable productions of 1984, a year in which women were making their voices heard.[22]

Siren had already been speaking as women, as feminists, as radical feminists, since 1980. In 1985 they concluded that it was time to speak unambiguously as lesbians. Their work had always been informed by a radical lesbian consciousness but they had never openly publicized themselves as a lesbian group. The mid-1980s seemed the right time to 'come out' with a lesbian thriller. The works of Ann Bannon, written in the 1950s, had just been republished, resulting in a revival of interest in club life, 'low' life. There were nervous discussions about whether the use of the word 'lesbian' might jeopardize their chances of being taken by certain venues. It was decided that the words 'Lesbian Thriller' should appear on posters and flyers.

Set in mid 1950s New York at the time of the McCarthy purges of all those guilty of 'un-American' activities and also thirty years later in London in 1985, influenced by films of Raymond Chandler novels and British spy films, *Pulp* is about secrecy, deception and betrayal. All the characters are women, all lesbians. The Americans are Magda, of Czech origin, a former film star with a very shady past, sexually and politically, a victim of McCarthyism, now working for an unspecified organization as a hired killer; Heddy, a journalist in search of the 'simple truth'; Dolores, a waitress in a bar in love with Magda, who is the spitting image of her pin-up, Lana; and Kay, an incompetent detective. It is Kay who provides the link between the two countries, the two decades, by finding herself mysteriously transported from New York to London, where she becomes involved with Dagmar and Ella, both spies for the British government, one of them having been given the job of checking out the other's lesbianism, since dykes are not acceptable in the Secret Service. Therefore they are both closeted, both reporting on each other, both mistaking the identity of the odd American stranger who suddenly appears on the scene to prevent Dagmar being mown down by a car.

Kay, Dolores and Heddy are all attracted to Magda, the heartless villain of the piece. She is a Garbo-like figure, dangerously sexual, a killer. She shoots her employer; then, under orders, she shoots her lover Dolores because Dolores knows too much. She is the femme that every butch lusts after.

HEDDY: (*staring after Magda*) They just walked out of the door. Magda and all my dreams.

KAY: Put the two together and you wind up with the same thing in the end.

HEDDY: What do you mean?

KAY: Magda is the great Hollywood dream made flesh.

HEDDY: Magda's real.

KAY: Uhuh like all dreams, she seduced you.

HEDDY: The great Hollywood dream, is that all desire is?

KAY: All this one was.[23]

She is also the femme who divides butch brothers against each other, who wreaks havoc in the bosom of the 'family'. We have seen how the heterosexual nuclear family was satirized in *Now Wash Your Hands Please*; in *Pulp* we are offered the possibility of a family of a different sort, on the occasion of Dolores's birthday.

DOLORES: Hmm, hmm (*poses theatrically, as though at the Oscars*) Darlings. ... (*laughter*) I'd just like to say, I love you all. (*becomes more extravagant, more laughter*) I feel like we're all part of one big, happy family. (*becoming more serious, but still drunk and giggly*) No, seriously. I do, I do. I feel we're more family than a real family ... than my proper ... (*poshly*) ever so proper family ... (*laughter*) in whose ... whoops, to whose reluctant bosom I was born into.

KAY: (*with the bottle of bourbon*) I do solemnly re-baptise you into this holy spirit. (*pours some over her head*)

DOLORES: Now Magda. And Heddy. Do it to everyone. Go on. (*Kay does, to more laughter*) That's right.

(*They dance*)

DOLORES: There. Now we're all family, aren't we?

HEDDY: I guess we do have certain bonds between us.

MAGDA: Do we? How? Besides the obvious one. (*An intimacy becomes apparent between them that grows throughout the evening.*)

HEDDY: I suppose the bonds of people who have no bonds.

MAGDA: The loners of the earth.

HEDDY: In our different ways.[24]

These bonds are slender, since the position of an outsider is a vulnerable one which means that in the last analysis you will betray a friend to save your own skin: it is a matter of survival. Lesbians in the 1950s in the USA, especially if they had left-wing tendencies, had to look out for themselves.

In 1985 in London, Dagmar and Ella learn that lesbian lust may lead them into a trap, but it also leads them into love. They fall in love with each other. Dagmar is expected to denounce Ella, who tries to turn the tables on her by demonstrating that Dagmar herself is a dyke. Love gets in the way; they are unsure what to do. Dagmar leaves to agonize over her report; Ella announces to her German neighbour, Monika, that she is going to give up spying. In the final scene of the play Monika reveals her own secret – she had always given Ella to understand that she was a prisoner in a Nazi camp, in fact she was a guard. It was the only way she could remain alive. Another Judas, she nevertheless represents the wisdom of sad experience. She is able to see that Ella will free herself of conventions, prejudices, fears, in order to be her 'true' self:

MONIKA: ... You are capable of great love. And what you love you
           will love with passion. Somewhere deep down the ice
           begins to melt and will become a flood. Goodnight, Miss
           Ford.[25]

The resolution of both situations is that one character decides to have done with subterfuge, with hiding one's real opinions or one's real sexuality. Ella will go on to acknowledge lesbian passion; Heddy the journalist decides to come clean about her views on the present attitude of the US government by publishing a provocative article, which she knows will bring her to McCarthy's attention. Real and supportive friendship is offered to both – from Monika to Ella, from Kay to Heddy. The call to end the lying and concealment is the same as we heard in Jackie Kay's *Twice Over*.

According to Jane Boston, *Pulp* was profoundly influenced by the world of publishing, the stereotypes of pulp fiction, their relationship to readers, and the problem of trying to write 'the simple facts' for the popular press.[26] The language is the language of the American detective story, with a Bogart-like narrator, Heddy, whose opening monologue is reminiscent of *Sunset Boulevard*. The role is that of the male hero in this popular genre, but all the characters in *Pulp* are lesbians. The narration is dependent on the fact that women can desire women, the characters being essentially different from heterosexual men and women. Heddy and Kay only sound like a male reporter and detective; they do not behave like men.

Joyce Devlin considers *Pulp* to be Siren's best work, taken as an artistic whole. The company now had an administrator as well as using guest directors, which released the performers to concentrate on the design, acting and music. Tash Fairbank's script is remarkable in its mastery of different sorts of language. The dialogue in the English scenes is so different from those set in New York that at first one has the impression that there are two different writers at work. It is not simply a question of borrowing American slang from the movies: the deep structure of English and American cultures is faithfully and sensitively conveyed through speech patterns. The English scenes seem much more 'serious', perhaps because there is less immediately recognizable parody. Even Monika's incredible admission, that she was a prison guard, could be played either in high-camp fashion or as a truly emotional moment. Perhaps this accounts for the review in *City Limits*:

> If you're looking for a show that's daft, daffy and deliciously dizzy, see *Pulp*. If you're looking for a show that's serious, sinister and sad, see *Pulp*. This ambitious new play from the multi-talented Siren Theatre Company is two plays in one.[27]

Gender and desire were further explored in the next production, *Hotel Destiny*, directed by Bryony Lavery, who was already a well-established writer herself. I have been unable to consult a script of this, so the best comments are those made by Jane Boston on working on the production with a director external to the group:

'There was a conflict between Tash's writing, Bryony's writing and our vision of ourselves. We weren't easily directable. I don't think we were at all. I think we were notorious for saying "Yes" but we control all of those things, we've always done it. So there was no acquiescence for the process because we couldn't afford to. We couldn't give ourselves the peace of mind to go through a process and be led. We wanted too many contradictory things [from a director], we wanted someone to make us amazing and successful, someone who knew intimately our physical and emotional desires, who could read that script exactly as we thought it and work on all the levels that we always did. We always worked on far too many levels, I think, for an audience to digest at once.... We would make our theatre multi-layered and we would expect people to understand that immediately, and to know it and take pleasure in it.'[28]

The company had already worked for many weeks on a show before the director was brought in. A show was usually six months in preparation, the director being involved only during the last six weeks, at which stage the music was still being written, the choreography still undecided. It was difficult for a director to know how much control she would actually have.

'For *Hotel Destiny*, we also took up the idea of genre again.... We were always trying to find other forms to express our ideas that weren't necessarily rooted in Theatre but came from film or popular culture, so *Hotel Destiny* was very much country western, because we were interested in what it gave us – the flavour of the costume, the flavour of the song, the flavour of its world. It's hard to say why we did it, except that it gave us an instant form to subvert. It gave potential for theatricality, it gave us a popular culture world to play in perhaps.... Although we had these radical feminist origins, and were known to be pretty hard in a lot of ways, I think we were much more sponge-like as we went on through the eighties. I think it just seemed to be the thing to be aware of stylistics, and they were coming through in publishing more than theatre, and they were coming through in popular music more than theatre.'[29]

The publicity leaflet for the Oval House read as follows:

This Women's theatre company promise a wild west evening in South London. It was high noon. The sun was howling like a coyote. The horizon was dust and heat as four strangers rode into Town. Each woman rode alone to Hotel Destiny. Run your eyes down the guest list – they are all there. Rough Crockett, Chance Earp, Blame 'The Kid' Cassidy and (who the hell is) Miss Evans. Rough had bullets for eyes and a six-shooter for a mouth. No-one saw her arrive, but a tequila was waiting for her at the bar. In the corner Miss Evans slid quietly to the floor ... but who would lay the blame?[30]

The emphasis on style led to a diversification of talents within the group in the late 1980s. There was a return to the importance of music in *Hotel Destiny*; at the same time there were cabaret performances in *Chic to Chic*, Jane Boston and Jude Winter did a two-hander, *Les Les*, on the nature of lesbian relationships, and an extremely experimental piece, *Bubbly*, about the nature and construction of reality. To some extent this marked the beginning of a disintegration. After the success of *Pulp* they had all expected somehow that everything would be easier, that they would be 'looked after', that there might be major funding which would enable them to have the proper working conditions they wanted. That they might have a 'home' or base, rather than relying totally on tours and *ad hoc* rehearsal spaces. It was disappointing that none of this happened. Having an efficient administrator certainly helped to keep the company going. There was still a sense of excitement in the process of creating a play and a loyalty to the collective lesbian group, but it was all hard work for little reward.

Jane Boston used the image of a sponge soaking up the flavours of the moment. Towards the end of the 1980s physical theatre was becoming increasingly important in Britain, mainly through the Théâtre de Complicité, whose style of training, and performance was very influential. Hilary Ramsden had attended workshops organized by the Complicité group – her comic persona was largely 'physical', agility and play being basic to her performance. Jane comments:

'I was very probably threatened by that, in the sense that I couldn't control play. Play was spontaneous.... When we went to the workshops one had to, I felt, learn how to play, but I felt so serious about the issue, and I remember I found it quite painful being in the physical theatre workshops, because I didn't have the kind of freedom to let go that was required by that training. The game "le jeu" is about finding a joy and a kind of rapport and a sensitivity that is child-like, in a sense. It's sophisticated, but I'd been too used to being part of controlling a process, controlling ideas, and being involved with language, to undo that and to simply be, was very, very hard for me. In differing degrees, members of the company found they were skilled to approach that or not.'[31]

Out of this workshop experience came what was to be Siren's final show, *Swamp*. At last a proper sum had been granted by the Arts Council for the project. There were long arguments over the script. By then tensions over power and control were at their height. In physical theatre the script was secondary; Jane and Tash tended to hang on to the notion of writing and ideas. There was a clear schism over this issue. The script and the performance always seemed to be in conflict.

'We were really attempting to live on stage in a very different way, make the stage come alive in a very different way. We worked with someone who had worked with Complicité, who I personally found very threatening. Looking at the piece I could see the dynamics of the schism, and it never really worked as a total piece.'[32]

It was a failure, as far as the audiences were concerned. Those present on the opening night at the Gardner Centre for the Arts in Brighton were mystified. What they were presented with was a post-holocaust world in which three women are trapped in a swamp, metaphorically and physically. There was none of the usual humour, nor the political bite.

'I would read it psycho-dynamically and say it was actually where we were.... From that point of view it's totally fascinating. That's my way of finding fascination in what was pretty much a theatrical mess. Tash wasn't in it. She was missed as a performer and frustrated as a writer and I was frustrated as a performer and Jude [Winter] and

Hilary [Ramsden] were finding the rapport in the performance mode.'[33]

In spite of all the problems, the company was working on the next idea – a collaboration with gay men on the theme of restoration. Siren would start from a play by one of the little-known seventeenth-century dramatists and explore cross-dressing. They were refused funding on the basis of a bad report on *Swamp*. As usual by the time the Arts Council gave its verdict a good deal of research had already been done, the play had been chosen and the adaptation was under way. Without a grant the project was impossible, so the company was disbanded. Jude Winter and Hilary Ramsden went on to perform as a cabaret duo, Dorothy Talk and Jane Boston to teaching of drama and voice, Tash Fairbanks to concentrate on writing. Their administrator, Rose Sharp, subsequently became the administrator for Gay Sweatshop.

If Siren had been able to continue, their agenda might have been radically changed. Cross-dressing had been a natural part of most of their shows; they had played men in order to be able to represent male characters. The three or four performers were able to play an extraordinary range of parts. In *From the Divine* Tash played Harry playing younger and older men. The audience read Harry as a man, not as a cross-dressed woman. Bert in *Now Wash Your Hands Please* is first read as a man, then revealed as a woman disguised as a man in order to succeed in a man's world. The disguise does not reflect an aspect of the character's sexuality, but expresses her vulnerability as a member of the lower classes. The exploration of sexuality conveyed through dress, playing around with notions of gender with gay men, could well have demonstrated a marked shift from their original radical feminist position. Such a shift might have been necessary for their survival in the 1990s when 'queer' politics began to dominate the Gay Liberation Movement, and feminism became unfashionable.

Siren were always on the fringe. Their early shows played either in Brighton, at the Pavilion Theatre or the Nightingale, or at the Oval House in South London. When they became better known they were able to move north of the Thames to the Drill Hall for their London venue. They played small touring venues, attracting favourable reviews without becoming known to a wider audience. Lack of recognition and lack of money went hand in hand. Working as a collective was ultimately exhausting when differences of intention became hard to reconcile. Life on the fringe is tough at the best of times; when a group's *raison d'être* is called into question survival is unlikely.

Notes

1. Joyce Devlin, 'Siren Theatre Company: politics in performance', in Lynda Hart and Peggy Phelan (eds), *Acting Out: Feminist Performances* (Ann Arbor, MI: University of Michigan Press, 1995).
2. By the time this book is published, more definitive works may well have appeared, as they are already in preparation.
3. Interview with Jane Boston, February 1995.
4. Quoted by Devlin, 'Siren Theatre Company', p. 186.
5. *Ibid.*, p. 189.
6. Derek Paget, 'Oh what a lovely postmodern war: drama and the Falklands', in Graham Holderness (ed.), *The Politics of Theatre and Drama* (London: Macmillan, 1992), pp. 154–79.
7. *Ibid.*, p. 158.
8. Siren, *From the Divine*, unpublished script.
9. ENSA = Entertainments National Services Association.
10. Siren, *From the Divine*, p. 50.
11. *Ibid.*, p. 50.
12. *Ibid.*, p. 53.
13. *Ibid.*, p. 63.
14. *Ibid.*, p. 68.
15. Siren, *Now Wash Your Hands Please*, unpublished script, p. 10.
16. *Ibid.*, p. 2.
17. *Ibid.*, p. 37.
18. *Ibid.*, p. 41.
19. *Ibid.*, p. 37.
20. *Ibid.*, p. 47.
21. *Ibid.*, p. 2.
22. *City Limits,* quoted in Devlin, 'Siren Theatre Company', p. 193.
23. Siren, *Pulp*, unpublished script, p. 61.
24. *Ibid.*, p. 17.
25. *Ibid.*, p. 64.
26. Interview with Jane Boston, February 1995.
27. Barney Bardsley, 'Theatre', *City Limits*, 8–14 November 1985.
28. Interview with Jane Boston, February 1995.
29. *Ibid.*
30. Oval House publicity leaflet.
31. Interview with Jane Boston, February 1995.
32. *Ibid.*
33. *Ibid.*

Chapter 5

Coventry Lesbian Theatre Group: Hormone Imbalance, Hard Corps and Double Vision

Between 1976 and 1979 Jane Boston and Tash Fairbanks were involved in feminist politics in Brighton, in the University of Sussex and the town. During the same period in Coventry a group of women in their early or late twenties became interested in creating theatre that was quite specifically lesbian.

'We began out of a boredom with doing very traditional political activities. We'd been in all sorts of women's groups at university, talking about all sorts of things and working on very conventional women's movement things like abortion. We were all quite dispirited by it. We were interested in doing something that was a LESBIAN thing. Although we'd been in lesbian groups, there hadn't been a sense of direction, and it had been very theoretical, in that political way. We wanted to do something that was more interesting. At the time we were all in a very strong extended friendship group. We wanted to do something that was all together and that was fun.'[1]

They met at Warwick University, through the university lesbian group. They started to get together to play music, make up songs, changing the words of old songs to give them a lesbian meaning. The Coventry Lesbian Theatre Group (CLTG) was a formalization of their informal performances for each other. Their identity as lesbians was of paramount importance. They objected to venues advertising them as Coventry Women's Theatre Group, since they had broken away from 'mixed' (i.e. heterosexual women and lesbian) consciousness-raising groups, finding them unsatisfactory for lesbian-consciousness raising. This reflected a general dissatisfaction with lesbians in the Women's Liberation (WL) Movement. What happened in Coventry was symptomatic of what was happening throughout the UK:

'Our WL group actually had a massive split. The whole of the town group – which was THE group – split up and turned into one lot of lesbians and one lot who called themselves the Socialist Feminist group. We started to organize on our own because we had to.'[2]

They wanted to project a positive image of lesbians as fun-loving and funny. They based most of their sketches on their own experiences, including consciousness-raising. Their material was aimed at a lesbian audience, who would recognize the situation and the jokes. Within the security of the lesbian 'family' they could afford to be scathing about each other although they were aware that such sarcasm could make them very vulnerable in front of a straight female audience, who could not read them in the same way.

LOU: Some of the response was complete misunderstanding.

JANE: Do you remember Reading?

                     [*Laughter*]

LOU: Yes, Reading and the other one was Sheffield.... Where
there was a total silence at some point, a complete
misunderstanding about what we were doing. They all very
politely clapped at the END but they didn't know what
was going on.

                       ...

SUZANNE: I think there are things you can say within a lesbian
community like 'lezzie', and you can laugh at that because
you're a lesbian. But to do that with a heterosexual
audience ... it could be misunderstood or misinterpreted.[3]

They had no budget and no rehearsal space apart from their own homes. They had a particular way of inventing their shows.

VICKY: We would think of something that would possibly be funny
if just entertaining or interesting. Then we'd go out into
the kitchen in twos and threes and we'd have to makc
something up and come back and do it for the others. If
the others thought it was funny then we kept it. Literally
that was it. We didn't have any props, we had a suitcase.[4]

Performances in public were partly improvised. They all wanted to do everything – sing, dance, tell jokes, play instruments. They were close enough to feel free to talk about each other on stage, without working out any off-stage tensions, which was strictly against their rules. During the two years of their existence they felt compelled to stick together, whatever their disagreements or emotional involvements might be. Since there were no more than twenty 'out' lesbians in Coventry, membership of the minority imposed loyalty.

SUZANNE: I think in Coventry we felt it was US and THEM. THEM was society and the world outside, and there was us, a small group, and quite a vulnerable group – I mean we occasionally got beaten up and things like that.... So it was very tight-knit and supportive.[5]

They never regarded themselves in any way as 'professional' performers. The payments they received from the organization who hired them never covered their expenses, which meant that they had to earn a living in other ways. Unlike Siren, theatre was not their whole life; they were simply 'good old dykes' having fun on stage. After two years they moved away from Coventry, some of them to London, where they stayed in touch as friends. Their last two shows were more difficult to organize since the group was already scattered.

JANE: The theatre group couldn't continue because we really weren't in and out of each other's lives or around just to chat each day about a new idea or whatever. We were in other bands and stuff and nearly all of us on some level have carried on doing 'artistic' things.[6]

The CLTG women were separatist, more defiantly 'out' than Siren, on and off-stage. They marched around the streets in gangs, wearing badges, boots, waistcoats, cutting their hair very short, provoking men. The fact that they were beaten up several times was no deterrent. Their friendship and their political ideals persisted well beyond the existence of their theatre group:

JANE: But because we brought our group to London from Coventry, in some ways it's still there. We were fortunate then. Even though you might not think it when you're in the middle of a terrible time like we've had recently. And I don't think we could've done it if we'd just met up in London – I really don't. Not to have gone through that bad a time and had to face up to that we probably all do still like each other.

VICKY: You don't necessarily see a future but you certainly don't see an end of it. I can't imagine it for ever.

LILIAN: Stopping?

VICKY: No. The kind of bond that was made then is not something that will ever disappear – not for me.

JANE: No, I don't think so.

SUZANNE: That's right.

JANE: Some of us had terrible rows and conflicts. That makes me
            think it will go on and on – because it's still there after all
            that.

VICKY: Most of us – in the combination of everyone – we have all
            LOVED each other – a lot!

OTHERS: Yeah. Yes. Mmm.

JANE: So we probably still will.[7]

The death of CLTG coincided more or less with the formation of
Hormone Imbalance, a lesbian company, taking their name from the
notion that lesbianism is caused by a hormonal imbalance in the body.
It was among the first of many lesbian groups to play at the Oval
House theatre. Their opening revue-style show was about control. In
one scene, lesbian actresses struggle against the dominance of their
director as they put a revue together; in another scene, lesbian characters in a short story try to escape from the control of the author; in
another, lesbians are subjected to aversion therapy. One of the scenes,
in which Ophelia is forced into a marriage with Hamlet, although she
was really in love with her maid, was developed by Melissa Murray
into a full-length verse play, *Ophelia*, performed in late 1979.
Unfortunately lack of funding obliged the company to disband after
the production.[8]

Three years later more than twenty women performed a play by Jill
Flemming, *Lovers and Other Enemies*, as part of the 1982 Pink
Festival. They called themselves Gauche for this production; subsequently a few of them stayed together as Hard Corps. Among them
were Jill Flemming, Adele Saleem, Sandy Lester, Karen Parker,
Debby Klein and Sarah McNair. The cast of *Lovers and Other
Enemies* was a mixed bunch: some had no training, some were at
drama school, some had just finished drama school and some already
had both training and professional experience. Some already knew
each other; others were complete strangers. They had been recruited
through a variety of means, including advertising. This is a very
different situation from that of Siren or CLTG because there is no
collective writing, or even exchange of initial ideas, the script being
complete before the actresses are found.

Sarah McNair had arrived in London two years previously from
South Africa, where she had been performing a show with two other
women in the Market Theatre, Johannesburg, and in Cape Town. It
was a review about singing sisters which they took to the Edinburgh

Festival, calling themselves Skirted Issue. It was so successful that they were engaged to play for six weeks at the Mayfair Theatre in the West End. Sarah received a script of *Lovers and Other Enemies* through the post, with the suggestion that she might like a part in it. Having read it, she felt that the content was too 'dykey' for her to be able to handle, her previous work having been feminist rather than lesbian. She decided to return the script to the writer by hand with an explanation of why she had to decline the offer. As she was about to put it through the author's letter box, the door opened and Jill Flemming said 'Can you come up and do the reading because somebody has dropped out as Cleopatra?'[9]

Needless to say the reading led to a complete involvement, the idea of working with so many lesbians being very attractive, in spite of Sarah's suspicion that this might be detrimental to her theatrical career:

'I kind of sensed that it might be the kiss of death, and I still think that it probably is for a lot of actors, because once you're branded a lesbian, it gets a bit ... I mean, not that it matters for a lot of people, you know, I certainly didn't care when I decided to get into it, because the audiences are so amazing. You always have full houses, all these women just loving everything you do.... But I think the difficulty in casting sometimes, and why people don't come out, is because they know that'll be it, they might not be touched again.'[10]

Gauche's committed core, Hard Corps, went on to revive a slimmed-down latent pantomime version of *Lovers and Other Enemies*, described in its publicity as:

The bizarre, passionate and hilarious attempts of the characters to find the answer to the eternal question, 'which comes first – the sex or the politics?' The strengths of individuals who don't give a damn or have trouble remembering what the question was in the first place. Set in Highgate Cemetery, Lesbian Nation, Hampstead Heath and a desert, The Communist Prevention of Natural Death Party is the vehicle through which each character thinks she might continue her search for this elusive Truth. Confusion is the name of the game and everybody's playing it.[11]

This alternated with a new Flemming play which was advertised under two titles, *For She's a Jolly Good Fellow* (the author's title) and *Running Out of Time* (the director, Sandy Lester's, title). This was 'a farce about political manipulation, artistic freedom, closet lesbians and small town communities'.[12]

The action centres on an exhibition of a young artist, Ingrid, whose lover, Thea, is determined she should win a substantial award. The final decision will be made by County Councillor Mrs Harriet Hatchet, a powerful figure who works the system to her own advantage. Thea persuades Harriet to visit the exhibition. The result is explosive as the diverse people in Ingrid's life are forced to confront the reality of power, and the manipulative games that inevitably ensue.

The core shrank further, leaving just four full members, Sarah McNair, Sandy Lester, Adele Saleem and the designer Catti Calthrop. They decided to focus on notorious lesbians, starting with Radclyffe Hall. Adele Saleem wrote the script of *John*, which Sarah describes as 'basically a biography'.

'Michele who directed it wasn't a lesbian, but she'd done a lot of stuff before. She worked with Adele on the script, because originally it was going to be all flash backs, not in chronological order, and she made her put it in chronological order.... It had songs....

We wanted to do entertainment for lesbians, we didn't want to stand on any soap boxes.'[13]

Entertainment, as opposed to political message, was emphasized in the flyer for the Oval House production in February 1985:

John is a lavatory ... a prostitute's client ... no, John is the Baptist, a boat, a fish, a typical Englishman, a plain man, a wild pansy, a black servant, a contraceptive, a brush-off dear.... Radclyffe Hall is John. (No, it's not another play about our feminist foremothers, it's a whodunit and who she did it with.) She wrote *The Well of Loneliness*, a sentimental melodramatic lesbian love story which was banned, but read under the bedclothes by boarding school girls, and in brown paper covers, by their mother.

Una is the friend of John. She likes Dachshunds, wears a monocle and smokes small green cigars.

Radclyffe Hall is the Queen of Broken Hearts.

John is a...

Hard Core is committed to theatrical hedonism and Torville and Dean emotion-packed spectacle. Their first productions ... were hailed as 'Lesbian high camp', '... a welcome antidote, zany, rampant and rude', with 'a few smart one-liners and much heavy puffing' and 'enough creative muscle to trash the closet door'.[14]

The show went on tour after opening at the Oval. At more or less the same time two original members, Karen Parker and Debby Klein, who had broken away to form their own cabaret duo, wrote a revue for themselves and Hard Corps. This was called *For Ever* and was described as centring around a 'lesbian feminist orgy'.

John was followed by *Les Autres (That Lot)* written by Sarah McNair, inspired by the 'women of the left bank', mainly British and American ex-patriots living in Paris at the beginning of the twentieth century, including Nathalie Barney, Romaine Brooks and the well-known lesbian poet Renée Vivien a.k.a. Pauline Tarn. As usual it was a loose-knit structure of sketches and songs, predominantly comic. The flyer reads:

LES AUTRES. A tango for three to a glorious celebratory beat
Yes – Hard Corps go poetry.
Do you love 'one alone' and 'all or nothing' like the ill-fated Renée Vivien (1877–1909) or do you believe in the love of turtles who bill and coo with many mates which increases all the more their store of love? Hard Corps cast aside Camp (honest) and bare their souls – or at the very least, the undersides of their feet in this turn of the century (plus three decades) drama.
CAST: Sarah McNair, Adele Saleem and Catti Calthrop.
Stage Manager – Corrine Mackavoy.
PLUS! 20 Rue Jacob
Nathalie Barney presided over the most famous salon in Paris for 50 years. We invite you to partake of the heady atmosphere, the tinkle of teacups, the grace, the wit, the dignified abandon – everything but the powdered perukes of an eighteenth century salon. Very special guests at this Oval only event to celebrate LES AUTRES. Including Colette, 'Henry King', 'Mata Hari', 'The Dolly Sisters', a different guest each night. Dress = 1920.[15]

In 1986, joined by Parker and Klein, Hard Corps performed a third play by Jill Flemming, *The Rug of Identity*, opening as usual at the Oval.[16] I shall discuss the script in detail since the play's themes, couched in fast-moving witty dialogue, represent some of the most common preoccupations of lesbian dramatists.

Two friends, Joanna and Laurie, who subsequently become lovers, are having serious problems with their mothers. Joanna's mother, Mona, is about to be hanged for murder, having worked as a hired assassin to supplement her meagre income. For her part Joanna has made money out of publishing the violent stories her mother told her. The fact that these stories were actually based on 'truth' comes as a revelation when she visits her mother in prison. Nevertheless, out of filial loyalty she promises to seek out her mother's last 'employer', who informed the police. This employer is a woman who has a bank account in Milton Keynes under the name of Mrs Gambell. She carried around one of the victim's fingers, rolled in gold.

Laurie's mother, Mrs Proctor, descends on her daughter unexpectedly, having been thrown out by Laurie's brother, David. It soon becomes evident that she is a double sex change who is trying to extort money from her children to have the operation reversed yet again. She is an unruly, riotous woman, a sponger, a nymphomaniac and a liar. At some point she had a husband – the father of her children – to whom she refers on a couple of occasions, but who has disappeared from the picture, presumably confused by her gender dysphoria. We learn that David has banished her because he associates her with the murder of his fiancée. In fact in the final scene she is revealed as the Mrs Gambell who hired Joanna's mother. She is also revealed as Joanna's father. As well as confessing to her infamous profession, Mona had confessed to Joanna that the latter was *not*, as she had always believed, the fruit of AID,[17] but the product of a passionate moment over a seat in Charing Cross Gents' Lavatory. All of a sudden the idea of 'father' had taken on a concrete reality for Joanna. She is now convinced that she must find out the identity of her progenitor to establish her own identity. What she discovers, of course, merely adds to the confusion, since her father turns out to be Laurie's mother, which places her in an odd relationship with Laurie herself. What is identity anyhow? Is it established by naming, by sexuality, by one's status within the family, or by documents? The end of the play poses all these questions.

LAURIE: Mother (*to Joanna*) I've brought you your papers.

JOANNA: Darling, that shows you validate my existence.

LAURIE: What I bring you is stronger than a locker, mightier than maternal love, and more powerful still than the stench of the sewers that draws you here.

MRS PROCTOR:
Did you bring me anything to eat?

JOANNA: Laurie, this is my father.

MRS PROCTOR:
Haven't I got a name?

JOANNA: Laurie, this is my father, Mrs Proctor.

LAURIE: Impossible.

(*Mona enters. She sees money in Mrs Proctor's hands*)

MONA: My maintenance!

JOANNA: Mummy!

MRS PROCTOR:

   (*money taken out of her hands by Mona*) Dearest?

JOANNA: (*to Laurie*) Sister.

LAURIE: Lover!

MRS PROCTOR:

   Incest.

LAURIE: (*to Mrs Proctor*) Sisterhood!

   (*Prison Officer turns round from urinal with keys in hand*)

PRISON OFFICER· (*making a clicking noise as if unlocking a door*)
   Cosy!
   (*Lights two freeze shots of Victorian family. Bow.
   Blackout*)[18]

An identity as mother is established by giving birth, as father by providing the necessary sperm. However, these would seem to be the simple facts of parenthood which do not provide what we require from an 'identity', that is a clear image of ourselves. Such minimal facts would seem to be meaningless without associated roles. Joanna believes that if she discovers who her father is, she will 'find herself'. Finding a father who is biologically someone else's mother but who does not fit the stereotype of either parent, is merely disappointing.

Neither mother behaves in the way we expect a mother to behave. Both are more anarchic than their daughters, with no sense of responsibility. Mona claims that she started her life of crime because it was the only way she could support them both; however, it did not take her long to get a taste for it. Selfish to the end, she puts a clause in her will which makes it impossible for Joanna to inherit her property until she has written her mother's 'autobiography'.

MONA: Time's up. Better go now, sweet (*she gives her the
   portfolio, the document with ribbons that she has just
   signed*). I'm putting my legacy in your hands. In a few
   minutes I shall be a human pendulum. Think, is that how
   you want to remember your mother?

JOANNA: God no! I shall have enough trouble altering my birth
   certificate as it is.

MONA: All my love, Jo, this will be a test of yours.[19]

To Mona her daughter seems boringly 'straight', restricted by current notions of political correctness, unable simply to let go and be relaxed. She is quite happy for Joanna to be a lesbian (although heterosexual herself, she is having an affair with the female prison officer); she is unhappy about her solemnity. In fact, part of Joanna's anxiety in the opening scenes is due to having discovered through a urine test that she is not actually lesbian, in spite of having had 'all the right contractions and swellings'. She is on the point of giving up sex when Laurie seduces her. Mona doesn't have the slightest problem with any variety of sex, since 'we all make the same sounds in bed'; celibacy, on the other hand, fills her with dismay:

MONA: ... You'll find yourself standing in a corner of one of those awful bars, wishing you could ... pop out of your body. You can't abstain for the rest of your life. You've got to take the responsibility for your swellings and contractions like everyone else.[20]

The unprincipled, fun-loving, sexually uninhibited mother is thus set against the anxious, politically conscious, sexually confused daughter.

The most unprincipled character of all is Mrs Proctor, whose 'love' for her children is nothing more than economic dependency. She needs them to provide her with a roof over her head, with all the food she wants and with the price of another sex-change operation. She is obsessed with eating and with penises. She's had one taken away, now she wants it back. Her dilemma seems to be whether she really prefers to have one attached or whether she likes them best on other people. When she gives so-called motherly advice about relationships we see a parody of 'normal' mother–daughter exchanges:

MRS PROCTOR:
          Honestly Laurie, all this jumping from one Harvey to another, it's not proper for a woman.
LAURIE: Oh, so it's okay if you're a man, eh?
MRS PROCTOR:
          A man has to have experience.
LAURIE: That's what I'm getting – experience.
MRS PROCTOR:
          ... And a woman has to get pregnant.
LAURIE: Really?
(*Mrs Proctor thumps the sofa for Laurie to sit next to her*)
MRS PROCTOR:
          Who do you think's going to look after you when you're old? Your dummy? You've got your looks now, but just

you wait till you're an ageing woman and there is no pair
of slippers panting after you. I'll tell you what men are
like – quite happy to wear women's clothes, but none of
them would ever want to be one and I should know.[21]

To keep her mother quiet, Laurie pretends to have a male flatmate
called Harvey, whereas all she actually has is a tailor's dummy, on
which she models clothes to sell in her chic boutique in Covent
Garden. When Joanna becomes 'available', Laurie is free to explore
her latent lesbianism.

LAURIE: (*pause*) Really, I should be the lesbian not you.
JOANNA: Why shouldn't I be? I'm a woman, I've a right to be a
lesbian like everybody else. Try if you think it's so easy.
I'd have thought you'd have tried everything.
LAURIE: You'd think so, wouldn't you? I mix with enough women.
But no, I'm still a Harvey Wallbanger. It's the only way I
can do it. Lying down seems like such a commitment. I
think I could do it with a woman, but I'm not sure there'd
be much difference. Take you and Marilyn, for instance.
JOANNA: For WHAT instance? How would you know what the
difference is?
LAURIE: Well I can only speak for myself, but ...
JOANNA: That's all you can do, speak and talk for yourself. I have
been traumatised today more times than I care to relate,
and all you can do is criticise my sexuality ... and I
thought you were attracted to me.[22]

Lesbianism is something which Mrs Proctor claims to find completely
baffling. She can't imagine what women do with each other.

MRS PROCTOR:
Carnal knowledge? Are you trying to tell me you lust after
your own sex?
LAURIE: Is that so very strange to you?
MRS PROCTOR:
No matter what I've been in the past, I've always been
one thing, and that's consistent. But a *woman*? What do
you do? Do you play with each other's breasts?
LAURIE: We don't play with each other's breasts, we make love.[23]

The mother–daughter bond is strange but real enough to cause jealousy, both on the part of Mrs Proctor, of her daughter's lesbian lover,
and on the part of Joanna, of Mrs Proctor.

MRS PROCTOR:
> You only get the scraps of her affection. My daughter
> would do more for me than for anybody else in the whole
> wide world, and when the time comes when she'll have to
> choose between us, I know who she'll put first.[24]

JOANNA: What about your mother? I insist there be no other women
in your life.

LAURIE: A night without sheets and blankets will have cooled her
maternal passion.

JOANNA: Her name must never come between us. My problems
must consume you utterly. Oh Laurie, I could not even
bear it if you were breastfed.[25]

Mona and Mrs Proctor expect much of their daughters. Meeting
Mona's ghost in the men's lavatory, Mrs Proctor announces that sex
is more satisfactory than motherhood, she always got more out of it.
Mona's ghost bewails her own single-minded dedication to Joanna,
who has ultimately failed her, by considering the search for her father
more important than the publication of her mother's biography. *The
Rug of Identity* demonstrates that the control the very idea of family
exerts, in spite of its contradictions, can be opposed by sisterhood, by
lesbian feminism.

Hard Corps disbanded after this production; however, several of
their members had been used, and continued to be used, by other
companies. In 1985 Parker and Klein presented *Coming Soon* at the
Oval, with a cast that included Sarah McNair, with Catti Calthrop as
one of the costume designers. It was almost the original Hard Corps
team. Parker and Klein wanted to continue to provide lesbians with a
good night out. Debby Klein, the author, describes her intentions
thus:

> As a writer I've never wanted to explain or justify gay sexuality, or dwell
> on how oppressed we are.... I also wanted to reclaim the trivial, and to
> crush, once and for all, the myth that only gay men can be camp.
>
> ...
>
> We performed it on a bright pink set presided over by a photograph of Joan
> Collins in her underwear, lit by a glowing pink triangle. Maggie Nichols
> used her improvisational genius to create a 'live sound track', giving each
> character an individual theme tune and enhancing the dramatic moment.
> We issued every member of the audience with a square of pink toilet paper,
> inviting them to weep copiously into it should the distressing emotional
> realism of the piece overcome them.[26]

Obviously the relationship between audience and performers at the Oval House was special, being one of enthusiastic, supportive sisterhood. Ironically this militated against Arts Council funding, since the two major criticisms of the Drama Panel representative were first, he felt alienated in the Oval café, and second, the cast were obviously playing to an audience of friends. Debby Klein comments, ruefully: 'Presumably making lesbians laugh doesn't merit an Arts Council grant'.[27]

Coming Soon, as its title suggests, is about sex and sexual attraction. Inspired by American soap operas such as *Dynasty*, the family is also a central element of the plot. Ginny (a sculptress) and Kay (a psychosexual counsellor) share a house which belongs to Kay's mother. They have advertised for a lodger to take the spare room, but unknown to Kay, Ginny has changed the advertisement from 'Two socialist feminists seek considerate woman for house share' to 'Gorgeous blonde and tempestuous redhead want rampant dyke for spare room'. Bentley, a swimming-pool attendant, is the only suitable applicant – a more rampant dyke could scarcely be found. Not only is she rampant but also she is irresistible, her animal magnetism working its spell on every one of the other characters.

Complication begins to pile on complication. Ginny falls madly in love with Bernie, an ex-nun wanted by the Mafia for uncovering their dealings with the Roman Catholic Church. Bernie fled to the convent in the first place to atone for what she thought was the death of her girlfriend, caught in a fire started accidentally by Bernie in a jealous rage. Needless to say, Bernie's girlfriend is not dead after all; in fact she turns out to be the sexy swimming-pool attendant, Bentley, rescued from the blaze in the nick of time, by the woman with whom she was having an affair. Bernie is still in love with Bentley, Kay has fallen in love with Bentley, Ginny falls out of love with Bernie and in love with Bentley, who finally heads off into the blue with the next-door neighbour who has been left a fortune and discovered sapphic love in Amsterdam. Making all this more difficult is Kay's twin sister Jade, the rich, wicked half who has all the bad qualities that Kay does not possess. Jade has manipulated her mother into signing over the house to her. She is a married woman, a closet lesbian. In an unexpected final twist Jade loses everything, Bernie's debt to the Mafia is paid off and Kay inherits the house. Kay and Ginny are left alone wondering how to phrase their next advertisement for a lodger, appreciating the comfort of solid friendship after the ravages of passion:

GINNY: What I love about you is that on the surface you're
           together, mature and completely sussed out ...

KAY: ... Yes ...
GINNY: And underneath you're as big a mess as I am.
KAY: Thanks a lot.
GINNY: You're welcome. I think we should drink a toast.
KAY: To us!
GINNY: To us!
KAY: To the women of our dreams.
GINNY: To our insane fantasies.
KAY: To friendship.
GINNY: Yes ... lovers come and go but where would we be
          without friends?
KAY: Is that the message?
GINNY *shrugs.*
          (*Blackout*)[28]

Coming Soon takes a heterosexual dramatic form, the soap opera, the descendant of nineteenth-century melodrama, and turns it into a highly camp lesbian version in which every emotion is clearly false. The handkerchiefs distributed before the performance would be used by the audience in a flamboyant symbolic way, a pretence of sympathy, just as the boos and hisses greeting a pantomime villain (which, I imagine, greeted Jade's appearance) are a conventional symbol of our condemnation of wickedness. The message is not 'friends are more faithful than lovers'. If there is a message at all, it is rather 'we have appropriated this form of entertainment and given it a meaning for us. We too can have our soaps'. The discomfort of the Arts Council representative was due to a feeling of exclusion, the exclusion of the heterosexual from lesbian culture. The *Dynasty* and *Dallas* references were part of his own cultural background, the lesbian references were not. For a 'straight' audience member who can recognize and not recognize at the same time, the experience is disorientating; for lesbians it is exhilarating. The following speech, for example, could be taken very seriously whereas, like the rest of the play, it is imbued with camp irony:

KAY: Do you know what I did last night? I went on the town. If you
          can't beat her, I thought, join her. Can you imagine – me!
          The epitome of discretion – cruising in a downtown women's
          bar. I sat in a corner drinking a lot and not knowing what to
          do – I felt out of place. When anyone smiled at me, I looked
          away. The last dance came – the slow one – everyone hit the
          dance floor like a herd of lemmings. I sat in my corner and
          tried to feel superior. I couldn't. I wanted you and failing that

I wanted anyone. Then came the tap on my shoulder. She asked me to dance. We danced. She asked me to go back with her. I went.

Oh we had a wild night Bentley. Her name was Ruth – her lover had walked out on her a month ago. They'd been together eight years. It all came out, the insecurity, the pain, the rejection. She talked and I listened and also facilitated the process using my not inconsiderable counselling skills. And finally, I grabbed a couple of hours' sleep – on her sofa. In the morning she was so grateful, said I'd really helped her to face up to herself again. She felt so positive I felt like shit.[29]

Compare this with the description of a pick-up in Jill Posener's *Any Woman Can*:

GINNY: The air is close, closets are usually stale, the lighting theatrically tasteless – we see each other glamorised in the reddish gleam. Tinted flesh with half light. Dancing couples, foursomes drinking in corners, some chatting up at the bar, some deft rebuffs. Haven't I seen all this before, down the ol' meat market of the straight scene? (*Music is playing. The Older Woman appears beside Ginny. Their talk is overheard over the music. The music stops.*)

OLDER WOMAN:
Your place?
(*They leave the 'club' area*)
Not a palace, is it?

GINNY: It's my home.

OLDER WOMAN:
Come on then, let's get to bed. Why are you shaking? Nervous? No need to be nervous. You'll like it. Haven't you ever been picked up in a bar before?

GINNY: No, and I'm not exactly ... I'm not sure this is what I want.

OLDER WOMAN:
Come on, what's up with you? Of course it's what you want.

GINNY: I'm not sure.

OLDER WOMAN:
Look, you're wasting my time. You gave me the come-on in the club and now you're playing hard to get.

GINNY: Leave me alone.

OLDER WOMAN:

Oh grow up. You know what it's all about. I'm going.[30]

The beginning is similar, the unhappy woman on her own goes out looking for something, for somebody, makes contact, but the subsequent turn of events is completely different. However, both women end up with the conclusion that the evening was fairly catastrophic. We feel truly sympathetic towards Ginny; we laugh at Kay.

By the time *Coming Soon* was produced, Karen Parker and Debby Klein were a well-known double act in lesbian venues. The Oval audience would therefore recognize them not simply as characters but as themselves, in the roles of Ginny and Kay. The fact that they are alone together, raising their glasses to friendship at the end of the play, would therefore have another layer of meaning for their 'fans'.

Neither Hard Corps nor Parker and Klein had funding, which is one of the reasons that they could survive for only a few years at most. When things became tense between company members there was no reason to stay together. Sarah McNair says:

'We didn't ever have any funding. The Traverse [Edinburgh] paid us a fee which covered us going up there and back. Never enough for wages and when we went to Holland they paid expenses, so it meant it didn't cost anything to go there and they put us in a hotel, which was lovely, but, yes, you had to do it on the dole....

When we formed the company, it took up all your time basically, until it sort of crumbled and we didn't do any more; we did a few combinations with Parker and Klein and that was it really. After that we all worked with the Sadista Sisters on *Madonna in Slag City*.'[31]

Sarah's answer to my question 'Had Hard Corps run out of material, of things it wanted to say?' was as follows:

'No. There are lots more notorious lesbians that it could have explored. But it was hard, because you had to write these things, you know, as well. I'd never written anything before. I don't think Adele had, either, although we'd been in devised things in past experience from way back, but actively writing a play, especially if it's based on someone's life, it's very difficult to find ... it just sort of warbles on, through their life. Unless you're an experienced playwright, I think it's hard work and you're just swimming.'[32]

To end this chapter I shall discuss *Double Vision*, one of the works that Adele Saleem, the author of *John*, was involved in devising before she joined Hard Corps. *Double Vision*, performed in 1982 by the Women's Theatre Group, was part of a season which, to quote the director, Libby Mason, 'was intended to examine the ways in which women have struggled through the ages to find a positive dynamic between their personal and political lives'.[33]

The director's description of the collaborative process is interestingly reminiscent of the way Siren worked in its early days:

> The earliest stage was workshops involving the whole company – the cast, the director, the stage manager, the administrator and two performers who were not, in the end, to perform the piece. Out of these workshops certain content areas were synthesised – class differences between women, attitude towards child-bearing, ideological purity, lifestyles, to name but a few!
>
> The next stage was for the unit which would perform the play – two performers, a performer-musician and the director – to decide through improvisation and discussion, on characters and a story. More improvisation, discussion and scripting (by all four of us) followed, with collaboration and comment at certain points from other company members.
>
> ... The script of the original production was, of course, one of the last things to emerge. So when we came to work on it *as* a script, most of the foundation work, in terms of characterisation, the objectives of the scenes, the humour had already been done in improvisation.
>
> ... I have left the script more or less in the state to which it had evolved by the time the piece was performed because I believe it is important that it should be read as a record of the final stage of a devising process, rather than the kind of script a writer might present to a company for consideration.[34]

Throughout, *Double Vision* represents the different points of view of two women drawn to each other by some form of magnetism, who are unable to find a way to live harmoniously, happily, ever afterwards. The director is at pains to point out that their problems are not those which arise from their lesbianism. In that sense it is not a 'lesbian' play:

> What we wanted to say about relationships would, we hoped, have a resonance for heterosexual and gay women and men who experience the area of relationships as a significant political battlefield.[35]

Nevertheless, many of the problems highlighted in the songs and short scenes would not occur in a heterosexual couple. The absence of any fixed role-models leads the pair to agonized indecision:

CHUM: I just have to go now and have a think. It's all a bit – I
       don't quite know what's going on.

SPARKY: Frightened in case I ask you to move in? I won't.

CHUM: Well, you must feel a bit strange, too.

SPARKY: No. I feel like I'd really like to see you again – like in about half an hour. Can't see you then, you're seeing the other woman. All right, I'll see you at lunch time – if you can't make it then, well, this evening. This evening you're seeing Tricky Dicky, so I'll say 'Let the little lady go': so let the little lady go.

CHUM: I'd rather you didn't call me the little lady. It's incredibly patronising. Oh, don't freeze.

SPARKY: All right then. Big Fat Momma.

CHUM: There's nothing wrong with being fat – if the rest of the world happens to regard the perfect shape for women to conform to.

    . . .

SPARKY: Do you want to do it again?

CHUM: No, maybe.

SPARKY: Sometime?

CHUM: I liked it, I really did.

SPARKY: What did you like?

CHUM: Oh that would take too long to explain.

SPARKY: I've got time. I liked this bit, and this bit and this bit.

CHUM: Yes, shh.[36]

This is the start of a relationship which is characterized by misunderstandings, by opposing positions. Sparky is the non-political one who becomes a militant activist. Chum is the political idealist who becomes the housewife longing for motherhood. Sparky has actually known motherhood; now she wants to play the child, with no sibling rivals. Nor can she stand the idea of Chum having sexual relations with a man, albeit gay, in order to produce a baby. The necessity to bring in an outsider as father, even if only via a syringe, is not a part of the lives of most heterosexual couples. This is what finally breaks up the Sparky–Chum couple. The creators of the drama wanted to leave several subsequent possibilities open. Instead of a neat rounding off, the narrator gives us alternatives to choose from:

NARRATOR:

    They found it impossible to live together, so they decided to live apart. But that's not the end of the story. There are at least three possible and plausible endings. In the first ending, the two decided that whatever it was that they had

was worth preserving, or working on in some forms, and
they tried to practicalise their politics....

In the second ending they hardly ever met at all, each
receding into her own world, occasionally meeting at
single sex parties or conferences....

In the third ending, Sparky came to believe that the way
forward was through direct action and that the time for
talking was past, while Chum continued working
methodically at her papers and poems, eventually
achieving minor success as an author.[37]

I have included this play because of its lesbian content, but mainly
as the kind of creation through improvisation that Adele Saleem,
playing Chum, had participated in before joining Hard Corps in 1983
As far as Women's Theatre Group were concerned, they were established on a different footing from the radical feminist co-operatives
we have so far examined, their concerns being feminist but not generally lesbian.

Notes

1. Interview with Jane Skeates, in Lilian Mohin, 'Interview with members of
   Coventry Lesbian Theatre Group', *Gossip 4* (London: Onlywomen Press, 1987),
   p. 59. This interview is the source of all my information about the CLTG.
2. *Ibid.*
3. Lou Hart, Jane Skeates, Suzanne Ciechomski, *ibid.*, p. 64.
4. Vicky Ryder, *ibid.*, p. 65.
5. Suzanne Ciechomski, *ibid.*, p. 71.
6. Jane Skeates, *ibid.*, p. 76.
7. Jane Skeates, Vicky Ryder, Lilian Mohin, Suzanne Ciechomski, *ibid.*, pp. 83–4.
8. This information is taken from Rose Collis, 'Sister George is dead', in Trevor
   R. Griffiths and Margaret Llewellyn-Jones (eds), *British and Irish Women
   Dramatists since 1958: A Critical Handbook* (Buckingham: Open University
   Press, 1993), p. 79.
9. Recounted in an interview with Sarah McNair, December 1994.
10. *Ibid.*
11. Oval House publicity leaflet, October 1985.
12. *Ibid.*
13. Interview with Sarah McNair, December 1994.
14. Oval House publicity leaflet, February 1985.
15. *Ibid.*
16. Jill Flemming, *The Rug of Identity*, in Jill Davis (ed.), *Lesbian Plays*
    (London: Methuen, 1987).
17. AID = artificial insemination by donor.
18. Flemming, *The Rug of Identity*, p. 110.
19. *Ibid.*, p. 91.
20. *Ibid.*, p. 88.

21. *Ibid.*, p. 97.
22. *Ibid.*, p. 94.
23. *Ibid.*, p. 104.
24. *Ibid.*, p. 102.
25. *Ibid.*, p. 101.
26. Debby Klein, *Coming Soon*, in Jill Davis (ed.), *Lesbian Plays: Two* (London: Methuen, 1989), p. 33.
27. *Ibid.*, p. 34.
28. *Ibid.*, p. 32.
29. *Ibid.*, p. 24.
30. Jill Posener, *Any Woman Can*, in Davis (ed.), *Lesbian Plays*, pp. 20–1.
31. Interview with Sarah McNair, December 1994.
32. *Ibid.*
33. Women's Theatre Group, *Double Vision*, in Davis (ed.), *Lesbian Plays*, p. 52.
34. *Ibid.*
35. *Ibid.*, p. 53.
36. *Ibid.*, pp. 34–5.
37. *Ibid.*, p. 49.

Chapter 6

Nitty Gritty and Shameful Practice

NITTY GRITTY

I have already mentioned Maro Green and Caroline Griffin's play *More* in Chapter 3 on Gay Sweatshop. I shall talk in a little more detail about Maro Green, who is the actress Penny Casdagli. My sources are an interview with her and her article, 'The Whole Nine Yards'.[1]

Penny Casdagli was born in Greece, so that English is not her native language. When she returns to Greece, her Greek is rusty enough for her to be identified as a foreigner. Therefore she feels that she does not belong to either culture. The only culture which is her own is lesbian; her only home is her identity as lesbian, which she discovered as an adolescent at her theatre school, a girls' boarding-school. Unfortunately all her professional experience in the theatre – as a drama student, as an actress, as a tutor in two major London drama schools – has reinforced her conviction that it is compulsory for women in the theatre to be heterosexual, which puts closeted lesbians at a great disadvantage from the moment they start their training.

> The burden of compulsory heterosexuality on the lesbian drama student is very great. She has to constantly imagine, in all situations from the formal text to 'free' improvisation, to watching her back at the coffee bar, *what if* she were straight, and act accordingly. Everything she does has to go through an extra imagination, and since much of the work in drama schools is designed to 'release the authentic self', she may never, unless through the disguise of metaphor, emotional substitution or other techniques, ever be able to do that. Because she finds herself subject to intolerable pressures to simulate heterosexuality, to survive she is most likely to resort to and engage in paradoxes: to reveal herself as a performer while protecting herself as a person; to dissemble in order to keep some integrity; and to feign an authentic spontaneous self whilst simultaneously giving it away. And it is very hard to get back.[2]

For gay men, because there will be a number of openly gay

members of staff, they will have 'a continuum to key into'. For the women there are no role-models, no curriculum provision. When Penny left drama school in the late 1960s, it was 'mandatory to be a dolly bird'. The odd lesbian who might appear would cause great excitement and would be the subject of much fascination.

During the ten years after drama school, in spite of having had lesbian relationships previously, for all the reasons given above Penny functioned as a heterosexual. Her main turning-point was the Women Live festival in 1980, inspired by a feminist-motivated movement within the theatre, which showed that instead of competing with each other professional actresses could co-operate. This was the dawning of her real political awareness, although her work at the Unicorn Children's Theatre had brought her into contact with a powerful lesbian role-model, Caryl Jenner, who ran the company.

At the time of Women Live, Penny was writing as well as acting. Her contact with other feminist lesbians encouraged her to think that it was no longer necessary to conceal her lesbianism from her straight fellow-performers in a touring production of an Alan Ayckbourn play. The result was more than disappointing.

> Opening out of town, in a university city, snowbound in a pub after the show, I told the man acting as my stage husband I was a lesbian feminist. The following Monday, in a new town, on stage, he shoved his tongue down my throat in what was blocked to be a casual peck on the cheek. This was the start of a campaign of extreme harassment. In the interval the Company Manager, who was gay, told me I was sabotaging the comedy of the play by changing the moves. After the performance, they took me into an empty dressing-room, which they prevented me leaving – the C.M. put his chair against it and got out his knitting and they humiliated me verbally. After they let me out I 'phoned the director to talk to them. They told him there was no problem. I was just upset. He believed them. No one in the company spoke to me after that. In the weeks that followed the harassment got worse. By then all the men had joined in to different extents: I was pinched on stage, they changed their entrances to trick me, hid my props (and what is Ayckbourn without props!), turned away visitors and would not allow any friends backstage.[3]

She fought back by refusing to go on stage one night unless, in the presence of the director, the company manager gave her an assurance that the harassment would stop. She resolved not to act in mainstream theatre ever again, a decision she has never regretted.

Penny Casdagli's first experience of presenting a piece of lesbian writing to a heterosexual workshop funded by the Gulbenkian

Foundation in the mid-1970s had been as discouraging as her 'coming out' as an actress. The reaction of the other members of the workshop was to attack and dismiss. Now, in the early 1980s, separatism in order to be able to express herself honestly and openly seemed the only way – separation from the mainstream, separation from hetero-sexual value systems.

I have included the description of Penny's experiences in a non-lesbian theatrical environment to emphasize the difficulty for those who had professional training before the 1970s to have the courage to declare their difference, thereby drastically reducing their chances of employment. It took more than ten years for Penny to dare to leave the closet; many are still in there.

The rehearsal reading of *More* at the Drill Hall as part of the Sweatshop Times Ten Festival in 1984 was a major theatrical break-through for Penny Casdagli, who had decided to write under the name of Maro Green. This was the first of three collaborations with Caroline Griffin (described more fully in Chapter 3). It became a full Sweatshop touring production. Penny describes it as lesbian theatre, as opposed to a lesbian play. She makes these distinctions:

> My definition of lesbian theatre ... is theatre made by lesbians, informed by their perspective, ... and performed within their control. ... The salient point is that its intentions and impetus are lesbian. It is *owned* by lesbians. ... Non-lesbian companies and mixed gay companies have done lesbian plays or performing pieces but this is just what it is: lesbian work not lesbian theatre.[4]

Everyone involved in *More* was lesbian; everyone 'owned' the decisions and process. The audience response was good, the reviews too; the collaboration was such a success that Caroline Griffin and Penny Casdagli founded their own theatre company, Nitty Gritty, to perform *Memorial Gardens*, a play about lesbians self-inseminating, creativity and the effects of child abuse. The Arts Council refused funding on the grounds of the director's inexperience. Most of the money needed for the production (which had additional costs because one of the actresses was in a wheelchair and lived in the North of England) was raised by writing to well-known theatre people asking for their support.

The lesbian play (as opposed to lesbian theatre) which was the final Green/Griffin piece was *Mortal*, performed by the Women's Theatre Group. It was 'about death and dying, passion and love, featuring three women and an angel on a raft'.[5] When the work was commis-sioned Women's Theatre Group was a collective; by the time it was produced two years later its structure was hierarchical, in response to Arts Council requirements:

> It had been workshopped on three different occasions by more than twenty different women, and it had been inherited by the Company's new artistic director, who said at the first read-through 'does anyone know how to direct this, because I don't!' Every joke was misunderstood, every idea was so hostilely questioned that the intuitive layer of the play was obliterated, and it was hell. Having seen all the previews, I attended the first night wearing ear plugs so as not to hear the text getting more and more mangled. Inevitably, it was trashed by the papers, yet still the gallant performers had to go on in it every night and try to make something of it, while scraping the egg off their faces. It was this experience which made me think very deeply about content and process and about how the means need to be identical with the aims and content of a play.[6]

Of course this kind of misreading of a text with a subsequent breakdown of significance can arise with any play. There are often changes of cast which interrupt the rapport which has already been established between the actors. Misunderstandings and misinterpretations are most likely to occur, however, when a text which has been written by two lesbians, from a totally lesbian point of view, passes into the hands of a series of heterosexual women, who are given leave to read their own preconceptions into the characterization. When lesbians lose control the play will take on a whole new meaning, or have no meaning at all.

Nitty Gritty was unfunded; its sister company, Neti Neti, established at more or less the same time by Penny Casdagli and Caroline Griffin to provide young people's theatre, was considered more favourably. This was not overtly lesbian, but was described as 'integrated': half the company are black, half white; half differently abled, often deaf or partially hearing; half lesbian and gay, half straight; half having a first language which is not English. Caroline was a teacher as well as a writer; Penny had worked with young people since 1975, had developed theatre for deaf and hearing children and in 1987, the year Neti Neti was founded, she had been given the British Drama Award for the Best Young People's Play, *Pardon Mr Punch*. Although the company did not produce any explicitly lesbian work, Penny maintains that everything they undertook was basically informed by their identities and the struggle to be allowed to express these identities.

In May 1995 when I interviewed her she had abandoned Neti Neti for all kinds of internal political reasons. In spite of attracting more attention than Nitty Gritty, obtaining money from the Arts Council had been difficult. In 1992 after many awards and appearing on thirteen television programmes, the company was refused a project grant on the grounds of an unfavourable show report (which is now becoming a familiar story!). It was concluded that the company had failed to fulfil its own aspirations. Upon asking to see the report in question they discovered that no one on the panel had been to see any of their shows for four years; the decision had been taken on show reports dating back to 1989. After they had organized an intensive campaign of protest they received their grant.

At this point in her creative life Penny no longer writes under the name Maro Green, not wishing to make divisions any more between 'lesbian' work and 'other' work. On reflection most of her plays from *The Green Ginger Smuggler*, a feminist children's play, have had a lesbian subtext. She is suspicious of labels, of definitions. She would not want to be too precise about her own identity at the moment. In a climate which is dominated by marketing and the language of marketing, she would rather remain silent and introspective than join in a game which is quite alien to her deeper self.

'One's definitions of oneself change all the time, which is quite right. Because of my own recent history, where I thought my roots were, these roots have been dislodged, one way and another through conflict or strife or other painful tactics. It's slaughtered the dogma out of me and even now I would hesitate to say that I am a lesbian. It's not going back into the closet – I think all these terms are up for grabs again. There'd be a big question mark for me over definitions now. I think that's quite a sad note to have to sound, but that would be it.'[7]

SHAMEFUL PRACTICE

Sue Frumin began her career in the theatre as an administrator at the Albany Empire, Deptford, in 1975. When she started to work at the Soho Poly, which she described as a 'writers' theatre' she decided to become more actively involved by writing a play. 'Coming out', after a year spent in Canada, was accompanied by a surge of creative energy. Inspired by meeting Kate Crutchley, Nancy Diuguid and members of Gay Sweatshop, she wrote *Bohemian Rhapsody*, based on a paragraph or so she had read about a women's revolution in Bohemia. Since her mother was from Bohemia, the subject seemed most appropriate. Sue Frumin chose to describe the revolution as a rebellion against the drunkards there who had stolen power from the women, thereby destroying the peace and harmony which had reigned in Mother Earth's favourite kingdom. Mother Earth and Father Sky are the male and female deities struggling for control over human destiny. It is Father Sky who decrees that his son Boleslav the Bold will defeat Mother Earth's daughter, Queen Libussa, because the women of Bohemia, who have founded the golden city of Prague, have interfered with his universal plan:

FATHER SKY:

> She is messing up my galaxy! Look, it's horrible, they're having bizarre rites and wearing strange clothes. I shall call on my sons, the warriors, to bring back order.

MOTHER EARTH:

> Stop setting our standards for us. These people grew as they would wish to be. There is no plan for the human race.[8]

The war which Father Sky unleashes is too much for the pacifist women to tolerate. They finally capitulate to patriarchal rule because they cannot bear the sight of the bloodshed and destruction of the countryside. However, life with men who are constantly befuddled by drink (Sue had read that many Czech kings died from an over-indulgence in alcohol) being no more tolerable than war, with renewed feelings of sisterhood they take to the hills to form a resistance organization. Through superior intelligence and magic, they gain control once more, accepting a king, but a gay one, the gentle, effeminate Wenceslaus instead of the boorish Boleslav. The new society will be a 'commune of friends', an agricultural, teetotal, vegetarian nation in which marriage will have no place.

Sue Frumin showed the play to Noel Greig of Gay Sweatshop, who advised her to pass it on to Kate Crutchley. The result was a modestly funded production at the Oval House in 1980, performed in a broadly comic style. The excellent reviews encouraged Sue to write *Rabbit in a Trap*, a two-hander, also directed by Kate Crutchley in the Oval House Upstairs Theatre.

'It was a play about class.... It was a play about two women, one of whom was working class and lived in Deptford, and one of them was very middle class.... It was about the sort of things that people weren't actually talking about, because they weren't talking about class divisions amongst women.'[9]

The working-class character, Doris, narrates the story of her meeting with middle-class but unconventional Stephanie in their local supermarket. Doris immediately falls in love; Stephanie is too preoccupied with family and money problems to notice the attraction until well into the play. Doris gives Stephanie support, helping her with the children, even offering to use money she has earned through gambling as a deposit on a house, so that Stephanie can leave her sixteenth-century renovated property, because inexplicable and terrible things happen there. There are in fact ghosts – the benign spirit of Stephanie's black ballet-dancer husband, drowned in the lake in Central Park, New York, when his boat sank and his roller skates stuck in the mud, and malignant souls of Negro slaves locked in the cellar and left to die. The bad ghosts are finally liberated, again mainly through Doris, who finds the lost key to the cellar, and the two women decide to move away to the country, near the sea. Class barriers are transcended.

This play was even more enthusiastically reviewed than the first. It moved to the King's Head and other venues, always playing to appreciative audiences. It was described by its author as a very happy production in which everyone gave both time and services generously for almost no financial reward.

A piece for television followed, then the formation of a comedy team The Red Bucket (a deliberate reference to the well-known fringe company Red Ladder), specializing in what Sue Frumin describes as 'camp little numbers' such as an adaptation of Peter Pan called *The Great Wendy*. When the team disbanded, Sue decided to train properly as an actor at Rose Bruford College, an experience which destroyed a lot of her confidence rather than providing her with new insights and skills. At the end of her course she wrote and performed *The Housetrample*, inspired by the emigration of her Czechoslovakian mother to England before the war. The story, narrated in Brechtian fashion, is of two friends, who may or may not be lesbian, one of whom stays behind when the Nazis invade Czechoslovakia, while the other goes to Manchester, where she becomes a bus-conductress. Twenty-two characters and a factory are portrayed by the narrator. Deep and lasting friendship is the main theme, a depth of emotion which some may claim could sit happily within the lesbian continuum. She considers it her best play, but ironically she has not given a copy of the published version to her mother because it is included in *Lesbian Plays: Two*, and she thinks that her mother might be alarmed or disturbed by this.[10]

The Housetrample toured for three or four years, not only in Britain but also in the Netherlands and the USA, always by invitation. However, in spite of the play's obvious success, it was not a production which Sue was prepared to tour indefinitely, as a one-woman show throws a lot of responsibility on to the shoulders of a single actress, there being no one else to share the work or the fun.

Sue Frumin's next work, *Raising the Wreck*, was discussed in Chapter 3. After working with Sweatshop she became writer in residence with Live Theatre in Newcastle upon Tyne, recommended by Tony Kendall at the Albany. It was a difficult year, not least because she was the first lesbian that members of the theatre group had ever met. The result, as she describes it, was not a lot of work but a lot of drinking.[11] The resultant play, which got very bad reviews, concerned a young girl who went to work in a laundry, a choice of occupation mainly dictated by the fact that a laundry was sponsoring the production. The sponsors and the writer unfortunately did not see eye to eye as Sue told a *Times* reporter that she thought working conditions in the laundry were dreadful. Consequently a scrap-yard in Sunderland became the main focus, the heroine having left the laundry to work in the scrap-yard. The theme was corruption, inspired by the T. Dan Smith and John Poulson affair in 1972, a celebrated case at the time, concerning the wheeler-dealing of the two men largely responsible for rebuilding a major part of Newcastle. The main characters in the play were women whose men had died in mysterious circumstances, the final scene being a dinner party which the women all attended dressed as their dead husbands. It is described by the author as 'absolutely dripping in subtext'.[12] Despite the fact that the audiences loved it, the reviews were terrible because the journalists objected to the inclusion of a lesbian character (who was, in fact, played by a lesbian). Only the *Guardian* was enthusiastic. Sue sums up the response of the press as pure prejudice.

'Most of the critics in the North East were men and they got really upset by it. Everybody seemed to think I was just a very middle-class woman who'd gone from London up to Newcastle, and that was how I was reviewed. That's ridiculous, that's prejudice because they didn't know where I'm from.'[13]

On her return to London, Sue formed her own company, Shameful Practice. She decided on the name after reading an article in the *Hackney Gazette* in which it was asserted that there were no such things as Jewish lesbians, and if there were, they had better stop 'this shameful practice'. The first production, *Home, Sweet Home*, opened in 1987 at the Duke of Wellington pub, Balls Pond Road, London, and subsequently transferred to the Broadway Studio (Catford Broadway), and the Oval House in Kennington. The flyer describes it thus:

Sandy Beech, a struggling squatter, moves into a cosy two-up, one-down fleapit, right next door to heartbroken home-owner Katy Devine, with disastrously rib-tickling results! The play not only takes on the present problems of life in the none-too-glamorous gentrified ghetto, but also takes us into the past – to a wartime romance between Dorothy and Ilse, two women caught up in the struggles of the blitz.[14]

Sandy is a playwright, determined to write her politically correct lesbian feminist masterpieces, who finally gets inspiration from the love affair between Dorothy and Ilse, a German immigrant, as recorded in their wartime diaries. Katy is a costume designer, a 'lumpy' (lesbian upwardly-mobile professional). Needless to say, after a difficult start the two manage to get together. Sandy writes frequent letters to a woman from her past known as Goddess, commenting on things that happen to her. The first letter is a rueful description of life since 'coming out'.

Dear Goddess,

I have not written to you since 1978 when I thanked you for urging me to come out of the closet and 'be as one' with my sister. You promised me a life free of heartache, misery and men. Since then I have come a long way. I have been physically attacked twice, hissed at, spat at in the street, rejected by my family, lost touch with my friends and had my heart broken 365 times in the last year.[15]

One of the major themes of this work is the transcendence of difference, a theme which was also fundamentally important in *Rabbit in a Trap*. Joining together in adverse circumstances, women forgot barriers of class and nationality.

Fanny Whittington was the group's next show, at the Oval in December 1988, a spoof on the well-known English pantomime *Dick Whittington*. In the traditional version Dick, a poor country boy, arrives in London, with his cat, to seek his fortune. After a series of adventures he finally becomes Lord Mayor, Sir Richard Whittington, largely through the efforts of his cat, who slays the scourge of the docks and navy, King Rat. This version tells the story of a North of England young dyke who brings her cat to London for a Gay Pride march and gets separated from the rest of her party. The big city is a dangerous place, where those who look like friends turn out to be enemies in a society dominated by free enterprise and each woman for herself:

In the face of the destruction of the Lesbian Liberation Movement many of our sisters took to Free Enterprise, meaning property ownership, investment and the ownership of BMWs. In the Well of Loveliness café we find a babble of clones making dates in their filofaxes, discussing the overwhelming rise in house prices, remembering the old days and tucking into La Nouvelle Cuisine Vegetarienne at a price only they can afford.[16]

Having found a job washing dishes in the Well of Loveliness café, Fanny looks for lodgings. Following up an advert in a scrap of paper, she arrives at a 'Fabulously comfortable squat in Finsbury Park, Fully Furnished, Fashionable and Friction Free, Friendly Feminist Flat';[17] this is in fact a squalid collective inhabited by Virus, Fungus and Margret aka Magg-ot, who welcomes Fanny as an unpaid servant. Like the original Dick Whittington, Fanny finds herself shipped off to foreign parts, the Kingdom of Lesberania, ruled by Sultana, who gives her subjects magic potions to ensure their adoration. The cat becomes involved with Big Ratty, King of the London Underworld, who in the end turns out to be Little Mousey Wousey in disguise. Magg-ot, impersonating Fanny, is made Lady Mayor of Evenup, but is unmasked, leaving a happy ending similar to that of *Bohemian Rhapsody*.

The next project was a difficult one, so difficult that it saw the end of Shameful Practice. *The Beggar's Opry* was a lesbian rewriting of John Gay's eighteenth-century musical, *The Beggar's Opera*, reworked by Brecht in *The Threepenny Opera*. The darker aspects of the original, the deep divisions between rich and poor, greed and selfishness were still relevant today even in the lesbian community:

'It's very difficult to take a play with a difficult theme, *The Beggar's Opera*, or *The Threepenny Opera*, and change it into a play about lesbians. But it had all that dark stuff in it about some people being very, very poor and some people being very well-off and never the twain shall meet, and there being hostilities. Basically that's what's happening in the real world now, there's an underclass. And I think amongst lesbians there's an underclass of people who have no money, have never had any money and get exploited by the system. I wanted to exaggerate all that, but it was difficult because it isn't funny. People were used to my plays being a funny, jolly romp, and this wasn't a funny, jolly romp.'[18]

There were problems with funding. Shameful Practice had been led to expect a large grant from Greater London Arts to pay for the musical director, set, costumes, etc. Before the show had properly taken off, Greater London Arts collapsed. There were long discussions between the author, director and actors about the meaning and suitability of the text, which led to major changes. Sue Frumin herself became uncomfortable with her part as a grasping elderly woman because a Jewish actress playing such a role could seem like anti-Semitism. There were doubts about the musical style – country and western – since it had not yet become popular and fashionable, although the lyrics and songs were nominated for a Fringe First award. The break away from hilarious comedy to a more serious and subtle mode proved impossible to handle successfully, and gave rise to almost universally bad reviews. The following speech delivered by Jenny Devere, owner of the Deadly Nightshade lesbian bar, who has just shopped her lover Mo McHeath to Theresa (Tiger) Brown, corrupt head of the Criminal Investigation Department, gives an idea of the complexity of the script:

(JENNY *faces the audience.*)

JENNY: There you go ... sitting in judgement again. Wondering how I could betray the woman I loved. Well I did ... and it's not the first time ... I suppose you think I'm a cheat and a crook and a liar ... well, I might be ... and so might you. I suppose you're thinking ... I know why she wasn't invited to the wedding. She's not 'the right type', she's the sort that might steal your credit cards when you're not looking. Maybe she's not enough of a lesbian to fit into your scene. ... She once lived with a man you know ... doesn't that make her woman enough for you? I suppose you think I'm about as low as you can go. Well I can go much, much lower. ... I'm the sort of woman you have nightmares about turning up at your party ... the one who doesn't quite fit ... the one whose clothes are more than five years out of date ... the lesbian woman that even the lesbians hate. ... I've been a prostitute, my kids are in and out of care a lot, I have to get rid of them if things get hot ... and I do care about them, I care a lot ... I was the fool,
who was the mule, who brought the baggage back from Peru ... and then I served my time
on the inside ...
So where did I come from ... I came from the street, my education would just about cover the back of a five pence piece ... my father wanted a boy, and when he couldn't have one, he used me like a boy. ... Until I came out ...
I didn't think I would ever be

happy. ... And now I think that's probably true, that I
won't ... I opened a club where I thought women could
be happy too, and I think I learned that dreams don't come
true however much you want them to ... and now the bills
are soaring, I'm falling into disrepair and I feel like my
time is all running out ... so I sit and watch the world
going by like that worn old moon in the sky ... I don't
feel sorry for myself ... I'm too busy counting my
pennies, laying the cards
on the table and watching the wheels turn around.[19]

Disheartened by her first real failure Sue Frumin wrote nothing more
except a one-woman show about herself and her twin sister. She now
has a very demanding teaching job which leaves her with no time to
do anything except to recover from the rigours of the day. She does
not completely rule out being professionally involved in theatre once
more, but she may well concentrate on working with young people
and forget lesbian theatrical involvement. At the end of her interview
she paid tribute to Lois Weaver (see Chapter 3).

'Although I'd done quite a lot of work, I'd never had much confidence about that work and how to do it. I did some workshops with
Lois and Split Britches and it completely affected how I did my work
and gave me an awful lot of confidence. She's one of those people
who teaches you that you should actually trust your ideas, which made
a great change because most lesbians go around, like most teenagers
I work with, saying what crap they are and that's a very British thing.
The American thing is to say how good you are. And I find that if we
really had that in this country and people felt better about what they
are doing instead of either putting everybody else down around them
or putting themselves down, we would have a much healthier lesbian
theatre in this country. Most British people won't take that on, so they
go around thinking that Americans are wonderful because Americans
themselves think they're wonderful. They don't actually believe in
themselves or that people in Britain can produce good work. And I
think we've really got to change that for the future.'[20]

Notes

1. Penny Casdagli, 'The whole nine yards', in Susan Raitt (ed.), *Volcanoes and Pearl Divers* (London: Onlywomen Press, 1995).
2. *Ibid.*, p. 274.
3. *Ibid.*, p. 276.
4. *Ibid.*, p. 265.

5. *Ibid.*
6. Casdagli, 'The whole nine yards', p. 285.
7. Interview with Penny Casdagli, May 1995.
8. Sue Frumin, *Bohemian Rhapsody*, unpublished script, pages not numbered.
9. Interview with Sue Frumin, February 1996.
10. Sue Frumin, *The Housetrample*, in Jill Davis (ed.), *Lesbian Plays: Two* (London: Methuen, 1989).
11. Interview with Sue Frumin, February 1996.
12. *Ibid.*
13. *Ibid.*
14. Publicity flyer, June 1987.
15. Sue Frumin, *Home, Sweet Home*, unpublished script, p. 2.
16. Sue Frumin, *Fanny Whittington*, unpublished script, p. 11.
17. *Ibid.*
10. Interview with Sue Frumin, February 1996.
19. Sue Frumin, *The Beggar's Opry*, unpublished script.
20. Interview with Sue Frumin, February 1996.

Chapter 7
Red Rag, Spin/Stir and
Mrs Worthington's Daughters

RED RAG

Jill Davis lectures in drama at the University of Kent at Canterbury; she also writes about women's theatre and has edited the only two anthologies of lesbian plays published in the UK. She has been a member of the Arts Council Drama Panel, chaired its New Applications and Projects Committee, and been Chair of South East Arts Drama Panel. She has been a key figure in supporting lesbian theatre, not least through the influence she has had on her students. Much of this chapter concerns the work of two companies who, at different times, studied drama at the University of Kent, where their feminist consciousness was raised, where they were able to express their political commitment in their projects.

Red Rag was set up in 1987 by Winnie Elliott, Lois Charlton and Carole Noble. Having been taught by Jill Davis on a Women's Theatre course they decided in their fourth and final year to form a company which produced work for their practical assessment. Even before they graduated they had performed at the Oval House and met Kate Crutchley, thereby establishing a future professional link. Red Rag was founded after their graduation, a formalization of their already existing group. The name was suggestive of confrontation – 'a red rag to a bull' – and of menstruation. Their agenda was to be a socialist feminist one. Their first engagement, at the Oval, was in March 1987 just a few weeks after the formation of the company.

The Infamous Life and Times of Nell Undermine traced 500 years in the life of a bag lady, Nell Undermine, who became a fool at the Elizabethan court. She was a highway woman, a suffragette-representative of the group's fantasies. They were all women who went against convention, most of them being cross-dressed and anti-marriage. The show also contained a pastiche of Emily Brontë's *Wuthering Heights*, since pastiche was one of their favourite forms.

'Artistically our growth had been starting off with real popular forms and pastiching them. A lot of time that's when our work was best, because all the structures were set up and we could just bring our humour and our theatricality to it. Also we were very good comedians; comedy was a driving force behind all those early productions.'[1]

The response to *Nell Undermine*, performed in the studio theatre at the Oval, was encouraging, with the audience gradually building. Red Rag's second play, *Stockings and Shares* (October 1988), was also a pastiche of a well-known piece of nineteenth-century literature, Dickens's *A Christmas Carol*; this was a feminist version, obviously, in which the ghost of feminism past, present and future visits a post-feminist (a successful business-woman complete with Filofax) in order to take her back to her 1970s feminist roots. It was a broad parody, with songs, a lot of music and retro dance sequences and costumes. Bernadine Coverley in *City Limits* commented:

> A clever witty look at women's aspirations and the ongoing clash between money and morals, exploitation and equal opportunities, with some affectionate self-mockery in the characters of Marxist feminist Sarah and mystical Frizzy. A neat set of songs enhance some sharp acting. Red Rag move at a cracking pace and the jokes fly home.[2]

In the third production, *Seven Sins for Seven Sisters* (April 1989), Red Rag took each of the deadly sins and made them positive in a series of sketches.

'It was a topical subject – there was a lot going round in the media about the seven deadly sins. Sarah Maitland had just published something on them and that was in the *Guardian*, there was something on a radio programme about the seven deadly sins and how they related to today. We looked at that and how they affected us as women, today.'[3]

'Pride' was a Raymond Chandler-inspired piece about a woman who lost her pride and had to go to a detective to find it; 'Gluttony' was about enjoying food. This latter piece went beyond pastiche to become surreal – having a woman at a dinner party who ate like a bird turning into a bird and one who ate like a pig turning into a pig. They all played many different characters, describing the whole thing as manic. It was cartoon-strip feminism, publicized by the Oval House in the following manner:

> The time has come ... it had to happen, by popular demand Red Rag goes raunchy! Feeling wicked? Then join Red Ragsters and writhe in rage filled

with wrath, envelop yourselves in enticing envy, cavort in callous covetousness, savour the sublime serenity of sloth, give licence to the unbridled lust of lechery, preening pride, gorge yourselves in gargantuan gluttony. And above all resign yourselves willingly to the decadent debauchery and bacchanalian revelry of the supremely sumptuous and salaciously saucy SEVEN DEADLY SINS, a frantical musical comedy of sinner versus sinned and mayhem versus morals. Can you cope.... Are you alive or deadly ... well if you've accepted the alliteration, throw caution to the wind and yourselves with wild abandon to the Oval.[4]

As a student group Red Rag had been subject to certain constraints; when they were on their own they went somewhat wild in their first four productions, enjoying the totally farcical side of their work. Subsequently they wanted more structure, a story, and more permanent characters. Discussing this evolution, they suggested that it might have been common to many lesbian groups:

'Talking to people like Karen Parker, they've said a similar thing, "Oh you did a farce – we did a farce" and it sounds like you start off taking things off the hook. "Let's do a lesbian farce, or let's do a lesbian this, that or the other", then, like we did, you start to think let's go beyond that, let's have a story, let's find a lesbian aesthetic, although you don't think about it in these words, just write our thing and not do a lesbian version of all the things that have ever been done. ... We did very, very funny lesbian or feminist versions of things and then we got to the point where we wanted a story, and then we did Ellen Galford's *The Fires of Bride*, which was a novel adaptation, and that really took off. That was our most successful production, theatrically and in every way, it was leaps and bounds ahead of anything we'd done before.'[5]

Fires of Bride was the company's coming out, since it was their first production in which the story was centred on lesbian characters. Their work prior to this was feminist, with lesbian cameos. This time the word 'lesbian' was on all the publicity and the audience was largely lesbian. The writers, Carol Noble and Bridget Hurst, who also directed, were pleased to be working with a structured, complicated story after the cabaret-style form of the previous shows, in which set pieces had been drawn loosely together by a simple linear plot. Ellen Galford's novel sparked off ideas leading to an inventive, well-crafted piece of theatre. Everything came together, with everyone in the company learning new skills through being able to concentrate on particular roles, which also gave more strength to the production.

There was immense enthusiasm among the company and the audience, it being a time when actors and stage crew were still idealistic and willing to work for love.

The opening on 2 May 1990, in the theatre downstairs at the Oval House, was a great success and Red Rag's following increased rapidly. Acting in a larger space (the upstairs theatre at the Oval, where they had previously performed, was small) they were able to be more daring, promenading around the audience, recreating the Scottish landscape. The whole thing finished with a ceilidh – a nightly party when performers shared drams of whisky with the audience. The blend of myth, magic, humour and music was very attractive. They took the show on their most extensive tour, including a venue in Edinburgh and two in Glasgow. The Scottish public was appreciative of the English, not minding the performers' pseudo-Scottish accent.

The fires of bride referred to in the title are the sacred flames kept alive by medieval nuns in Cailleach, an imaginary place in the remotest Outer Hebrides. The nuns had in their possession a sacred book dating from the time of Christ's birth, illustrating the Nativity, showing that Christ had a twin sister who was spirited away by a mysterious old woman in a purple cloak to Scotland, where she lives in peace until soldiers come looking for her. The woman protects her, she is transformed into a bird and flies off to heaven. The nuns were massacred but the book survived. The ruins of the convent are being excavated by a lesbian archaeologist, who finds evidence of the book in the form of a few extra pages drawn by one of the last living nuns, Mhairi, hidden in a dungeon under the kitchen at the time of the slaughter. Mhairi had already entrusted the sacred book to her sister, who entrusted it to her daughter, and so it was handed down through the generations until it came into the hands of the head of the clan, Catriona McEochan, a doctor who dabbles in magic and a ruthless lesbian who seduces anyone who takes her fancy. And her fancy is very much taken at the beginning of the story by a young artist, Maria Milleny, whom she lures to the island from London. Maria is seduced, then spurned, but finds her place on the island making junk sculpture out of bits of old cars. In the last scene we learn that her mother was from Cailleach, the sister of the local minister, Murdo, who spends much of his time fulminating against the heathen ways of the clan chief, observed by him bathing naked with Maria.

The tone from the beginning is humorous, the content of the first speech tells us we are witnessing, amongst other things, the parody of a mystery story. The speaker is Ina, described in the stage directions as 'oral guidebook and purveyor of island lore and gossip'.

INA: You'll be wanting to know about the book, ah yes, the
        book of Pride. I don't pay any mind to it myself but it's a
        cracking good yarn all the same. Let me see, it all began
        in a pretentious art gallery in Clerkenwell, London. Our
        clan chieftain, G.P. and, some say, 'witch' Catriona
        McEochan was visiting an exhibition called 'Lives of the
        Saints' by a talented young artist named Maria Milleny.
        She's a rare old bird for the arts is our Catriona. Just as
        she was tipping her glass of cheap red wine into a nearby
        pot plant, her gaze was drawn to the picture entitled 'St.
        Bridget'. It bore an uncanny resemblance to the view from
        her own castle window. With no further ado Catriona
        wrote a cheque and arranged for the picture to be sent.
        She told me later she'd written a wee invitation on the
        back of that cheque. Maria was to visit Cailleach as soon
        as she could. The reply, eagerly awaited, was some two
        years in coming. But when it came, none could have
        foretold what effect that young artist would have on this
        island. ... Now, who would like another scone?[6]

The reviews in *Time Out*, *What's On* and *City Limits* were full of
praise, mainly for the comic performances and the fun of the production:

> This is the antithesis of those rather flat, dour productions where the
> emphasis has been placed in the text rather than the joy of live theatre.
> There is such a whirl of exuberance, colour and humour in Red Rag's
> performance that it runs the risk of turning into a series of set pieces.
> However, the cast do manage to keep one eye on the storyline, despite the
> crowds of people on stage (including most of the audience), smoke and
> costume changes.[7]

> The play's strong suit, both in the action and the music, is its comedy,
> largely situated somewhere between panto and cabaret. The jokes are
> good and the double entendres salty; memorable set pieces include a very
> witty parody of pretentious wine-tasting and a novel rendering of the
> twenty-third psalm. The small all-women cast (five players sharing
> fifteen roles) boasts more than its fair share of true comic talent.[8]

Claudia Woolgar described the show as 'a wonderful celebration of
all that is mystic and female – and a brilliant night out'.[9]

Another farce, *Ooh Missus*, followed *Fires of Bride* in October
1991; not a pastiche this time, however, but an original story dealing
with a topical subject – lesbians' motherhood through donor insem-

ination. Because only lesbians (seventeen of them) were involved in the production, it was permissible to 'send up' different sorts of dykes – therapists, scene dykes, baby dykes, earth mothers. The Oval House audience loved it.

> Purportedly the work of Lois Charlton and Winnie Elliott, *Ooh Missus* is surely the forgotten literary offspring of a drunken brief encounter between Ray Cooney and Andrea Dworkin.[10] On a set of Ayckbourn-like suburban splendour, the familiar conventions of farce and sit-com are acted out from a sisterly angle. Lovey-dovey yuppie couple Penny and Jenny are hoping for some peace and quiet in which to make a baby (by inseminating Jenny with the sperm they've just biked over in an old mayonnaise jar). Naturally, there are all manner of interruptions, including a nosy neighbour, prospective flatmates whose identities get confused, and Jenny's Tory-harridan mother, who must be kept in the dark regarding her daughter's sexual preference.
>
> All this works best when subverting, rather than simply imitating, the form. The coming-out of a Baby Dyke (an attractively nerdy Maureen Philbert) and the implications of the oh-so-proper neighbour's interest in lesbian sex, are made to work in a way that is both genuinely funny and telling. ... *Ooh Missus* is one of those occasions where enthusiastic playing to the gallery wins the day. Red Rag's impressively confident ensemble rarely falter, and are rewarded with the highly vocal appreciation of the Oval House audience. The enjoyment is catching.[11]

Desire by Design followed in October 1992. Binnie Greer called it 'a version of the Frankenstein story via *Being There* and *Fatal Attraction*'.[12] Cherry Smyth was more expansive:

> If you could create your perfect lover, would you want her? *Desire by Design* introduces an ambitious scientist (played excellently with sexy aplomb and dashing evil, by Jackie Clune) who moulds the ideal woman from the tastiest bits of her other lovers. At first her Eve (captured by a versatile Alison Seddon) mirrors her so completely that she can conjure up a favourite fantasy, from simpering secretary to underwear saleswoman, and Eve becomes it. However, perfection becomes predictable, so Eve is dished into a dyke world of pool-players, agenda setters and therapists until she absorbs a life of her own and seeks revenge against her creator.... Red Rag have converted a cold-blooded Jacobean tragedy for contemporary queers.[13]

Red Rag always worked as a team on a production, the final scripting being done by two people, a different two for each play. Like Siren, they start by discussing an idea with the whole company, using personal experience as a part of the creative process, for example using the notion of difference and diversity between the five lesbians in the group as a basis for the 1994 production *Sexual Orienteering*.

'*Sexual Orienteering* was based in the group, in the group dynamics. We hit the point as a company where we felt we had nothing in common and we started to think "Is this what's happening in the lesbian community? This is where we've got to be, this is what we've got to write from...." Winnie came up with the idea of an outdoor pursuits course. Once we'd got the issue we then had to think of a setting – where can we put this, where can we place this political issue?'[14]

This led to the creation of more realistic characters and realistic situations, particularly since the whole cast actually went on an outdoors activities course to experience the physical and emotional pressures. In an interview with Sophia Chauchard-Stuart, Winnie Elliott explained:

Well, it's a potentially volatile situation to put five dykes into, isn't it? We thought that physical challenges of the activities, the strange environment and the close proximity of the women being together for a weekend would leave us room to show the differences and similarities between dykes today.[15]

In the same interview, Jackie Clune remembers the good moments of their actual weekend.

It really sexualised the physical experience in the play that we had been working on in rehearsal. We had to wear harnesses for the abseiling and refused to take them off for the canoeing – we loved the feeling of wearing wetsuits as well; we all looked fab in those. There was lots of bottom slapping that day.[16]

The final piece received the usual enthusiastic response from the Oval audience and praise from *What's On* and *Time Out*.

Sexual Orienteering is set in the dark drizzly depths of Eva's Mount, where five dykes are forced to survive the elements in a stimulant-free environment – no fags, no fucking, no running water. If the thought of spending a wet week in Wales sends you scuttling towards the nearest radiator, then this lusty, loamy adventure might not be your cup of tea, but you'd be a chump to miss it.

The most obvious strands of lesbian culture are plainly displayed, with an old mother lesbian, a masochistic model, a devious journalist, a pedantic P.E. instructor and an unemployed club bunny. Their common calling and personal philosophies are severely tested, the only things that match are the cagoules.... The actors use every inch of performance space. The audience perch and squat, helping out where they can.... The audience contained a complete cross-section, and even those who clearly saw themselves in the various characters laughed hard and long when stereotypical mannerisms were employed. Whether it's five dykes in harnesses and rubber who fumble around in wet crevices that intrigues you, or just the prospect of having a night of dashed fine entertainment, this show is a feisty and piquant play.[17]

Sexual Orienteering had received Arts Council funding on condition that there was a director from outside the company. Red Rag had no objection to this provided she was a dyke. Sarah Frankom, already experienced in the mainstream, was chosen. There was by now an insistence on collectives bringing in outsiders, as directors and writers. A writer who came from within the company would not be given a writer's award. Since part of the writer's fee had to come from the company itself, an additional expense was added to a slender budget. It was suggested that Red Rag might work with, for example, Bryony Lavery, Lois Weaver or Sarah Daniels. In spite of feeling that their own writing was undervalued, they were willing to do this, but when I talked to them at the end of 1994, one arrangement had already fallen through because they had failed to obtain the writer's bursary from the Arts Council. They felt under pressure from funding bodies to produce seriously 'artistic' work, from audiences to give them broad comedy and lots of songs. Comedy and music were in fact included in their policy statement.

'We have a total commitment to new writing. Plays are produced by employing co-operatives devising processes within the creation of new scripts. We have a commitment to theatre which is comic as well as pertinent to our community, and we are equally committed to the creation of original music for our productions (in the form of songs or soundtracks).'[18]

Their strength, they all agree, is in their comic performance; they find pastiche very easy, but they sometimes question whether taking heterosexual forms and lesbianizing them in a farcical way is sufficient as a *raison d'être*. There are issues they would like to tackle in a more serious way – the relationship of older lesbians to their extended families, for example, yet their audiences do not 'allow' them to do that, applauding them only when they are 'jolly' and keeping all the troops entertained in the ghetto.

In 1994, the production they were working on in a collaborative way with a writer (rather than commissioning one, which they cannot now afford) was to be called *Strumpets*, dealing with lesbian pirates, working from real historical figures, rather than totally invented characters like their first creation, the 500-year-old bag lady Nell Undermine. There were to be 'big production numbers' and a lot of sexual references. They had tried for sponsorship, sending fifty letters out to gay and lesbian businesses asking for support. The only response was a £50 cheque from Shush, the lesbian sex shop. Generally speaking lesbians were poorer than gay men, so they could not afford to donate money to the arts.

Since its foundation Red Rag has gone through various administrative changes. Three newcomers were added to the original three members during the first year. This led to a discussion of whether they should still continue as a collective or whether the founder members should be the management. For good political reasons they opted to be a collective. They now operate under a management system because only three are committed enough to run the company without proper remuneration. Unable to pay an administrator, the management have to spend all their spare time on administration, at the same time working in full-time paid jobs in order to survive. For each production they pay themselves less than anyone else, sometimes nothing at all. Their survival as a group has depended on the support they have had from lesbians willing to give their services free. Seventeen women, with professional experience, recruited through advertising or contacts, worked for them on the technical side of *Ooh Missus* without any payment.

Strumpets was scheduled to open at the Drill Hall, not the Oval, a move closer to the mainstream, since it is a bigger venue, close to the West End, visited regularly by reviewers, with a wider audience. Perhaps this is an indication of rising fortunes, perhaps not – time will tell.

'It's a very small world, obviously, lesbian theatre is extremely small, there's probably not many people you could name that we haven't met, or heard of, or worked with, or owed a lot, or fallen out with, whatever. To be a lesbian dramatist or a lesbian actress, to stand up and hold your head high, is quite hard to do. And to find somewhere to work as such, you've got to be in with a very tiny group of people – you've got to be in with Red Rag, or you've got to get into Red Rag, or you've got to get into Sweatshop or the Drill Hall pantomime, you've got to get into these to do anything lesbian. A few people make a leap, like Sarah Daniels, say.... Your book in the end will tell the story of quite a lot of really talented people, who give up in the end, just run down....

Why is it that it's much more difficult for us, that it takes us much longer? Is it because the men are the ones who are always defining the criteria, setting the goal posts?[19]

SPIN/STIR

Joelle Taylor, the joint artistic director of Spin/Stir, graduated more recently than Red Rag from the University of Kent. She too had been very influenced by the teaching of Jill Davis. In 1993 she and Vanessa Lee, also a Kent graduate, formed a women's physical theatre collective which began work on father–daughter rape, a theme which interested them both personally. Joelle had already written a script on this subject as a surviving victim, which had aroused the interest of Sphynx theatre company, but was refused the money needed for development on the grounds that 'no theatre in London would be interested in it'. Trying a different route, the collective wrote to schools and colleges offering workshops on the same subject. They were somewhat surprised at its 'marketability'. They concluded that not only was the theme of widespread interest but also they were alone in providing space for experiment in feminist and lesbian theatre. Students found the workshop challenging on a cultural and political level, three or four of them 'coming out' as having been raped by their fathers.

Spin/Stir were concerned to explore gender as performance, 'the engenderment of performance', influenced by the work of Sande Zeig and Monique Wittig in the USA on the appropriateness of gesture according to sex or gender. Joelle gave the students sections of her script which she describes as 'performance poetry', as a starting-point for the development of their own materials, with an emphasis on the challenging, even harrowing. The success of this venture built up the company's reputation, as well as its confidence, which led to a performance of Joelle Taylor's play *Naming* at the Oval House in March 1994.

Naming was written in the first instance as a piece of poetry. Another text, the visual text, was added, so the production was built up in layers. The aim of the collective, including the stage manager/administrator Nicola Hayle, was to produce high art while remaining accessible; therefore child abuse was treated in a nonrealistic way. Realism was rejected as an inherently misogynistic form, with no space for women as subject. The preferred form was 'social surrealism', the use of metaphor to describe social reality, a blend of poetry and physical theatre which breaks away from the linear narrative while trying to make stories that the audience understand on some level or other. Cassandra, whose name recalls the Trojan princess, witness of her father's and brother's slaughter and the slaughter of their enemy who takes them captive, is the central character in *Naming*. She 'sprouts another woman', No-Name, representative of the womb, who releases all the women's stories within her, five or six different stories, with five or six different characters played by each of the two performers.

Naming is a literary as well as theatrical creation. The stage directions are more than an indication of the set or actions, they are written to be appreciated by a reader. Take, for example, the first page of the script:

The land beneath the Bed. A nursery. But no. Not quite. The performance space is a single bed, grotesquely enlarged and raked upstage. Everything happens here / it holds them hostage. The bed is a white wasteland. There are traces of sleep on its skin. Pillows the size of men struggle with each other at the head of the bed. There is the suggestion of another bed above this one and, by implication, a further bed below.

An armchair is suspended from the lighting grid, perhaps a foot above the bedcovers. It has swollen to four times its normal size / large enough for a shy woman to get lost in. It leans slightly forward on one arm like a late night drinker. Its back is broken. A leg has been scraped through in parts to the white wood bone. It smells of institutions. A child's Wendy house waits down stage. Its opening faces the audience. Its lips are sealed. A high chair, large enough to hold an adult, flounders on its side, the contents of something half-eaten licking the floor.

And there are other things; things which slip down the side of the bed and are never heard from again. A Little Mother tea service, bunches of clothing, curled books, naked dolls.

The colour is white.[20]

The references require a knowledge of European literary and philosophical heritage in order to be understood. The text is prefaced by two quotations, one from Nietzsche's *The Birth of Tragedy*, the other from Aeschylus' *Oresteia*. The metaphors are those of classical mythology, of fairy tales, of nursery rhymes. The educated reader/spectator remembers the novels of Angela Carter and Jeanette

Winterson or the well-read lesbian feminist thinks of Monique Wittig's *The Lesbian Body*.

The first story released by No-Name within Cassandra is Jenny's story. Jenny is sixty-two, an inmate of a psychiatric hospital, a north-erner institutionalized in alien southern territory, intensely suspicious of her therapy, yet dependent upon it.

JENNY: Therapist / the rapist / therapist / the rapist – do you know any good tongue-twisters? Or is it just that you are one? Give us a fag old love / old cocker / old chicken / old mate / my best fucking mate / give us a fag.[21]

The story Jenny tells to her new ward therapist is that the police brought her to the hospital for protection from persecutors who sent her anonymous letters, which in the end frightened her into a state which an outsider would describe as paranoia. Later we find her reverted to twelve years old, her menstrual cycle having just begun, visited by 'Father Xmas' who rapes her:

JENNY: (*Fighting for breath through the pain. The only way she will be able to survive this experience is by depersonalising herself.*) Beard in my mouth. He steals my sex and wears it on his face to hide his lying lips / he has taught it a dead language / he pulls and stretches it around like rotten syllables / inseminates it with silence. He wears red / he wears red / the colour of syphered sexuality drained from us before we can even spell the word.[22]

Father Xmas gives her a baby, then an abortion. The dead child is still inside the old woman:

JENNY: Do you want to see? (*Very slowly lifts dress. Underneath is a dome bird cage. Inside it / on the perch / is the carcass of a baby*) I had to, see ... (*opens door of cage / strokes the cheek of child*) It were carnivorous.[23]

Catherine's story is of attempted suicide after rape by her step-father. It tells not only of the man's abuse but also of the mother, Claire's, dilemma, her attachment to her daughter, her fear of her husband, her refusal to believe what is happening because of her own damaged condition. Catherine sits lacerating herself in a pool of blood while Claire, turned away from her, washes up in a tank of fighting fish. In this story Cassandra plays the mother unable to achieve the proper mother–daughter bonding, which is always, in any case, intensely problematic.

N.N.:   You would make a wonderful mother, Cassandra. Sticking plasters across the generation gap, over the Gulf/War. Band Aids as bridges. Splendid.

CASS: I feel sick ... that isn't what really happened, is it?

N.N.:   It is the view between the school railings. This is what Catherine recalls when she falls awake on these last ditch days before the term starts. She will spend the rest of her life waiting for the morning assembly bell to gather her together again.

CASS: But none of this is Claire's fault ...

N.N.:   In her dreams Catherine sees the apron strings snake out from around her mother's hips, sway silently in front of her for a moment and then strike, blinding her with domestic poisons and cleaning fluids. Mothers are always blamed ...

CASS: It's part of their job description –

N.N.:   And Catherine has read all the right books, wept through all the right films. Shirley Template. The wicked witch of the washing up bowl. The stories of King Solomon: mothers who would rather rip their children neatly in half than lose them to another. Old Husband's Tales.

CASS: We should be careful what we say to our children. They have this disgusting habit of listening to us.[24]

Catherine's accusations against her stepfather are dismissed as fantasies, a product of False Memory Syndrome.

After Catherine comes Poppy, a well-spoken down-and-out drug addict, retreating totally from reality into her own fictions, full of nightmare reminders of her past – alarming images of self instilled by her childhood reading.

OLD WOMAN:

How a girl became a Fairy Story. In the fairy tale books they have wide pictures / and somewhere between the Prince and the Princess, the Wicked Witch and Kindly Old Man, there are all of these background People / staring stagnant from the page with hatted faces. And do you know where they came from? Well, read between the lines on my face. They are what is left of little girls who lean too close to the story / and slip on a stray sentence skin and just stumble in. And the Kindly Old Man in the next room comes in and says 'Dirty / Messy / Unnecessary Little Girls' – and slams the doors of the book shut.[25]

Poppy was abused at four years old by a preacher, who turned on her as the temptress, the source of evil. Her identity is caught between saint and whore.

Jill is a twenty-six-year-old Mancunian. She is also Jill of the nursery rhyme *Jack and Jill*, who went up the hill to fetch a pail of water. Jack fell down and broke his crown and Jill came tumbling after. Jack was Uncle Jack, the rapist who passed on a disease to the adolescent girl. Again when she is asked who she has had sex with, her answer is dismissed. Jill the adult regularly gets drunk, goes out looking for sex, makes a suicide attempt and is taken to hospital. She has a friend, who is her life support, who loves her. She cannot love back; she is driven by a nymphomaniac urge to pick up any woman.

FRIEND: (*Takes a slow drink from her can. She is impassive / the way that sad people often are*) I've already ordered the taxi back from the hospital. We have a routine. I meet her in here at 8 p.m. We have a few beers. We have a few words. By about 9.30 she is ready for her monologue. This comes in five easy stages: Wit, Lust, Loss, Anger, Suicide. Well: everyone has to have a hobby. At 10.15, she starts to get anxious because the pubs will be closing soon. So she gets louder. She doesn't want anyone falling asleep. Or she will be alone (*a pause / head lowered / breathes out, looks at Jill, still trying to pick up women in the audience*) By 12.30 we are ready to leave the hospital. I take her home. I post her into her blankets. I stay with her for an hour or so while she drowses.[26]

This is an inadequate lesbian relationship, unable to work because of the seriousness of the harm caused by Uncle Jack to the fourteen-year-old Jill. Another even less successful, more overtly lesbian relationship is between Aischa and Sarah, who meet at Greenham Common. Aischa falls in love with Sarah, who appeared to her like a saviour goddess.

AISCHA: I loved her from the first moment I arrived. She made me a cup of tea. She rolled me a cigarette. She made me forget about hating myself. Five foot six / tall enough to peer over the edge of the world / back brave enough to carry her own weight / shoulder blades like sharks. I sleep in the branch of her arms. Go fishing in her eyes. Sweet Harbour.[27]

No-Name, listening to this recitation of the ideal, puts the other woman's point of view.

NO-NAME:

> She pulls the legs off her lovers / to see if they grow back again. She has a history, you see. I was warned. She warned me / when she was still living where her body stood she said: It is inevitable. Unchangeable. I will punish you for your love of me.[28]
>
> ...
>
> She wears her sex like a purple scar. She shows me her war wounds but won't let me dress them. She needs them. (*Pause/a resolution*) I know this much. I am not a skip. I am not a dumping ground for all these women who did not survive the war. I am a lesbian. And that. Is. It.[29]

These are women's stories, mothers' stories, daughters' stories, all questioning the meaning of those names 'mother', 'daughter'. There are no male characters yet each tale recounts the oppression, the violence, of the patriarch, the father, the stepfather, the uncle, Father Xmas. These men come in friendly disguises, bearing false gifts in order to take their own pleasure, tearing their wives and daughters apart. The myth of the kindly protective father is a terrible deception; no man is to be trusted:

CASS: The oldest protection racket.

N.N.: Men protecting women from other men.

CASS: Therapists.

N.N.: Fathers standing in front of boy friends.

CASS: Social Workers.

N.N.: Husbands standing in front of fathers.

CASS: Judiciary.

N.N.: Did you hear?

CASS: The streets are unsafe.

N.N.: So she calls a taxi.

CASS: And is driven home by a male taxi driver.

N.N.: Taxi drivers are never rapists.

CASS: On the way inside the front porch.

N.N.: She sees a man scuttering through the bushes.

CASS: So she calls the police.

N.N.: Policemen are never rapists.

CASS: Waiting for the police, she becomes lonely and afraid.

N.N.: So she calls her neighbour.

CASS: Neighbours are never rapists.

N.N.: Anyway.

CASS:	The scuttering man
N.N.:	Turns out to
CASS:	Be her neighbour.
N.N.:	He is an ex-police sergeant.
CASS:	He now works for the local taxi firm.
N.N.:	And she is married to him.[30]

As a result of the success of *Naming*, Spin/Stir received funding of £8,030 from the London Arts Board, to develop a second project which would use more contemporary dance and movement. As with other companies, funding changed the structure from a collective to a hierarchy. Working production meetings were held to delegate different roles. The group worked on a basis of skills sharing. Auditions took the form of a four-hour workshop and participants were asked to fill in a form stating whether they wished to be considered for a part and what their second choice of job would be. This way they found a network of lesbians with various skills, working in the theatre. They also took in people with very little experience, asking them to 'shadow' other more experienced members of the company, to learn new skills.

A cheap rehearsal room had been found in Brixton, a derelict room in an under-resourced arts centre. It was unheated and dirty. In spite of these drawbacks and the fact that it was frequented by all kinds of unstable, threatening people, they worked there for six weeks, until the arrival of funds allowed them to have their own rehearsal space in 'safe' surroundings, where they could pursue the 'radical exploration of women's bodies'. It was not considered necessary for the actors to have had previous training in dance, nor to have perfect bodies, although the performance would be physically demanding.

Joelle Taylor's *Whorror Stories* opened at the Oval House at the end of May 1995 as part of the Pride Arts Festival. Like *Naming*, it was a loosely knit series of stories, played out by spiders transforming themselves into different characters.

> The central theme ... is facing the most horrific things in ourselves and undergoing cleaning through self acceptance, warts and all. In the play, the catalyst for release and change in the characters' lives is a tarantula. ... Joelle uses spiders metaphorically as well as literally. She makes parallels between her reaction to spiders and her confrontation with traumas that have taken place in her own life in the past. Spiders are powerful symbols in many different cultures, usually representing danger and female sexuality. And this is the sub-text of the play, exploring the fear of women's sexuality from men and from women themselves.[31]

On the question of lesbianism, Joelle insists that it is not stated in terms of 'I am other'; there are no journeys made from heterosexuality to lesbianism; it is a given, accepted from the beginning. She is trying to defend a third sex which is not man and is not woman, but can be critical of both. Characters are played as excess in a way which critiques them, thus demonstrating that gender is performance.[32] One of the characters, Billy, the Drug King, is a stone butch, injecting herself with male hormones, who at one point becomes her girlfriend Flick, who becomes Billy. The instability of gender is emphasized by Flick, as she shaves Billy's head:

FLICK: She is / of course / entirely fictional. We must be careful around water / wouldn't want her to smudge ... would we? It started in such a small way. Stomach exercises. I think that's where it began. She inverted. Pushed too hard and gave birth to herself. Nightmare. The last thing a lady needs is a burgeoning butch. And she doesn't even own a tie. Or even a pipe. A pipe would do. And nine months later / I have her head in my hands / I can scratch my name on her scalp / I can carve her in my own image – and she doesn't even notice. I have all the responsibility in this relationship / and none of the power. One of us isn't here really.

Billy was always the kind of girl who rolled her own tampons. Unfiltered / of course. And she was quite good at balling up bits of paper and flicking them across the room too. It's in her jeans. Not that she'd wear them / of course. She also tried pool / but it's too unfashionable. And never went with her hair.[33]

Billy is terrorized by the fantasy of her mother as a spider, The Tarantula, who eventually kills Flick and forces Billy to submit, as a woman, to her spider/mother's rape in order to become pregnant and continue the female line. This is sexual terrorism, imposed gender, in order to retain power. The horror story is the story of the mother refusing to acknowledge the identity of the butch.

Heather's horror story is that of the anorexic. She has inherited her father's house on condition that she stays in it for three weeks without going out. There is a hamper of food, which turns out to be full of spiders, even the tins. She sits, watching the spiders weave their webs around her, not eating, unable to eat as a funnel spider is living in her throat, convinced that if she becomes thin enough she will be able to walk across the webs. The words 'skinny bitch' echo through her thoughts, yet she still wants to be thinner, lighter, insubstantial, in defiance of her father, Farmer Frank, who tries to force-feed her like an animal destined for the table.

Lindsay's tormentor is a serial killer, Mr Webster, who abuses young girls. Fourteen-year-old Lindsay comes to him when three months pregnant and he prepares her for a slow death, just as a spider would. In his turn he is paralysed by all the women he killed who rise from the dead to bring him to trial. He becomes a baby; he is taken back to the scene of his obsessions, to the reason for his revenge against all women, the denigration of men in the female household in which he was raised.

Both Farmer Frank and Mr Webster appear on stage played by the spiders. The Tarantula, the most threatening of all spiders, plays the serial killer and the vicious mother figure. In both roles she is defeated, since Billy finally kills her with Flick's high-heeled shoe. The final line of the play repeats a catch phrase of Mr Webster's, a phrase already used in *Naming*:

BILLY: *(Stands on dead spider's back. Poses with tea cup. Places it solemnly / like a coronation ceremony on the spider's head.)* There.
It's easier if you just lie still.
Shall I be mother?[34]

The publicity flyer for *Whorror Stories* ends with the words 'Be afreud. Be very afreud'.[35] These are the nightmare images which lurk in our unconscious. They are also images we are more used to seeing on television and in the cinema than in the theatre. In the tradition of Artaud, Joelle Taylor wants to use the theatre to shock our sensibilities by presenting us with violent images, with 'the impossible'.

> She wants to offer the impossible 'because' that's what I find missing from theatre, the impossible. We learned to accept it in television and film but not in theatre. I want to see a horror play that is truly terrifying in British Theatre. This is frightening because it's real life, how we feel as women, how I feel as a stone butch, not being able to be touched, and how victimised you feel by that. And yet how in turn I victimise the women who want to touch me.[36]

'The impossible' in the cinema is often represented by extraordinary physical transformations – people become animals, animals become monsters, the ordinary turns into the extraordinary. This happens throughout horror stories, for example a spider becomes a fifteen-year-old girl, who having been brought up as a dog becomes a dog, becomes a wolf, an avaricious, sexually terrifying creature who stalks the audience and murders her mother in front of the audience. She rips her mother's skin and hair off, makes up her lips with her mother's blood and becomes a woman.

During the rehearsal period performers had been asked to articulate their own worst fears, their own personal horror stories, which were incorporated into the final piece, with its complicated structure of five characters' stories, each broken down into three parts, making fifteen stories and an 'outer-narrative' about spiders. Arachnaphobia was chosen because it is a secondary fear, a displacement. The feeling experienced when seeing a spider – loneliness, cold, sickness – is the same as the feeling after being raped. It was considered important that phobias, post-traumatic stress disorders, should be made funny, for if you laugh at a story, you own it.

Spin/Stir plan to experiment and grow in as many ways as possible, stretching their minds and bodies. They believe it is important for lesbians in particular to work on the body, in a world which is often trying to 'get at' that body. However, the poetic text will still be there, providing the verbal metaphors, the literary intertextuality. They also hope to progress 'beyond the ghetto', attracting different and wider audiences, whose support is needed in any career structure. It is not regarded as part of mainstream fringe by agents and casting agents.

'What we found during this production [*Whorror Stories*] was that our audience was actually minimized by being part of Pride Arts Festival, whereas we'd assumed it was going to widen. We just did. I mean who wants to go and see a play about father–daughter rape [*Naming*]? Well, we sold out. There we were doing *Whorror Stories* as part of an enormous festival, we did a two-week run instead of a three-week. By the end of the second week we were selling out but we didn't make our hire charge. So what we're trying to do without watering down any of our work, any of our principles in the least, is to try to break out ... to expose people to the underbelly of fringe theatre and women's performance.[37]

MRS WORTHINGTON'S DAUGHTERS

There are certain English place-names which recur when one is discussing the development of lesbian theatre. Apart from London, we have already seen that the University of Kent at Canterbury was the cradle of two important companies. Canterbury itself is not particularly known as a home of theatrical innovation, however, whereas the town of Brighton, which has a large gay and lesbian population and a 'theatrical' population of actors who prefer to live outside London, has encouraged artistic experiment. Siren began in Brighton, their shows often opening there. There have been several small venues in pubs which have made the development of new writing their priority. Brighton Actors' Workshop, founded in 1975, inhabited a series of rooms above bars – the Marlborough, the Sea House, the Nightingale – where they stayed to change their name to Brighton Actors. They produced their own shows with a small annual subsidy from South East Arts, and played host to incoming companies, including Siren, and Hard Corps. In May 1995 a newly formed lesbian company, Mrs Worthington's Daughters, put on a play by Charlie Hughes-D'Aeth, *Any Marks or Deviations*, at the Nightingale. This was:

> A chilling ghost story in the tradition of Edgar Allan Poe, Stephen King, and Jennifer Saunders, which balances powerful imagery with incisive humour to reveal an intriguing network of passion and womanhood spanning the ages.[38]

The references are to horror stories and women's comedy. In fact, the play is neither particularly horrifying nor extremely comic. It is one of the few pieces I have come across which is a real love story – a double love story, comparing the fate of lesbian lovers in the seventeenth century condemned as witches, and a parallel couple in the twentieth century, who are out and proud. Hen and Kate, middle-class professional lesbians – Kate is a painting tutor, Hen works for a publishing company – have their life disrupted by the appearance of a ghost, Bethan, a servant girl burned as a witch 365 years previously. Bethan needs to make amends for the cowardly acceptance of the accusation of witchcraft which led to her execution. Her lesbian lover, Katherine, was spared because she was perceived as being under a spell. She was also from the ruling class, the daughter of the landowning vicar for whom Bethan worked. Twentieth-century Kate discovers during the course of the play that she is a descendant of Katherine and that she resembles her physically. For this reason Bethan has chosen to haunt and to seduce her. The seduction happens in so far as it is possible. Kate falls in love with the ghost, becoming obsessed. Her partner Hen is at first sceptical, then jealous and frightened. She stops Kate attempting to join Bethan by taking an overdose, suggesting instead that more meaningful contact will be made if she allows Bethan to possess her, Hen's body. This is an act of self-sacrifice which allows Kate to force Bethan to go back in history to deny the false accusations of witchcraft, rather than accepting them to save her soul:

KATE: But it didn't save you did it? Who were these so-called God-fearing people to tell you how your soul was to be saved? They didn't want to hear your truth, the truth about your love for Katherine, they couldn't accept that truth. All they could cope with was what they wanted to hear: that you were evil. If you confessed to evil, it made them feel all the more righteous. Their pride was all you saved by confessing, not your soul.

BETHAN: (*Pause*) 'Tis true, Katherine, all you say is true. Yet I am always in mind of it having been wrong for me to love my Katherine so, it did leave us in such torment.

KATE: It was never wrong for you to love Katherine and for she to love you. You have to accept that Bethan. You have to know that's true. What was wrong, what was so, so perverse was your being treated the way you were purely because of that love.[39]

Bethan's spirit leaves Hen's body to return to reshape her history. The play ends with the juxtaposition of two declarations of love:

HEN: I've been so scared Kate ... I mean ... I could cope if you left me, but not very well.

KATE: But I'm not going to leave you, Hen. Not now, not ever. Look at Bethan and Katherine, they loved each other for nigh on four hundred years and they've been through more trauma than we ever will.

HEN: I love you more than anything, Kate.

KATE: And I love you my darling.
          (*They kiss.*)

          . . .

VOICES: Why did you become a witch?
          Who was the one you chose to be your incubus?
          What was his name?
          What was the name of your master among the evil demons?
          What was the oath you were forced to render him?
          Who were your accomplices in evil?
          (*Crescending* [sic] *to:*)
          Denounce your evil ways and your soul shall be saved.
          (*Pause*)

BETHAN: I have no dealings with witchcraft. There is no devil I
serve and well you know.

My love for Katherine Hoxted is real. My love for her is
right. The pride I take in that love will travel with me far
beyond the reach of your grasping hands. I command you,
do not squander these feelings. I command you, do not
turn these pleasures of love into a torment of guilt and
anguish. These are feelings on which your ungodly souls
thrive, but not mine. It is not for you to take two lives
here today. Katherine's life may be fair spent in firm
assurance that I did proclaim my love for her beyond my
final breath. For myself, I seek not your paths to
righteousness, I languish not in your coward's servitude to
repentance. I seek only the truth which did bring me here
before you. I love Katherine Hoxted and do delight in
dying with that proclamation on my lips.[40]

Even in the seventeenth century, there was more to gain by coming
out than by denial, sentiments which the Nightingale audience heartily
applauded.

Like Red Rag and Spin/Stir, Mrs Worthington's Daughters draw on
cultural references well known to a young contemporary audience,
sometimes including innuendo specially for lesbians, for example:

HEN: I'll have you know that that story was told to me by one
Katriona MacCarthy on a long, tempestuous wet night in
Winter '82.

KATE: Don't try to blind me with details about the weather – you
just don't want to admit you're a traditionalist at heart.

HEN: Who said anything about the weather?[41]

And:

HEN: Well, I can see you're taking it terribly seriously. So what
the hell eh? If you can't beat 'em ... sell your bondage
gear.[42]

Catherine Deneuve, a lesbian icon, is described as being the right idea
in *Hunger*, a film known to many lesbians in which Deneuve plays a
vampire. Two films dealing with ghosts are mentioned in the script –
Ghost and *Truly, Madly, Deeply*.

Like many a girl in lesbian theatre, Hen has been to boarding-
school, an experience which has marked her for life, in more ways
than one.

HEN: I don't know what scurrilous innuendos you're trying to scurrilously innuend – but I like to think they're all true. I just adapted to my surroundings, that's all. Who am I to rail against time-honoured tradition? No, the good convent did me proud in more ways than they'd ever care to admit.

KATE: Oh very Malory Towers. Your ruling classes are so pitiably loyal.[43]

Very few British women would fail to recognize the name of the school from a popular schoolgirl series, by that most popular of writers for British children and adolescents, Enid Blyton. The popularity of boarding-school adventure stories is such that every schoolgirl feels she has been there.[44]

Charlie Hughes-D'Aeth was much encouraged by the unexpected support she received for this production. The group were not in receipt of a grant but they were overwhelmed by offers of help and by gifts of props and costumes. When it was all over she felt that the show had served to consolidate a community which until then had been somewhat fragmented. The play was no longer simply 'her baby', it was a 'community baby'.[45] When I talked to her in July 1995, she was hoping to find sponsorship for a tour. She had been contacted by a Canadian company, which recycled cable, offering to fund a Canadian tour provided that the audience paid for their tickets in used cable. This would have the advantage of attracting a lot of publicity. Negotiations were in process.

Notes

1. Interview with Lois Charlton, Winnie Elliott and Jackie Clune, November 1994.
2. Bernadine Coverley, *City Limits*, 6 October 1988.
3. Interview with Lois Charlton, Winnie Elliott and Jackie Clune, November 1994.
4. Oval House publicity leaflet.
5. Interview with Lois Charlton, Winnie Elliott and Jackie Clune, November 1994.
6. Red Rag, *Fires of Bride*, unpublished script.
7. Steve Malins, *Time Out*, 9–16 May 1990.
8. Sam Willets, *What's On*, 9–16 May 1990.
9. Claudia Woolgar, *City Limits*, 10–17 May 1996.
10. Ray Cooney is a well-known farce writer and Andrea Dworkin is a well-known feminist.
11. *What's On*, 9–16 October 1991.
12. Binnie Greer, *Time Out*, 20 October 1992.
13. Cherry Smyth, *City Limits*, 8–15 October 1992.
14. Interview with Lois Charlton, Winnie Elliott and Jackie Clune, November 1994.
15. Sophia Chauchard-Stuart, *Mapping the Lesbian 90s*, January 1994.
16. *Ibid.*
17. Megan Radclyffe, *Time Out*, February 1994.

18. Lois Charlton, Winnie Elliott and Jackie Clune, policy statement.
19. *Ibid.*
20. Joelle Taylor, *Naming*, unpublished script, p. 1.
21. *Ibid.*, p. 7.
22. *Ibid.*, p. 25.
23. *Ibid.*, p. 55.
24. *Ibid.*, p. 15.
25. *Ibid.*, p. 44.
26. *Ibid.*, p. 21.
27. *Ibid.*, p. 35.
28. *Ibid.*
29. *Ibid.*, p. 38.
30. *Ibid.*, p. 31.
31. Nina Rapi, *Diva*, June–July 1995.
32. Interview with Joelle Taylor, July 1995.
33. Joelle Taylor, *Whorror Stories*, unpublished script, p. 14.
34. *Ibid.*
35. Publicity leaflet.
36. Nina Rapi, *Diva*, June–July 1995.
37. Interview with Joelle Taylor, July 1995.
38. Publicity leaflet.
39 Charlie Hughes-D'Aeth, *Any Marks or Deviations*, unpublished script, p. 48.
40. *Ibid.*, pp. 49–50.
41. *Ibid.*, p. 3.
42. *Ibid.*, p. 19.
43. *Ibid.*, p. 2.
44. Of course, it may well be that I am not speaking for the current generation of schoolgirls. I have not done any research into this matter!
45. Interview with Charlie Hughes-D'Aeth, July 1995.

Chapter 8

A Look at Venues:
Kate Crutchley, the Oval House and Character Ladies; Julie Parker and the Drill Hall

By now it will be clear that there are two venues, and only two, which have been consistently associated with lesbian theatre – the Oval House and the Drill Hall in London. Neither venue is exclusively devoted to feminist, lesbian or gay theatre; both are community arts centres offering opportunities to a wide spectrum of different groups and providing space for workshops. The Oval House, partly because of its situation in South London, has encouraged black theatre. The association of both places with lesbian theatre has been because of the two women who organized the programmes, Kate Crutchley at the Oval House and Julie Parker at the Drill Hall.

THE OVAL HOUSE

Before Kate took over as programmer in 1981, the Oval House was already well known as an experimental venue devoted to new work. She herself had already worked there as director of Sue Frumin's play *Bohemian Rhapsody*. However, from 1981 to 1991 her background in feminist, gay and lesbian theatre led her to widen the opportunities for women. We have already discussed her work with Gay Sweatshop, as administrator and director of *Any Woman Can* and *Care and Control* (see Chapter 3). In 1977 she and Nancy Diuguid left Sweatshop to form Women's Project Company, a group subsidized by the Arts Council to encourage women writers. One of their productions was Michelene Wandor's *Aid Thy Neighbour*, the first feminist play on the subject of artificial insemination by donor (AID). As director Kate wanted to make the play a rather serious examination of the topic, inspired by an article in the London *Evening News* on lesbians and artificial insemination; Michelene herself preferred to imitate a situation comedy style, taking off traditional West End comedy, since it was to be performed in the New End Theatre in Hampstead, almost

West End. Rose Collis describes it as a political comedy of manners involving two couples, one lesbian and one heterosexual, who are trying to have children.[1] She comments:

> The play's happy ending, with the lesbian couple being successful and the heterosexual woman realising that she doesn't actually want a child, is an ironic reversal of 'normal' values.[2]

The play received good reviews, most of the audiences liking it in spite of the problem of style for the actors: the exaggerated playing intended as a critique of commercial comedy was taken seriously.

After a spell as artistic director of the Writers' Theatre Company at Birmingham Arts Lab, Kate Crutchley came to the Oval as a free-lance director in 1980 and was appointed as full-time programmer the following year, with somewhat less freedom than an artistic director since she was responsible to the committee running the Community Centre. However, she had the opportunity to commission new work, provided that the funding came from the Arts Council or Greater London Arts. One of her first commissions was an adaptation of Isobel Millar's *Patience and Sarah*, a 'cult' lesbian novel, based on a true love story between a woman painter and a farmer's daughter in nineteenth-century America. Permission was sought from the author, who was delighted. Joyce Halliday, whom Kate had met while playing in *The Changeling* at Stoke-on-Trent, was asked to write the script, although she was not herself a lesbian. Casting, which could have been difficult, was made easy by the fact that Split Britches happened to be in London for the season and had always wanted to play *Patience and Sarah*. In performance they put in the explicitly physical relationship which the heterosexual author had chosen not to include, Kate's argument being that the audience would expect it. Split Britches subsequently performed their own adaptation in their New York venue, the WOW Café, after the success of the London version, played at the Oval House and also at the Cockpit Theatre, London.

Kate's main satisfaction came from acting and directing, which had to some extent to be seen to be quite separate from her role as administrator. As the Oval House had no resident company, it could not mount its own productions, so Kate formed her own company, Character Ladies, in 1986, which performed at the Oval but received funding from elsewhere. There were three directors – Kate Crutchley, Susan Hayes and Dee Berwick – whose aim was 'to present new work by women writers, in particular to ensure that a lesbian consciousness is represented in the area of women's theatre.'[3]

The first production was my own play, *Supporting Roles*, in 1986. I had met Kate when my company New Plays and Players took a production into the Oval. She knew something of my work already since she had read my scripts for the Arts Council Drama panel. We talked, she asked to see some more work, and I gave her, among other things, an unperformed piece called *Sharing* based on a gay couple taking in lodgers. This should have been produced by Brighton Actors' Workshop, but as has often happened with my plays, a suitable cast could not be found. Kate asked why I had written a play about men rather than women. My reply was that a play about lesbians would have posed too many problems of political correctness. My doubts were not without foundation: the play which Kate commissioned, on the theme of the menopause, was found by some members of the audience to be ideologically unsound, in that two of the central characters had lived together for fourteen years in what might seem to be a mere imitation of heterosexual couplism!

One of the most important questions in *Sharing* had been the fulfilment of the protective, 'parental' impulse towards young people that gays and lesbians experience. This is not the same as actually wanting to have children; in the case of the male couple in *Sharing*, parenting a child was never a consideration. Confronted by a young man and woman who arrive at their house and prove to have all kinds of connections with their past life, they are emotionally disturbed. In *Supporting Roles* I returned to a similar sort of situation. One of the characters, Jo, lived for some years with a single mother, becoming a parent to her child. When they split up under traumatic circumstances, Jo lost a partner and a child. This child, years later, arrives on her doorstep, having run away from home, claiming love and affection, at a stage when Jo, on the threshold of her change of life, is trying to sort out a coherent plan for the future. The return of this lost child, the bond between the two, was written up somewhat melodramatically in the very first draft. I showed the reunion scene, which I felt was by far the best moment, to Kate, who, with the judgement of long experience, suggested that it was entirely wrong, too heavy. She was right. I scrapped it and the play took a different and much better turn, becoming lighter, developing into farce.

In her introduction to *Lesbian Plays: Two* Jill Davis describes *Supporting Roles* as a 'brave play', brave in its apparently reactionary stance. It has a traditional form (it was even written in three acts), it seems to uphold bourgeois values, there is no deconstruction, it is almost realistic, being 'a play set in probably the most common lesbian situation – the long-term domestic relationship'.[4] The characters are recognizable (too recognizable perhaps to some of my friends!); they are not caricatures or stereotypes. Three of them are 'middle-aged', one is 'old' and two are 'young'. Kate as director thought it important to cast actresses of the same age; they had to be 'convincing'. They had to have some inkling of what the menopause meant. When the play was performed by the Triangle Theatre Company in Boston, the cast, with one exception, were all young. The director, Kate Caffrey, invited an expert on the menopause from the local hospital to tell them what they could expect in later years. Somewhat shocked, they tried to incorporate this knowledge into their characterization. This kind of approach was not necessary for any of the plays previously discussed, as it was not important for the actors or the audience to 'believe in' the characters. Indeed, the empathy associated with naturalistic theatre was deliberately rejected in favour of what Joelle Taylor described as 'extreme performance' leading to a critique of the characters rather than any kind of psychological identification.[5] I shall return to the problem of 'realism' – 'classical realism', 'bourgeois realism' – in Chapter 10. Suffice it to say for the moment that it is regarded with immense suspicion by most lesbian feminist theorists, since it is misogynistic, and by obscuring the differences between lesbians and heterosexuals, it prevents political awareness. It is quite true that *Supporting Roles* does not emphasize lesbian difference – I don't think. I have to admit that I do not know from personal experience how heterosexual 'couples' work, because I have never been part of one. But I am part of a long-term lesbian couple and I want to write about *that*, whether it is considered to be politically correct or not!

Character Ladies' next production in 1987 was *Sappho and Aphrodite* by Karen Malpede. In her early days with Gay Sweatshop, Kate Crutchley had worked in a collective way, devising shows with the company (see Chapter 3 on *Care and Control*), which was an interesting experience that she preferred not to repeat with her own group. What she liked best was to work on a tight script, in a more or less finished form before the first rehearsal. The structure of the company to some extent dictated this, as different actresses were brought in for each production, with only a few weeks to prepare the show for performance. *Sappho and Aphrodite*, which had already been directed by Lois Weaver in New York, attracted Kate because it was entirely different from her previous productions, being a 'verse drama'. The New York version had been a sort of 'punk musical', the Oval House production was described by Kate as 'Swinburnian and beautiful'. 'It was all very pretty, but it got up people's noses because it was so beautiful! Wet, basically!'[6]

The following production was also beautiful visually, although not at all in the same way as *Sappho and Aphrodite*. While we were working on *Supporting Roles*, Kate and I had discussed a film treatment on the subject of the Ladies of Llangollen, famous for their romantic friendship at the end of the eighteenth and beginning of the nineteenth centuries. As no financial support could be found for a film, I proposed a stage version, *Ladies of the Vale*. It opened at the Oval House in 1988 directed by Tessa Schneidermann, with Kate playing the elder of the two 'Ladies', Eleanor Butler. I delivered a complete script which was reworked after rehearsal. The subject was quite difficult, being on the surface undramatic, apart from their initial 'elopement'. They left letters and diaries, all bearing witness to what would appear to be fifty years of harmonious togetherness in an idyllic country setting. They lived in the age of the Romantics, they were visited by Wordsworth, they became a legend in their lifetime on account of their love and loyalty to each other and their appreciation of the natural landscape. It was 'the good life' nineteenth-century style. It was essential to celebrate their devotion without ignoring the difficulties of settling in a foreign country (they came to Llangollen in North Wales from Ireland) among people who were not of their social class. They were both from an aristocratic background, Eleanor from an old Irish Catholic family, Sarah adopted by relatives of the Protestant ascendancy. They rented a modest cottage near a poor hill village, where the inhabitants spoke a different language. There were frictions with the local community apparent in their diaries: for example, their opposition to a new stone quarry which was to provide new jobs, on the grounds that it was ugly and unnecessary. There was the publication of an article in a national newspaper which suggested that their relationship was more unusual than the normal friendship between women, Eleanor being 'masculine' and Sarah 'feminine'. To the villagers, when they first arrived they must have seemed like haughty outsiders, foreign 'gentry', most definitely 'other'.

In *Ladies of the Vale* the village and heterosexual, country values are represented by a Welsh-speaking gardener, the common man! The 'common woman' is the ladies' maid, who accompanies them from Ireland. At her first meeting with the gardener he refuses to speak to her in English until she retaliates by addressing him in Irish. They subsequently become firm friends, treating each other with mutual respect. The gardener could have been played by a woman, but was in fact played by Welsh-speaking Fraser Cairns, described by Kate as a 'Character Laddie'. In spite of the fact that the director was heterosexual and there was a man in the cast, this play fits into Penny

Casdagli's definition of lesbian theatre as being controlled by lesbians (see Chapter 6).[7] Its basic theme is the negotiation of a lesbian couple's relationship with each other and with patriarchal society. It is impossible to know whether Eleanor and Sarah had a sexual relationship, although it is clear that they slept in the same bed and were physically uninhibited. Physical demonstrations of affection were fashionable among 'normal' women of the period. We, or rather Kate, decided that there should be no ambiguity for the Oval audiences, who would, after all, want to believe that the love was truly sexual as well as emotional.

This play, like so many other lesbian plays, in spite of being 'historical' had a close link with my own experience. At the time of writing my partner and I had just bought a cottage in an idyllic landscape, in a foreign country (France). I was particularly aware of all the aspects of 'otherness' which characterized us to the villagers, for the most part rooted in traditional Catholic family values.

After *Ladies of the Vale* Kate Crutchley looked around for something different again. She chose *Death on Lesbos* by Penny Gulliver, based on a real holiday, treated in the style of Agatha Christie's *Murder on the Orient Express*. Penny Gulliver had sent the script to Kate, who found it most entertaining. It was quite a rare event for her to receive a promising, unsolicited work, so she took it up gladly. It was set in a Greek taverna in summer, which fitted the weather at the time of the production, when both cast and audience were in shorts. It was such a happy production, that Kate thought she would commission another comedy from the same author.

Penny Gulliver's *The Sisters Mysteries* was inspired by Angela Brazil's school stories – back to the dormitory again! It was a rather complicated musical with 1950s-style song and dance routines. The story involved twins swapped at birth, a boy, the only boy at the school, whose name (a girl's name as well as a boy's name) had been put down to go there as soon as he was born. Set in Nunhead, it featured the ghost of a nun. Kate thought that the script was very clever. It would have worked better if she had concentrated on directing without also acting. At the time of production she had various health problems, which also prevented her giving the project the attention it deserved.

Another young writer that Kate Crutchley encouraged was one of the three directors of Character Ladies, Susan Hayes, an expatriate American who had been writing reviews of lesbian theatre since the days of Hard Corps. Her first play, *Byte*, was based on her adolescence. The first draft was fairly naturalistic, the second draft, influenced by Susan's exposure to absurdist theatre, changed form completely. It won first prize in the South London play competition, which meant that it had to be removed from the Oval House calendar, since Croydon Warehouse had an option to produce prize-winning plays. Susan then wrote a new work *Echo*, based again on her own experiences, she herself being cast by Kate as one of the main characters. As a member of the acting team she was willing for the script to undergo modification, to achieve a more dynamic form. Kate Crutchley described the process:

'They were doing it one run-through and I thought this is so long, this first scene, I said "Stop! It can't go on like this, let's break it up." And we all got on the floor and we got the scripts and we looked for word associations, to switch from one bit of a scene to another, to make it into lots of little scenes. Out of that came the style of the production, which was to swap around and put people into scenes they weren't in. If somebody was in your mind's eye they appeared, and people would be embracing the wrong person.'[8]

This was a modification of style which led to a sensuality which had not at first been clear. The stage was draped in red velvet, the characters wore velvet dresses, emphasizing the claustrophobic feel of modern Jacobean tragedy. The publicity leaflet reads:

ECHO: Four women weave a web of predatory intrigue. Each is compelled by passion, pride or promiscuity; each driven to plot, to punish or practise dissemblance.

ECHO: Four women with a weakness in common. Each believes in free will; and each is certain that their life is at their command. None is aware of the tragedy close at hand.[9]

Centred around the production by a group of lesbian actresses of an actual Jacobean tragedy, *The Changeling* by Thomas Middleton and William Rowley, *Echo* ends with the deaths of the villain and the innocent victim, an 'unrealistic' ending to what would seem to be a fairly convincingly realistic play about seduction and jealousy. In the final scenes we learn that madness is in the air, inherited insanity, and the vile seductress and her prey are revealed to be sisters, daughters of an unstable mother. What the play would seem to demonstrate are the disastrous consequences of selfish passion, of using others as objects.[10] *The Changeling* shows that this leads to disaster in heterosexual society, similar behaviour in lesbian society leads to its destruction.

Jigsaws by Jennifer Rogers, an Australian writer, which had already been performed several times in Australia, in fringe venues, followed *Echo*. It was a comedy about three generations of women – a granny, her two middle-aged daughters and the two daughters of one of them. One of the granddaughters is gay and decides to come out at Christmas. The audiences responded so well that Kate asked Jennifer Rogers for more scripts. *True Love*, specially written for the Oval House, was unfortunately never able to be performed.

The story of the Ladies of Llangollen continued to fascinate Kate. She asked me to write a musical version of *Ladies of the Vale*. This I was reluctant to do, but I agreed to write a completely new musical about their meeting and flight, the part of the adventure I had omitted in *Ladies of the Vale*, which began with their arrival in Wales. There were no men this time round, although Sarah and Eleanor's fathers were referred to constantly. The conflicts were played out rather with their 'mothers', in Eleanor's case her real mother, in Sarah's her guardian. I tried to mix romance and comedy, in a kind of Mozartian romp. The music by Carol Sloman was beautiful, complicated and indeed Mozartian. *The Ladies – The Musical* did not work. Perhaps it will one day.

Before Kate left the Oval we talked about a project based on the work of the Scottish painter, Joan Eardley. I rewrote an earlier script; the play, *High Tide*, was programmed, then fell through because of casting difficulties. Character Ladies ceased to be.

The plays that Kate Crutchley chose to direct at the Oval all had a fairly strong story line, written in an entertaining way. She considered it essential to capture the audience's attention from the start and keep it by inventive plots, witty dialogue.

'I think you actually get further and to more people by a story that everyone can relate to in some way, or grabs people or makes them feel. It's all right shouting and haranguing at people, but if they're not with you, you shout and harangue and lose them further. Your words say at the beginning of the play that this is a journey you go on, and you must feel safe, but you must *feel*, and come with us and we'll take you and we'll enlighten you. ... You have to come out feeling better than when you went in, or knowing something about yourself, you can't just sit back and let it all happen in front of you. On the other hand, if it isn't entertaining and it doesn't tell it well, in some way, whether it be excitingly told or interestingly interpreted ... if it doesn't grab you, in whatever style it's playing, then you're not going to take in the politics.'[11]

As theatre co-ordinator for the Oval House Kate invited performance-based companies, often influenced by dance, extremely experimental theatre, and visiting companies from the USA, as well as those who produced more traditional narrative-based work. Split Britches appeared frequently bringing with them a particularly North American style associated with other groups such as Spiderwoman and Hot Peaches, wild imagistic characters. Kate sees a clear difference between the development of American and British lesbian theatres.

'You see American performance theatre has come out of deconstructing their own culture and making their own personal statements. My theory of it has always been that the European version is slightly influenced by Pina Bausch and dancers, but more by Polish theatre, and the whole thing has come about because of the iron curtain. People couldn't say things so they said them with visual images. When British people pick that up, it becomes a bit self-indulgent because you don't have to do it like that.'[12]

When Kate left the Oval her job description was rewritten specifically to encourage non-verbal sorts of theatre, as there was a feeling that she had been pushing too much towards writers' theatre. Words were regarded by some members of the Arts Council panels as the prerogative of the upper classes; to emphasize physical wordless theatre with an emphasis on the visual aspect was considered to cut across class and ethnic boundaries. Kate's policy throughout ten years she described as 'seed-bedding'.

'It was seed-bedding at the lowest level – getting somebody from Brighton Polytechnic, for example, and letting them splash a jug of water over themselves in the upstairs studio. It was subsidized for that. Very often there would be something new and different about a student's work. There wasn't anywhere else in London that you could do that without paying, or without having to get a big audience. A lot of small spaces were pub theatres which had no funding, or they were large spaces, like the Drill Hall, which had to keep up their huge audiences, so they couldn't afford that sort of seed-bed level.'[13]

Many of the lesbian performers appearing at the Oval worked with several groups, not always lesbian, since they felt that other sorts of theatre should be integrated into lesbian politics. There was, for example, Penny Casdagli's emphasis on different ethnic mixes and theatre for the differently abled.

'Feminist theatre and gay theatre in particular, I think, made the most inroads into integrated theatre of all different cultures. It didn't just stick to its western tradition. It was important, but you kept going backwards and forward, a bit backwards and a bit forwards. Every time you change what you're doing you lose a bit of ground with your audiences and also you're expanding what you do, expanding your skills and talents but you're not necessarily getting any better at the ones you started with. I think that's why things can seem a bit tatty. No money, but you've got high hopes.'[14]

THE DRILL HALL

Julie Parker at the Drill Hall, as Kate Crutchley pointed out, cannot afford to 'seed-bed' in the same way, but she too has been important in nurturing lesbian theatre. Like Kate she trained as an actress, in the early 1970s, having spent her adolescence seeing as much theatre as possible in Nottingham, Derby and Sheffield, where the menu had to be traditional enough to appeal to all palates. Her political awareness was aroused during her years at the Central School of Speech and Drama in London, through seeing productions on the London fringe and meeting other politically committed students such as Nancy Diuguid. She saw the earlier, Leicester Haymarket, version of Jill Posener's *Any Woman Can* before it became a fully fledged Gay Sweatshop production. She came out and joined Gay Sweatshop for their lesbian tour. She remembers it as an extremely exciting, if unnerving, time, playing to lesbian audiences all over Britain, even in remote rural places. She was impressed by the way that Nancy Diuguid and Jill Posener led the consciousness-raising sessions; indeed she felt quite intimidated by their experience and knowledge. She was also disillusioned by the 'collective' process, which she did not think was the best way of dealing with a touring company.

After *Any Woman Can*, Julie Parker concentrated more on the administrative side, doing the bookings for a Gay Sweatshop tour of *Jingle Ball*, with Drew Griffiths. She is anxious that Drew Griffiths' contribution to the opening up of Sweatshop to women should be acknowledged. He fought for the inclusion of lesbians at a time when lesbian and gay politics were going in separate directions. His role in the company as supporter of woman as performer and as founder was crucial.

Julie Parker was subsequently involved in the Women's Festival at the Drill Hall when it was a venue called the Action Space building. She worked also with Hormone Imbalance (see Chapter 5), and with the company which ran the Action Space, who were coming to the end of their artistic energies. At the end of 1980, the Arts Council cut their grant, so Julie took over the building with help from a brewery, from Greater London Arts, with the intention of providing a venue for all the work that had until then been happening in pubs and clubs and back-rooms. The theatre opened in 1981 with a show called *Pack of Women* by Robin Archer. The intention was never to run a purely lesbian and gay theatre. The policy was to have a much more broadly based arts provision. A lot of the work was women's work, as it happened; black theatre groups and differently abled theatre groups were welcomed. However, there has always been an insistence on artistic values standing side by side with political commitment.

When I talked to Julie she expressed the same kind of mistrust of labels as Penny Casdagli.

'Here we are now, working with various new generation performers, writers, who, I think, are split down the middle between people who very clearly bring political will to their work, and those people who are "artists" and who say "I'm interested in the art that goes on stage" and don't really realize that what they're doing is political anyway.'[15]

Like Kate Crutchley, Julie Parker perceives a distinct difference between North American lesbian and gay theatre and British lesbian theatre, although the influence of North American work has become more apparent. The two cultures have given rise to different sorts of artistic expression, and an emphasis on an 'Americanization of style' may be quite wrong for some English performers and writers, who do not naturally express themselves in that way.

Julie Parker has experienced a dearth of lesbian scripts from the 1980s onwards. On the one hand more doors have opened for women, on the other there seem to be fewer of them trying to go through. The reason may be mainly economic – the necessity to earn a living which is not possible through writing plays. One is reminded of Jill Flemming's terse afterword to *The Rug of Identity*: 'This is my third play and I still don't have a toaster'.[16]

In 1995 the Drill Hall received a three-year grant from the Arts Council to set up a programme called 'Introductions' to encourage new lesbian and gay writers. It is possible that this would produce more lesbian work, but there has been such a strong move away from text-based pieces that the young people may no longer be interested in writing dialogue.

'I don't know.... I think there is a greater confidence again, and a desire to put on work that comes from a lesbian soul, or a dyke soul.'[17]

The future is bright for the Drill Hall. By the year 2000 the building will be completely redeveloped. There will be a brand-new theatre, capable of seating up to 400, a studio theatre and all the ancillary services (a bar is always fundamental to the attraction of a venue). This will give real commercial potential in the West End, for what is now totally a producing venue. Julie Parker has initiated a popular pantomime at the Drill Hall over the past few years, not described as lesbian, but usually with a lesbian love story and popular with straight as well as gay and lesbian audiences. She judges these pantomimes to be quintessentially English and would hope to see more work of a truly 'English' nature as well as North American lesbian theatre in future.

'There is an English lesbian theatre desperate to get out.'[18]

Notes

1. Rose Collis, 'Sister George is dead', in Trevor R. Griffiths and Margaret Llewellyn-Jones (eds), *British and Irish Women Dramatists since 1958: A Critical Handbook* (Buckingham: Open University Press, 1993).
2. *Ibid.*, p. 79.
3. Interview with Kate Crutchley, October 1994.
4. Introduction, in Jill Davis (ed.), *Lesbian Plays: Two* (London: Methuen, 1989).
5. Interview with Joelle Taylor, July 1995.
6. Interview with Kate Crutchley, October 1994.
7. Penny Casdagli, 'The whole nine yards', in Susan Raitt (ed.), *Volcanoes and Pearl Divers* (London: Onlywomen Press, 1995), p. 265.
8. Interview with Kate Crutchley, October 1994.
9. Publicity leaflet, November 1990.
10. Sandra Freeman, 'Fluid lines', in Raitt (ed.), *Volcanoes and Pearl Divers*.
11. Interview with Kate Crutchley, October 1994.
12. *Ibid.*
13. *Ibid.*
14. *Ibid.*
15. Interview with Julie Parker, July 1995.
16. Jill Flemming, *The Rug of Identity*, in Jill Davis (ed.), *Lesbian Plays* (London: Methuen, 1987), p. 111.
17. Interview with Julie Parker, July 1995.
18. *Ibid.*

Chapter 9

A Handful of Authors:
Nina Rapi, Phyllis Nagy,
Bryony Lavery and Sarah Daniels

NINA RAPI

This chapter deals with women who have made, and are making, important contributions to the images of lesbians on stage through their writing, but who may not necessarily see themselves as part of lesbian theatre in England, nor even call themselves lesbian playwrights. Nina Rapi, like Penny Casdagli, is Greek, but she has lived and worked in London for some years. She is a lesbian who nevertheless prefers to describe herself for the moment simply as a playwright.

'I don't call my theatre lesbian theatre, simply from the point of view that I perceive lesbian theatre to be company-devised work. In terms of calling myself a lesbian playwright, I would only if it becomes acceptable to call heterosexual playwrights heterosexual playwrights. To make that difference, I would refuse to call myself a lesbian playwright if the heterosexual playwrights assume the generic 'playwright' definition or description.... I have always perceived lesbian theatre as primarily white and English, so in that sense I've always felt excluded from it.'[1]

Nina Rapi started writing as a result of participating in a writers' workshop at the Drill Hall. She completed a short story which was turned into performance and which she was asked to expand into a full-length play, for a rehearsed reading at the Riverside Studios, Hammersmith, London. She had never thought of writing plays before, being from a small town in northern Greece where she had no exposure to theatre. Nevertheless, *Ithaka*, the work she developed from her short story, was considered interesting enough for publication after its public reading. So far it has never had a full production, although many of those present at the reading in 1989 felt very close to the content.

The central character in *Ithaka*, Sula, a young Greek girl, finds herself under immense pressure from her parents and brother to marry a repulsive, wealthy older man, who will make all their lives comfortable. This unfortunate alliance is presented to her as a daughter's normal duty. Even her best friend sees nothing wrong in taking a repellent husband and having lovers for excitement. The rigidity of Greek family culture is symbolized by both parents being set in concrete, each claiming to have been buried by the other. Sula runs away to Paris in search of freedom, only to discover that 'aliens' are condemned to be servants. She experiences a period of bliss with a beautiful lover, Debora, who is a wealthy concert pianist. The two women shut themselves away from the outside world, playing out a multitude of roles until Sula needs to break out once more, to establish herself in a bedsit. She dreams of becoming an actress, but is suspicious of the motives of her director friend Louise when the latter offers her a major role. When her old Greek friend Lenna arrives to take her back to a life of political activism, she is overjoyed until she imagines all kinds of ulterior motives. Doubts are constantly put into her mind by a mysterious stranger dressed black, who appears every so often to warn her that things are not what they seem. In the final scene the stranger is revealed as Sula's shadow:

SHADOW: I am the one you can't run away from. I am none other than your Shadow.

SULA: Tell me what Shadow is.

SHADOW: Shadow is the edge of time, is the crack of dawn. Shadow is a fathomless depth where you can only hang suspended, never reaching the end. Shadow is thoughts never formed in words, dreams that won't go away, poems that refuse to be moulded. Shadow is unfettered desire and unconquered passion. Shadow is the time when every moment reveals a new possibility. It is the darkness that defines light, the hell that heaven is marked with. Shadow is the eyes that couldn't see, the lives that couldn't be, the chains that were never broken.[2]

Beautiful and fulfilling for a time, lesbian love is shown to be dangerously claustrophobic. Sula escapes from the bonds of the nuclear family to become involved in a different sort of 'family', equally entrapping. Love gives a sense of worth, of security; it also leads to dominance and dependence:

SULA: But what shall I do without her? And who can't be without
          her? And how can I live without her?
SHADOW: How impotence and sadism mingle and try to pass for
          love.[3]

Love is nothing without freedom, which Shadow defines as 'knowing
what you want and need and how to get it'. The play abounds in
images of bondage: Sula is tied up by her parents, tied up by her
lover, becomes trapped in the same cement-like matter that imprisons
her parents. She can begin to break away only when she accepts her
shadow.

Having discovered that she could express her creativity in the
theatre Nina followed an MA course in drama at the University of
Essex, during which time she wrote a one-woman show *Johnny Is
Dead*, later produced in London as part of the first one-person play
festival in 1991. From this came an unpaid commission to write a full-
length play, *Dream House*, to be performed at the Oval House. Out
of this company of between ten and twelve, only one actress was
lesbian, a situation which proved problematic. A kiss between a
'messenger', played by the dyke, and a mother, played by a straight
actress, gave rise to arguments and debates as to whether the two
characters were lesbian or not, in spite of the author's assertion that
they definitely were. Nina found it astonishing how much prejudice
and how many misconceptions about lesbianism exist in the theatre.
Even in *Johnny Is Dead*, when the director, the writer and the actress
playing a lesbian were all dykes, there had been some difficulties over
certain lines.

'There was a line where the daughter (lesbian) says to the mother
(straight, portrayed by a straight actress) said "I'm into women now."
And she said, "Rather than say it like that, can we not say 'I don't
fancy men?'" I said, "That's not the point, it's got nothing to do with
men."'[4]

In fact many heterosexual actresses had claimed to know more about
dykes than the lesbian author.

The brief for *Dream House* was vague – secrets and the subcon-
scious, which Nina interpreted as meditation on the nature of reality and
androgyny. It is a fantasy, a fairy story, about a mother who is not a
mother, who lives in a house which turns out not to be her house, with
three 'daughters' who are not in fact her own, where the only contact
with the outside world is through a messenger, Blue, an androgynous
woman and her lover. The mother keeps secrets, hides the truth from

her 'children', who play games of make-believe with each other, inventing romances which are less strange than the 'reality' of their births. We ask what a 'family' really is when absent, or virtually non-existent fathers, dead mothers, are less important than the woman who has taken in the orphans. 'Reality' is what we construct for ourselves, for each other. The women are all energized by the arrival of the Messenger, who brings them real objects such as paintbrushes, fabrics, books, as well as an account of the outside world; the 'real' world which exists for them only in so far as she creates it.

MESSENGER:

> There she is, waiting for me. Always waiting for me to come, And I always do, giving shape to her time ... reminding her of the passing of seasons , of the body she has and denies ... of the life she could have and doesn't.[5]

In a more symbolic sense the messenger *is* the outside world, yearned for in the isolation of the house of dreams.

Dream House led to another commission by a Greek Cypriot company. Nina Rapi attempted to write a realistic play about the Greek Civil War, but found her natural tendency to refer to the unconscious led her back to a more surrealistic approach. Once more, heterosexual actresses were worried about playing the two central lesbian characters, and attempted to deny their lesbianism, claiming that there were no lesbians involved in the Greek Civil War. Nina's attendance at rehearsals was even regarded as threatening, since there was an ignorance about, and a fear of, lesbian desire. The actresses' nervousness led Nina to be somewhat cold and remote, which in turn led to disappointment with an apparent *absence* of desire. However, at the end of the production, over a meal, there was a veritable explosion of curiosity about dykes and their way of life. Questions which the company had never dared to ask poured out: 'Do you think I'm butch or femme?' 'What is this about "Vanilla"?' 'Tell me about S and M', etc., etc.

This play, *Dance of Guns*, returns to the situation of a mother left to bring up three daughters. There is an absent brother, for whom Nina would like to have created a proper role, but who appears as a corpse only at the end of the play, as there were no men in the company with whom she was working. The first scene is a tender parting between Rosa, one of the daughters, and her lover Ellie. The stage directions read:

Their dynamic is playful, familiarly sexual, bonded – but with an element of tension.[6]

Rosa is returning home, having lost her job, unnerved by the tense atmosphere in Thessalonika. Greece is on the brink of a civil war, with the people exhausted after the Second World War but angry and rebellious. Ellie declares her intention of joining the rebels should the war happen; Rosa cannot believe that it will. Thus the main theme of the play from the outset is the way the relationship between the women is threatened by family ties and profound differences in political attitudes. When war does break out they become involved in a nightmare. Ellie becomes a guerrilla fighter, hiding out in the mountains; as far as Rosa's family is concerned, she is part of a monstrous band of outlaws. When she arrives on their doorstep, wounded, they nevertheless take her in, as Rosa's friend, until she has recovered. This leads to terrible nationalist retribution in the form of the multiple rape of Rosa's most religious sister Daphne, who loses her mind, withdrawing into silence. The youngest sister, Ismene, who had hoped to escape to Paris to become a singer, turns to prostitution. Rosa herself tries to purge her guilt by joining Ellie and the Communists in spite of her loathing for guns. The tragedy which was foreshadowed in a dream sequence, a prologue to the play, comes to pass: without recognizing him she shoots her own brother, Angelo, who is a Nationalist soldier.

Not only is the lesbian relationship doomed, but also the lovers themselves bring disaster to their families. Ellie's mother is tortured and dies because her daughter is a rebel, Rosa's involvement with Ellie ultimately leads to the rape of her sister and death of her brother. None of these tragedies would have occurred without the war, equally none would have happened had Rosa not fallen in love with Ellie. Lesbian love is a love which divides daughters from their families, thereby threatening the institution which is the most sacrosanct. A woman's role is to become a mother and a mother's to provide for her children, making sure they have economic security even if that security is the opposite of what they want:

MOTHER: As you know, having three girls is for a mother a mixed blessing.

ROSA: You needn't worry about me, mother, I can take care of myself. I have done for years.

MOTHER: What you do for yourself is one thing. But I as a mother have an obligation to provide for my children, leave something behind.

ROSA: It's quite simple really. Just split everything in four.

MOTHER: Well, it's not so simple. You know what a comfort Angelo has been to me since your father died. Without him both the sheep and the orchard would have finished.

ROSA: I know he's given his youth to you.

MOTHER: And he'll stay with me till my dying days, hopefully with a wife who isn't jealous of his love for his mother. So of course I must leave the house to him.

ROSA: I see, and the rest?

MOTHER: Well, he grew up at the shop, so it's rightfully his really. And I've invested in yours and Daphne's education, so I was thinking of splitting the orchard between you two.

ROSA: And what of Ismene?

MOTHER: I was thinking of finding a man who doesn't want a dowry.

ROSA: What man doesn't want a dowry?

MOTHER: An ... older man perhaps.

ROSA: Mother!

MOTHER: Shhhsss, you'll wake her up. I've already had two suitable proposals for her. Men with money, widowers, who just want a young and beautiful bride.

ROSA: But she wants to go to France![7]

The family is thus presented as the same oppressive force as it was in *Ithaka* but in a more direct, less symbolic way. The 'freedom' that Rosa finally achieves is limited, it is freedom in hiding.

ROSA: I luckily remain free. Of sorts. Hidden and underground but free. No iron bars around me. Most women political prisoners are now released, on furlough, thanks to international pressure. But no Amnesty yet.

         ...

         For me the hardest thing has been not being able to tell my family I killed Angelo. ... So, a permanent exile I am after all and in my home too. Strange what a total coward I become when it comes to telling the truth to my mother and sister.... Maybe one day ... maybe one day, I'll stop hiding.[8]

Nina sees the *Dance of Guns* as an interesting departure towards some sort of social realism with surreal elements.

Nina Rapi's latest play was *Dangerous Roses*, based on the life of Isabelle Eberhart, an adventuress who dressed up as a man at the beginning of the twentieth century. Although Isabelle was of Russian parentage she was brought up in Switzerland, where she learnt several languages. She ended up in North Africa, living as an Arab man. This was Nina's second paid commission, a vehicle for an actress to show off her talents to casting agents. She judges it an unfortunate project. The author's interests lay in the exploration of the double masquerade, the function of cross-dressing, the assumption of an identity twice removed from her origins; the straight actress and straight director had other interests, which meant that in the end the constraints they imposed as 'the paying customer' meant that it was more their product than the author's. Interesting questions are thus raised about the artistic control of paid commissions, and about the differences between the lesbian playwright and the straight actress in the way they see the script. Nina has often experienced homophobia among actresses wishing to redefine her lesbian characters for her. She has encountered archaic prejudices which are stronger than personal observations:

'There is something about performing lesbian characters that embrace masculinity that heterosexuals seem to have difficulty with.'[9]

Heterosexual women directors and heterosexual men have proved to be more supportive and understanding. When I talked with Nina she had written nothing for over a year because she wanted her next play to be 'all her own' with no interference. She had waited for her ideas to become crystal-clear before putting pen to paper. This had happened four days before our meeting, so she was set to begin. Her sights are now fixed on Off West End venues. It is a question of moving into a different cycle, changing form and content. By the year 2001 she may feel confident enough to move on again, into the West End itself. She believes that having confidence in what one is doing is the most important way to succeed.

PHYLLIS NAGY

In 1995 Phyllis Nagy was a stone's throw away from the West End as writer in residence at the Royal Court, London. A US citizen by birth, she has been associated with the Royal Court since 1991, settling permanently in England in 1992. She studied musical composition and theory and poetry in the USA and had intended to be a poet. Her earliest writing took the form of unfashionably long narrative poems. One of her lecturers suggested that she might try a dramatic form, so she enrolled in a playwriting course, which was of little help except in introducing her to a tutor, a playwright who became her mentor. At the same time she continued her studies in music, which was most useful since this taught her all she needed to know about structure and tone, which she would not have learnt from textual analysis. However, she considered that the work she produced at this period was not good enough; therefore at the end of her studies she travelled around North America taking a series of jobs until she was twenty-eight, always keeping open the possibility of maybe writing for the theatre one day.

Plaza Dolores was Phyllis Nagy's first actual play. It was a Gothic drama with Surrealist edges, set in the American South. It was written for a workshop run by a friend and producer in a small theatre in Vermont. In two weeks of working on the project she learnt more than she had from her playwriting classes or from seeing plays. Although it had no lesbian content, it dealt with themes which have subsequently run through much of her work: an obsession with time, the nature of time and how it passes, a fascination with the nature of sexuality, duplicity as it relates to the way we deal with sexuality, fate, coincidence and the nature of love. It also had a mother–daughter relationship which followed the same course as her later mother and daughter relationships but because it was following a Gothic, 'Tennessee Williamsesque' style, it was 'much less conclusively drawn out to the bone'.[10]

What followed was the very first draft of Phyllis Nagy's *Butterfly Kiss*, which took about four years to be written to her satisfaction. Afraid to send it out, she constantly altered it, a luxury she can now no longer afford. In the middle of 1990 it was given a workshop production in a professional theatre in Los Angeles and Phyllis was taken up by an agent. She joined a playwriting organization in New York where she met established playwrights, including several women writers. It was an exciting and disappointing experience: having been inspired by seeing *Cloud Nine* as a teenager, she expected women to write like Caryl Churchill. She found that in the USA in the 1980s women wrote about subjects that men expected them to be interested in, such as childbirth, divorce and breast cancer. She did not want to address these issues, at least not in overt, obvious ways.

One of the issues she *did* address was lesbian culture, in *Girl Bar*, at the end of the 1980s. Its setting is 'the Girl Bar of our dreams' where every night is Monday night, time and space not being really sequential. There are six women characters and no plot. It caused a complete uproar in the lesbian community of the USA because it dealt with themes which were normally not spoken about, such as the obsession with the straight girl, racism within the lesbian community, denigration of the pre-Stonewall Butch and the older lesbian. It was an articulation of an anger about the fact that the lesbian community was not learning from the past. Lesbians may not have liked it but it proved very popular with middle-aged straight women, playing for years in small theatres in small places. In 1994 there was a very successful production in Los Angeles, which would seem to indicate that the time was ripe for lesbians to listen and approve.

In 1990–91, New Dramatists, the playwrights' organization to which she belonged, was given money by the New York Times Foundation to fund an exchange of writers with the Royal Court, London. The result was that Phyllis Nagy came to London for a fortnight for a rehearsed reading of her play *Awake*, in 1991. This marked the beginning of her real professional career.

Returning to New York, she wrote *Weldon Rising*, very quickly. The subject which had been maturing in her mind for a while, concerned the erosion of gay life in the West Village, the incidence of gay bashing and the double standards in the community.

'The women in New York, who had been very supportive of the gay men's crisis, had been very supportive over AIDS, had once again taken on the traditional role of nurse and mother, suddenly started resenting it, because the boys weren't there for them and they never would be.'[11]

When the play was finished in February 1992, Phyllis returned to the UK permanently. Stephen Daldry, the artistic director of the Royal Court in London, organized its production jointly with Liverpool Playhouse. The whole event was intimidating and somewhat baffling. The critical response surprised her; reviewers did not treat her as a promising young playwright but a writer of much greater experience. There were vituperative reviews in the gay press. As an afterword to the published edition she wrote:

> It is much easier for audiences – both straight and gay – to accept lesbian and gay characters who obsess and fret about their gayness as an *issue* (and who, as a result, enable an audience to feel they are on solid ground) than it is to accept lesbians and gay characters who sometimes 'misbehave' and who do not present themselves as sexless, vaguely martyred but politically hip individuals who manipulate empathy and equate it with victimhood. That kind of characterisation creates a false empathy in good liberal audiences, and that empathy is built on guilt. *Weldon Rising* is not a politically correct gay issue play, nor does it trade on collective guilt, which is why I suspect it was either completely ignored or poorly received by the London gay press.[12]

She also gives her reason for writing the play as:

> My growing frustration over how we might best conduct our lives, and still
> manage to live in the midst of violence and its inevitable by-product, fear,
> led me finally to write *Weldon Rising*.[13]

The setting is a cobbled backstreet in New York's meat-packing
district. A huge map of the district covers one surface. The action
moves between the street and symbolically represented apartments. It
is hot, incredibly hot, and gets hotter throughout, until in the end the
whole world seems to be melting. Natty Weldon, a half-starved gay
man, Marcel, a transvestite, and Jaye and Tilly, lesbian lovers, all
live in this space. They all know that the heat started when Natty's
lover Jimmy was stabbed on the street by a young stranger, Boy, who
is 'so beautiful and dangerous that no two people can remember him
the same way.... The sum of all fears'.[14] All of them witnessed the
stabbing, all of them, apart from the victim, afraid of the threatening
outsider in a predominantly gay quarter. The encounter, the murder,
is replayed along with memories of Natty and Jimmy's life together,
including their first meeting. In his grief Natty becomes more and
more insubstantial, exciting the pity of the two women, who had seen
him and his lover often and wanted to make some sort of contact.

JAYE:　We saw you a lot, you and your lover. You shopped at all
the food stores we couldn't afford. We envied your
clothing. We fantasised about what art you'd collect. And
each time we saw you we said, we really must invite them
up for a drink.[15]

Natty and Jimmy had also noticed the women, keeping their
distance but feeling well-disposed towards them. Marcel, on the
contrary, is affronted by the idea of dykes in the area.

MARCEL:　... WHERE IS THAT DIZZY FAGGOT MUSIC
COMING FROM?
NATTY:　It's the lesbians above the poultry market. They like to
dance.
MARCEL:　There are DYKES in this neighbourhood?
NATTY:　Uh-huh. They're very cute. Serious types. I think they
drink a lot.
MARCEL:　Well. Marcel says this is BOYS' TOWN, honey. Marcel
says this is not the neighbourhood for LADIES' HOUR.
NATTY:　You've never seen them? Dragging groceries and laundry
behind them? They do an awful lot of laundry.

MARCEL: No fucking way. Marcel converses with MEN.

NATTY: Marcel never talked to me. Marcel never talked to Jimmy.

MARCEL: Listen here, Mister Sandman. Marcel can spot those who are worth conversing with. Marcel knows a dud when Marcel spots one. LISTEN UP MY LEZZIE SISTERS. CUT THE FUCKING MUSIC. DANCE TO YOUR OWN DIFFERENT FUCKING DRUMMER, BUT LEAVE MARCEL OUT OF IT.[16]

They all finally get together in the street when Jaye and Tilly return from a beer-stealing expedition. In the extraordinary temperatures the beer seems to be unable to quench their thirst or to make them drunk: they drink twenty-seven cans without being affected. They offer to share it with the other two in a sort of 'street party'. Bonding begins between Natty and the two women in spite of Marcel's hostility. Jaye and Tilly tell how they first met. Since they have introduced themselves as liars, there is no way of judging the truth of this version.

TILLY: I met Jaye at Kennedy Airport. She was to meet a cousin from Los Angeles. I flew into New York looking for a home. I was especially unattractive that day. I approached the ground transportation exit, I felt a hand grab my arm. I whirled around and it was Jaye. She said –

JAYE: You're ugly, but you must be the one.

TILLY: I couldn't tell if this was a compliment. She took my bags to her car, muttered something about an Uncle Roger.

JAYE: I passed on regards from Aunt Ida.

TILLY: I wondered where we were headed. She said –

JAYE: The barbecue's at three.

TILLY: I mean who could argue? I began to hallucinate. Maybe I was destined to be in the back seat of a stranger's Honda Civic with no idea of where I was being taken. All I could think about was her eyes. Her funny hat. The way she gripped the steering wheel.

JAYE: I stopped three times so she could vomit.

TILLY: Jesus was I sick. But I couldn't help it. This was completely unlike me, to be in a car with a sexy woman who was wearing a funny hat. A hat with a musical flower attached to its brim. Wow. And then, as I was about to pass out from the thrill of it, she said –

JAYE: I wish I'd known I had such a wacko cousin.

TILLY: I blurted out, but hey, I'm not your cousin. Stop the car, there's been a mistake.

JAYE: I stopped the car.

TILLY: But there was no mistake. She turned to me. I was a mess. Drool dangling from the corners of my mouth. Acne grew spontaneously, like spores. She said –

JAYE: I know you're not my cousin. I was just testing the quality of your imagination.

TILLY: Oh sure, I said. But I don't even *know* you.

JAYE: And why the fuck *don't* you know me? Said I.

TILLY: Well. So. Why not? It was true. She looked at me and there was a conspiracy of understanding.[17]

This echoes Jimmy and Natty's first meeting; love at first sight. In the final scene, Tilly and Jaye make love while Jaye holds tightly on to Natty's hand. Tilly and Natty are wearing each other's clothes, Natty is burning up with the heat; Tilly, who has cut herself on splinters of a perfume bottle, is bleeding herself clean, shedding herself. Jimmy appears dressed in white, holding a knife, and takes Natty in his arms; he cuts through the map of the district and disappears with his lover, leaving Jaye and Tilly for a moment a splendid sight amid the ruin, until they disappear too in a glorious flash. Marcel has already disappeared in the brilliant glow of a car's headlights. Love performs transcendence, transfiguration, purification; it should be stronger than shame, guilt and fear:

JAYE: And then one day, we get well. Shake the shame right outta our hair, and wonder, well why in the fuck did we ever let it get the best of us? The trick is to get rid of it. Before the point of implosion. Before it eats us to pieces.[18]

The move from suspicious separatism (in the first scene Tilly says, 'Men are violent. Even when they wear dresses. Let's stay home forever') to supportive friendship reflects the change in political attitude from radical feminism to 'queer' politics. Hostility is pointless:

MARCEL: I didn't think I'd live to see the day when a lesbian became my pimp.

TILLY: Times change.[19]

Before the production of *Weldon Rising*, Phyllis Nagy had already been commissioned by Lois Weaver to write a piece for Gay Sweatshop – *Entering Queens*. Working on this was a bad experience, because she felt that the actual production ruined the play; she admits that it was extremely difficult, in spite of being short, and that she should have written something much simpler, within the reach of most actors. Still relatively inexperienced, she thought that she should write the best play that she could from an artistic point of view, which would challenge and extend all concerned. She did not realize that Sweatshop's criteria were not, could not be, only artistic, that the company had other briefs. The experience taught her that the fringe was not for her.

'I don't write the kind of plays that support that kind of ethos. Some people do – if I wrote plays that took place in one room and required very little subtlety, finesse or irony from actors, then yes. It was troubling. Everyone was expected to work not for free, it wasn't that, it was the sort of aura "all for one, one for all", it was the process not the product, and anyone who makes a career in any field knows that it isn't the process that's important in building a career, it's the product, whether you're a teacher, a writer or a truck driver – if you don't deliver the goods, you have no career.'[20]

Phyllis Nagy considers that *Entering Queens* is a good play and regrets not having had a production which did it justice. This failure did not harm her career, perhaps because she is still young, and was able to transcend a temporary setback. Her 'media friendly' personality helps to counteract the expected image of the outrageous dyke, charming interviewers into forgiving her 'mistakes'.

Commissions came from several quarters – Royal Court, Hampstead Theatre Club, American theatres – an adaptation of *The Scarlet Letter*, *Trip's Cinch* for the Actors' Theatre of Louisville, a response to David Mamet's *Oleana*, which had filled her with dismay. She wrote *Disappeared* with a view to winning an award, and won the Mobil prize. It has a heterosexual man as a central character; it appears to be literal, logical, linear, which appealed to the critics who responded very well when it opened at the Leicester Haymarket and during the subsequent tour. It was the play she wanted to write, clothed in a more 'acceptable' form than she would normally choose. She is somewhat alarmed by the fact that in two weeks she could produce a work which was 'what the public wanted', opening up the temptation of commercialism.

Butterfly Kiss, conceived years previously, was performed at the Almeida Theatre, London, in 1994. Lily Ross, a woman in her twenties, has shot her mother Jenny. Lily's lover and her lawyer Jackson try to find a motive. We are faced with three generations of women, influencing and depending on each other – Sally, Lily's grandmother, her daughter Jenny and Lily herself. Sally dreams of going to live in Florida but needs Jenny to go with her, even though she is in the para-

doxical position of having to take care of her daughter. Jenny fantasizes about her own life as a famous singer and about her daughter
marrying a member of the Kennedy family. The mother's reality is a
woman despised and abandoned by her husband, dominated by her
mother, clinging on to her daughter who will never be what she
hopes. Lily breaks away from the enclosure of the nuclear family, by
taking a lesbian lover. All the pressures have been to live a 'normal'
heterosexual life: at the age of fourteen she took her first lover, a
friend of her father's, a sexual encounter on a beach which was engin-
eered and witnessed by her father. She is dazzled by her father's
mistress, a 'Countess' (by marriage), a dancer, the epitome of tawdry
sexuality. Her grandmother opens her eyes to the degradation that her
mother experiences in order to have any sexual relations with her
husband, to the fact that a woman's identity is largely in her ability
to please her man. Jenny is obsessed with becoming too fat, dressing
in black to appear slimmer and because Lily's father prefers her in
that colour. Lily herself equates slenderness with sexuality. Her first
remark to her lover on the beach was 'Hi there, Teddy, I'm Lily
Ross. Do you think I'm fat?'[21] When her lover visits her in prison she
says to her, 'Putting on some weight, aren't you?'[22]

A lesbian relationship is not enough to break the grandmother–
mother–daughter tyranny. Lily has found a way of escaping from
marriage; she cannot live her own life ignoring what is happening to
her mother. Lily enters a different life by becoming a lesbian; Jenny
has nowhere to escape to but death. By shooting her mother Lily
liberates her, at the same time liberating herself from the emotional
hold her mother has over her. At the end of the first act she tells her
lover that her mother asked her to kill her.

The bond between Lily and Jenny is physical as well as emotional.
At one point in the play Jenny persuades Lily into pretending to be
her father and dancing with her.

JENNY: Why don't you talk to me about dancing?
LILY: I've never been dancing.
JENNY: Don't be so *boring*, baby. That's what your daddy says to
    me. Why don't you talk to me about dancing, he says.
LILY: Mama, it's Lily. I'm here. Not him.
JENNY: It's not me any more, Jennifer. I'm not the fella you
    hitched up with. Why don't you wrap your arms round me
    and DANCE?
    (JENNY *wraps her arms around* LILY. *She kisses* LILY's
    neck. She begins to dance.)

JENNY:	Oh yeah. Yesss. Of course. So sweet, baby. So light on your feet. Teach me what you know.
	(LILY *pushes* JENNY *away*.)
LILY:	I can't do this, mama. It's not right.
JENNY:	What are you looking at? What? How come you're looking at me in that way?
LILY:	I don't know. I ... can't touch ... you that way.
JENNY:	Whatsa matter, Lily-pie? Too old to hold your mama? Too smart?
LILY:	I'm not him, mama.
JENNY:	Who loves you best? Who loves you more?
LILY:	I can't say.
JENNY:	WHO LOVES YOU BEST?
LILY:	You love me best.
JENNY:	Who loves you more?
LILY:	You. You, mama.
JENNY:	And who's your sweetheart?
LILY:	You're my sweetheart.
JENNY:	And I'm the nicest person you know.
LILY:	Yes.
JENNY:	So. What have you got to tell me?
LILY:	(*Hesitates, offers her hand to* JENNY) Would you.... Why don't you dance with me? Just a little.[23]

The fantasy of the happy nuclear family is contrasted with the reality of manipulation and emotional blackmail. It is the American dream which has such a hold on the imagination that it takes over from the bleakness of real life. In her prison cell, Lily invents an alternative scenario for her family, based on what each one of them wanted to happen.

LILY:	My father is a renowned lepidopterist. My mother attends each of his lectures and she understands everything he says. Of course, she's very busy herself, being as she's rather a good mezzo-soprano. Just a cut below super stardom, but she does well. She's in demand. My grandmother, once a famous mezzo herself, has retired to Fort Lauderdale. And because she's very wealthy, men pursue her. She's dazzling.[24]

In fact the last time we see the 'dazzling' Sally, she is scrubbing clean the blood splattered all over the kitchen:

(SALLY *crawls round the floor. She scrubs the floor with her palms.*)

SALLY: I had to scrub Jenny's blood from the floor. Look. See
          that? I'm scrubbing this spot, see? And it up and
          disappears on me. The blood is jumping around the
          linoleum and I can't catch it and I think I'm going crazy,
          but no. No. It's really happening. A blood vessel in my
          head pops. I hear it. Like it's mocking me. I'm having a
          fucking stroke. TAKE CARE OF ME.[25]

Before Lily murders Jenny, they both go along with Jenny's dream of
Lily being a proud wife and mother, a successful song-writer. These
lies are necessary between them, just as it is essential to repeat familiar actions to establish their closeness. Lily shoots Jenny as she
brushes her hair, holding her close in the intimacy of an exclusive
couple.

Phyllis Nagy's *The Strip*, first performed at the Royal Court,
London, in 1995, moves between the USA and Britain. No more
succinct summary of the play could be found than the one on the back
of the published edition:

> Opening with the memorable line, 'Female impersonation is a rather
> curious choice for a woman, Miss Coo', THE STRIP follows the fortunes
> of the aforementioned Ava Coo, along with a love-struck repo man and an
> obsessive lesbian journalist, as they cross America in search of fame and
> self-gratification at the Luxor Hotel, Las Vegas. Meanwhile in Earl's
> Court, an enterprising astrologer, a family of fugitive white supremacists
> and a gay pawnbroker set off to Liverpool in search of justice. Moving
> amongst them all is the mysterious Otto Mink.[26]

There are five American characters and five English. They are
all less 'real' and more 'surreal' than the characters in either *Weldon
Rising* or *Butterfly Kiss*. The 'reality' which is the springboard is
Las Vegas, particularly The Strip, a three-and-a-half-mile stretch of
Las Vegas boulevard lined by thirty casinos, including the spectac-
ular Luxor Hotel, a 2,526-room bronzed-glass pyramid, 350 feet
high and 561 feet along each side of the base. Through the hollow
centre runs the Nile River. Visitors have a choice of three attrac-
tions (besides the gambling and the variety shows) – a virtual reality
motion machine, 'In Search of the Obelisk', an interactive movie,
'Luxor Live', or 'Theater of Time' with three-dimensional special
effects. A capitalist Wonderland where dreams of wealth can be real-
ized and transformation can happen, it is represented in the stage
set of *The Strip* by an enormous three-dimensional Sphinx and
Pyramid.

Ava Coo's dream is to make the big time as an entertainer, a female impersonator. In a curious contortion of gender-bending she is a woman pretending to be a man pretending to be a woman. She is given a promise of employment if she manages to find a mysterious place called Tumbleweed Junction. She sets off on a quest accompanied by Calvin Higgins, who has been sent to repossess her car but who falls in love with her and, for part of the way, by Kate Buck, a lesbian journalist looking for a truck driver accused of the mass murder of other truck drivers. Kate and Ava have a sexual encounter, much to Ava's surprise, since she had not recognized lesbian tendencies within herself.

Tumbleweed Junction is in Las Vegas, an establishment owned by a god-like magician of a man, Otto Mink, who had promised Ava a job. For some time Otto has employed Ava's mother, Tina, as a lavatory cleaner. Ava is totally unaware of this fact since she has very little contact with her mother. Tina constantly thinks of her daughter, nevertheless, having an imaginary contact through cassette tapes which she records but never sends. In the recording she describes a happy life with her second husband, Mr Marshall:

TINA: Dear Ava, I probably didn't get your last letter because
        when I married Mr. Marshall, I moved house. Not that my
        split level wasn't nice enough for us but. ... Well now I
        live in a one-hundred and fifty acre ranch with Mr.
        Marshall.... You would like Mr. Marshall. He's tall and
        rarely speaks. But he opens doors for me and buys me
        bunches of daisies from the Seven-Eleven and really, Ava,
        that's more than good enough. I miss your voice honey.
        It's hard being a casino supervisor in Vegas, but it's
        rewarding. As you can imagine, I don't make many
        friends on the gaming floor, but I am a fair boss and last
        week I got Dolly Parton's autograph. Mr. Marshall breeds
        horses. I keep an eye out for promising colts.[27]

In fact, Tina lives alone in a caravan where she spends most of her non-working time obsessively chopping up mounds of salad vegetables. As in *Butterfly Kiss*, the mother builds the fantasy world which she expects her daughter to collude in.

Meanwhile in Earl's Court, a gay couple, Martin and Tom, and their straight astrologer friend Susy Bradfield find themselves involved with Lester and Loretta Marquette and their strangely silent baby. Lester and Loretta are Americans, on the run because Lester is the truck-driver who committed the murders. He is the innocent and unsuspecting tool of a powerful figure known as Mr Greene, who turns out to be Otto Mink. Like God, Otto moves in mysterious ways, his motives unfathomable, his actions unpredictable. All the characters are controlled by him.

OTTO: LORETTA, LORETTA, I NEED LORETTA. LORETTA, I WANT LORETTA. WHY LORETTA, WHY HAVE YOU BETRAYED ME?

OTTO *drops to his knees and lets out a quite unearthly and long cry of sorrow or deep deep pain. He flings the gorgeous bunch of flowers away. At the moment* OTTO *lets out his cry, these things happen simultaneously.*

KATE *about to plant a kiss on* AVA*'s lips covers her ears as if reacting to the most piercing painful sound she's ever heard.* AVA *faints quietly away.*

MARTIN, *squeezing* LESTER*'s balls ever tighter, hurls himself off* LESTER *and the multigym as if he's been hit in the stomach by some mammoth force.* LESTER *hyperventilates.*

TINA*'s tiny portable television set explodes.*

The Ouija board's pointer flies off violently and with great speed, up, up and away.

OTTO*'s bunch of flowers lands at* JFK*'s grave at Arlington National Cemetery. The eternal flame is suddenly extinguished.*

And without warning or prelude, the sound of a tremendous approaching storm, like a hurricane or a tornado-wind, like a portent, overwhelms the space. AVA *sits up suddenly, wide awake.*

The space darkens ominously, as if it's closing in on its inhabitants. Everybody looks to the sky as if it holds some kind of answer.

Blackout.

End of Act One.[28]

At the end of Act Two, Otto pushes apart the walls of the Sphinx and proclaims:

OTTO: What's your desire, what's the situation? I'll tell you the situation: I've got the booze, I've got the car stereos, I've got fax modems, I've got what you want. I've got what you want. I've got what you WANT.[29]

He does not, however, have the last word, or the last sound. This is left to Baby Ray, Loretta's child, who begins to cry for the first time.

Everyone is confused, everyone is in search of something better than what they have. Relationships shift and change with shifts in identity. Kate is fixated on Susy, with whom she has corresponded until she meets Ava. Susy firmly denies any possibility of a relationship until, in the last scene, she declares to Kate, 'It's you. It's really you. It's you. It's always been you.' Tom, who has been desperate to regain the esteem of his lover Martin, runs off with Loretta; Martin and his brother Calvin gravitate towards each other; Lester, a stereotypical swaggering cowboy, a homophobic member of 'the Klan', finds himself inevitably attracted to the sado-masochistic Martin. In the final tableau they all end up in yet another combination, the most unlikely pairs.

This is not lesbian theatre, nor is it a lesbian play. There are scenes of lesbian love, but they are part of a much more complicated emotional whole. It is a play by a lesbian and therefore, one might say, is reflective of a lesbian point of view. I shall discuss what this might mean in Chapter 10.

Phyllis Nagy considers *The Strip* to be the culmination of her first four and a half years in the theatre, the end of a cycle. When I interviewed her in May 1995 she was writing a play about a family in France, commissioned by Hampstead Theatre Club, London. The perspective is a more global one. She will never have a British perspective but as she spends more time away from the USA, her perspective on what American culture is inevitably changes. It is perhaps significant that this next work is 'European', set in neither Britain nor the USA, and concerns people who are looking at the English from the point of view of a 'foreigner' since this is her vision of English culture, the vision of an 'outsider'. She was also planning to write another play which would be entirely removed from English or American popular culture. It may well be that this second angle would be more concerned with ideas, would be more philosophically based and have less to do with contemporary life as she sees it, or would like to see it.

SARAH DANIELS

Like Phyllis Nagy, Sarah Daniels also started her playwriting career at the Royal Court, London. She had been encouraged to send off the script by a call for scripts in *Time Out*. Her first one was rejected, but nicely, with wise words of advice from the reader, who was careful to point out what he really liked as well as the shortcomings. She wrote a second play, *Ripen Our Darkness*, which was accepted and produced by the Royal Court in 1981. Her reasons for writing were, in the first instance, an increasing love of, and familiarity with, the theatre and a need to put her life in order. In her introduction to *Daniels Plays: One*, Sarah Daniels says she did not set out to be a feminist playwright, but feminist arguments run strongly through her work. She writes:

> I didn't set out to further the course of feminism. However I am proud if some of my plays have added to its influence.[30]

Ripen Our Darkness is a condemnation of marriage and what it does to women. It could be described as a black comedy, since some of the situations verge on the grotesque and much of the dialogue is witty. The tragic effect of the suicide of one of the wives, Mary, is undermined by a scene of Mary in Paradise, with a woman deity and a Holy Hostess, who tell her that only women have eternal lives, because men have no souls. Indeed, the three husbands – David, Mary's husband, a pillar of the local church; Roger, the vicar; Alf, a drunken wife-beater – show no evidence of a soul. They are all egocentric, dominating and totally insensitive. Mary's son Paul shows every sign of shaping up in the same way, referring to his mother as 'You old bag'. A wife's role is to fulfil every need of her husband first and her family second, or not at all, if there is conflict with the husband's needs. Rene's husband Alf is as brutal towards his daughter, particularly his younger daughter, as he is towards his wife. Rene's fear and loyalty lead her to defend her husband, when her daughter suggests they should leave home:

RENE: Where could I possibly go at my age? I know your
         father's not exactly gracious ... downright hostile ... but
         it's not his fault. He's done his best by you he has.[31]

When she is completely alone, however, she fantasizes a letter she could write to an agony aunt:

> Dear Mary Grant, I have a husband who drinks all my
> money away. I have two jobs and try to give him enough
> so he doesn't feel the need to slap me and my daughter
> around, but I usually fail. I have to lie in piss-soaked
> sheets, as my husband wets the bed every night. My
> daughter's severely handicapped baby has just died and I
> just can't stop fuckin' talking. I have dreams of doing
> myself in.[32]

Rene's eldest daughter, Julie, and Mary's daughter, Anna, are a lesbian 'couple'. Although they have their differences of opinion, of attitude, of behaviour, their relationship is loving and supportive. Neither of the mothers understands why her daughter has chosen to live with a woman, in spite of the failure of their own relationships with men.

RENE: You know what I think of that young lady – that's the wrong word – that young hermaphrodite more like, well I hope you don't pick up no bad habits, that's all I can say. Take it from me Susan, women like that are never 'appy, how can they be?[33]

Mary is altogether more sophisticated in her approach:

MARY: Mind you, you always had to be different, didn't you? I don't know what else I could have expected. You always were odd. Everybody else marries a man, but not you. It looks as though I've got to resign myself to being the only mother in Acacia Avenue with three sons and four daughters-in-law.[34]

The most prejudiced view of lesbianism, straight from Havelock Ellis, is elaborated by the psychiatrist who comes to examine Mary. It is so extreme that Mary at once rejects it as total nonsense. I quote it at length as it is a concentration of common prejudices even in the medical profession:

MARSHALL:

Yes, these people can only rarely achieve any degree of satisfaction, unless one of the two partners has unusually well-defined physical attributes. For example, occasionally, a woman may have an unusually large clitoris, maybe two or even more inches in length.

(MARSHALL *holds up his finger and thumb to show the size.*)

Now then, if the woman concerned happens to be a lesbian and her partner spreads her legs as wide as she can, well, they may just be able to attain some degree of penetration. Of course, this type of woman is hardly the average and the normally endowed woman may turn to the dildo, which in reality is no more than a sponge, rubber or plastic penis.

MARY: But I ...

MARSHALL:

Please let me finish. You must understand that this forever will be the curse of the homosexual, no matter how their tastes are developed, or the success rate they may claim –

> basically they all end up involved in some parody of
> normal heterosexual intercourse.

MARY: Are you sure about this? They seemed happy to me.

MARSHALL:

> True happiness depends on a lasting relationship, an option
> usually denied to homosexuals. Relationships between
> women do tend to last longer than they do for men –
> possibly this stems from the male's obsession with anal
> activities – but they are still full of unhappiness. But male
> or female, their eventual problem is common to both
> sexes. They are all looking for satisfaction where there can
> be no lasting satisfaction. They are all looking for love in
> a world where there can be no love.

MARY: (*very softly*) I think he's talking shit.[35]

This is another example of an authoritative male trying to dominate
the woman, this time with so-called 'superior' knowledge. Mary is
being blamed for her daughter's lesbianism, for ruining her life.
Immediately afterwards, in a crude Freudian-type diagnosis, Marshall
declares that she wanted to cannibalize her son's penis. Unable to
contend with overwhelming male oppression, Mary puts her head in
the gas oven. This final act of defiance is construed by the men in her
life as an unfortunate accident. Mary's ghost, lurking unperceived
during a Monopoly game between David and Roger the vicar, after a
vain attempt to make a last comment from the grave, gives up. Men
are a lost cause, heterosexual marriages are a lost cause, only the
lesbian couple have a chance of surviving.

Between *Ripen Our Darkness* and her latest play to be produced in
1994, *The Madness of Esme and Shaz*, Sarah Daniels has had eight
other plays performed, at the Royal Court, London, at the Crucible
Theatre in Sheffield, at the Manchester Royal Exchange Theatre, the
Albany Empire in London, and *Neaptide* at the Royal National
Theatre in 1986. She has thus bypassed the fringe and been performed
in the most prestigious of subsidized theatres. None of her plays has,
however, been transferred to the West End. Her work is more accessible than that of the other playwrights I have discussed, since nine of
her plays have been published. She may well, therefore, be the subject
of a more detailed analysis. Her uncompromising feminism, which
seems to take the form of an attack not only on patriarchal society but
also on men in general, has inevitably raised the hostility of male
critics. *Masterpieces*, first performed at the Royal Exchange Theatre
in Manchester in 1983 and subsequently at the Royal Court in

London, condemned pornography not only as a source of male violence but also as leading to a violent backlash from women. One of the leading characters, a social worker, incensed by a pornographic film she has just seen, pushes a man who approaches her in a tube station. He falls backwards on to the line and is killed. The description of the film she gives to a sympathetic policewoman is, one would hope, shocking and revolting to both male and female spectators. However, in the ongoing debate about pornography and whether it leads to violence in real life, the anti-pornographic faction was beginning to lose ground. The play caused a storm of protest.

Although all Daniels's performed works are worth lengthy examination as far as their feminist content is concerned, I shall confine my subsequent discussion to those in which lesbian relationships are important, *Neaptide* and *Byrthrite*.

Neaptide was first performed in 1986 at the Cottesloe in the Royal National Theatre, London, one of the most prestigious venues in Britain. If we categorize it as a lesbian play, then it is the only one to have been performed there before or since. It is interesting that one of the National's major productions of 1993 was Lillian Hellman's *The Children's Hour* (1934), one of the earliest plays in which the possibility of lesbian desire was suggested, but dismissed as leading to a fulfilling way of life. Both *Neaptide* and *The Children's Hour* are set in girls' schools, but the messages they contain are totally different. The very rumour of lesbianism totally destroys the life of one of the women involved in the latter play, which was described by those involved in the production as still relevant today, whereas the lesbian teacher in *Neaptide* decided to 'come out' to all her colleagues whatever the consequences.

Lizbeth Goodman lists Sarah Daniels's *Neaptide* under 'care and control' plays and comments that Daniels identifies with women's issues rather than lesbian issues, the issue of motherhood being at the heart of the matter:

> Here again, Claire is presented as a representative of 'womanhood' and 'motherhood'. Her lesbianism is incidental to her other roles, but is the lens through which her situation is focused. Lesbianism is the example but prejudice against women is the real issue of this issue play.[36]

'Here again' refers to the way that Daniels discusses the play, underlining the broad feminist base rather than defending a lesbian lifestyle. However, the right to be a lesbian is well and truly defended by three generations of women – Claire herself, her headmistress, who is in her fifties, and a seventeen-year-old schoolgirl. It is Diane, the sixth-former caught kissing her friend and suspected of writing graffiti on the lavatory walls, who sets an example to the older women by refusing to deny her sexuality under threat of expulsion. The disturbance caused in the school by the appearance of deviant sexuality is as essential to the plot, perhaps even more essential than Claire's husband's efforts to obtain custody of their seven-year-old daughter. Since Claire is sharing a flat with an indisputably heterosexual friend and has no current lover, she could remain in the closet, pretend to the judge to be 'normal' and thus ensure a verdict in her favour. She could deny her sexuality, as Peter denied Christ. She refers to herself at one point as 'Judas'. Ultimately her conscience will not allow her to remain closeted while her colleagues in the staff-room make the usual prejudiced remarks. Her consciousness is raised by the boldness of Diane, her pupil, who manages to have an inflammatory article printed in the school magazine:

CLAIRE: (*Reads*) Women should never again have to apologise for loving each other. How natural is it to spend your life in service to a man? When I deny through silence I am only reinforcing my isolation. I am a lesbian and I am not alone.[37]

In a confrontation with Claire, now the new assistant headmistress, Diane goes even further.

DIANE: (*Angrily*) No. I'm not going to try to be anything, least of all forcing myself to act normal. I hate the word. Normal is a lie. You're always on about change, well I don't know about you but I intend to change things.

    ...

CLAIRE: Standing in the dole queue won't change much. The only way to change the system is from within.

DIANE: (*Flatly*) Cop out.

CLAIRE: You think so?

DIANE: Every day making another compromise until you become so demoralised you hate yourself. (*Long pause*) What about all those thousands of women who were burnt as witches? It was you who told us that it was because they were independent and men were frightened of them. (*Silence.* CLAIRE *still doesn't respond*) What are you thinking?

CLAIRE: Something stupid, like how nice to be seventeen when the only dirty word is compromise![38]

Compromise is something that Claire realizes she can no longer do. This is the moment to stand up and be counted. Failing to persuade Bea, the headmistress, who lives with a 'companion', to do the same, she tenders her resignation. On the one hand she loses her custody case and her job, on the other she gains unexpected support from colleagues and, most surprisingly, from her mother Joyce, who, after consultation with a lesbian solicitor, organizes Claire's escape with her child to stay with her sister in New York. Like Demeter with her daughter (a myth which is used throughout the play) Joyce binds her family together, liberating them from male domination. By coming out, Claire has won, although she was prepared to lose everything.

Byrthrite, first performed at the Royal Court in 1986, takes up the theme of 'all those thousands of women who were burnt as witches' (see Diane's remark in previous quotation). The prosecution of women as witches has been the subject of several feminist plays, for example, *Any Marks or Deviations* by Charlie Hughes-D'Aeth, *Witchcraze* by Bryony Lavery and *Vinegar Tom* by Caryl Churchill. In *Byrthrite* Sarah Daniels makes the point that the persecution was mainly to do with the appropriation of power by male doctors jealous of the 'wise women' who knew how to heal sickness, how to help other women give birth. Daniels writes in her preface:

> I wanted to write a play about the implications and dangers of reproductive technology for women. I thought that setting it in the seventeenth century – the time when the role of the healer was taken out of the hands of women and established in the (male) profession of doctor – would give a poignancy to the ideas expressed in the play.[39]

The play is indeed poignant, but the theme of the dangers of reproductive technology gets lost in the stories of the various women characters. Towards the end of the play we are reminded that the use of forceps will eventually lead to dreadful manipulation by twentieth-century science:

LADY H: (*Sings*)
        Three centuries ago, they started with hooks,
        But the medicine man will next control our looks –
        For they have moved on from bleeding out our life
        To creating the next generation of perfect wife.
DOCTOR: (*Sings*)
        Fertilised in a Petri dish as a result of egg donation.
        Transplanted by the doctor, father of the future, perfect
            nation,

Completed the laparoscopy, done with amniocentesis,
Will abort if results show a less than first-rate foetus.

Have mastered the techniques of in vitro fertilisation,
Surrogacy, ectogenesis and super ovulation,
Won't stop now, intrauterine surgery will enrich our lives,
And cloning will ensure that males outnumber wives.[40]

Songs are used in a Brechtian way throughout, to convey the significance of the action, to make a link between the seventeenth and twentieth centuries and finally to stop the audience getting involved in an empathetic way with the action of the characters. This is epic theatre, using history to make us think. The lesbian line in the play is very strong: all the women are bonded in a sisterhood of esoteric knowledge which leads to particular emotional involvement and in some cases falling in love. Men are their enemies, jealous of their power and knowledge, they are all represented by one 'Man' among the eleven women, this 'man' being a 'pricker' (a witch-finder), a doctor, a soldier, a priest. By comparison with the man, the women are bold, wise, positively heroic. Two of them cross-dress to fight in the Civil War, another becomes a Quaker preacher. The oldest and wisest of them all, Grace, survives torture. It is all very stirring, a call for complete solidarity against patriarchal oppression:

Rosie's Song

. . .

The freedom to pass as man is a curse –
No woman would choose that for her life –
And marriage to men is no better or worse
For bearing the name of a wife.
The only way through is to stand out and strong,
And not wear disguise in their fight,
But to be with the women where I belong.

. . .

For they take the skills and the powers that we share
With women who trust in our healing.
For they cut and thrust and no-one will spare
So no woman dare speak what she's feeling.
But I shall take power and we'll start a war
Against doctors and soldiers and men
Who challenge our right and seize at the core
Of our birthright, our freedom. Fight again![41]

Spoken by Rosie, who is in love with dashing Jane and ready to dally for a while with an aristocrat, Bridget, this is not only militant feminism, but also radical lesbianism!

BRYONY LAVERY

Bryony Lavery's work for Gay Sweatshop has been mentioned in Chapter 3. She started writing, when a student, three plays with more parts for men than for women. These were her pre-feminist days, when writing was perceived by her as something she had to do in her spare time. To earn a living she became a teacher, until the combination of the work of the Women's Movement and the growth of fringe theatre gave her the confidence to form a collective group, Les Oeufs Malades, which performed her plays in small, under-equipped venues up and down Britain. These years of touring taught her that she had to be able to talk as well as write.

> If you want to write the plays you want *and* have them produced and performed how you want, you also have to learn how to direct, how to raise money, deal with the Arts Council, talk people into putting your plays on in their theatre, talk to the press, talk to actors, talk to the audience afterwards and talk talk talk talk talk talk talk.[42]

Bryony Lavery still would not call herself a feminist and her women characters, brave and strong though they were, were losers. It was not until she worked with Monstrous Regiment and The Women's Theatre Group that feminism began to have a real meaning. With these groups, plays grew not from a script but from experience. A new theatrical phase began with *Female Trouble*, the result of three women and Bryony working together to create a funny show which would make a positive statement about women. The show ended with *Yesbut Park* inspired by improvisations on two-way conversations in which one person made a statement and the other answered with 'Yes, but ...', casting doubts and destroying the positive. A matching exercise was 'Yes, and ...', in which the second person encouraged the first and reinforced her ideas. *Yesbut Park* was a scene in which women lived in a park created by a god who said 'Live in my park but don't walk on the grass, but don't pick the flowers, but don't step out of line'.[43] They are saved by a Yesand Angel who tells them to say 'Yes/and' to everything.

This sketch brought Bryony to a realization of how many of her women characters had lived in Yesbut Park. From then onwards she was increasingly aware of the way that women's view of the world has been distorted, how many of their fears arise from the propaganda of male-dominated literature. In 1983 she wrote:

I am a lesbian feminist writer
or in other words
I am the writer of *More Female Trouble*
or in other words
I am passionately dedicated to the rediscovery of women's
    strength through
positive theatrical presentation
or in other words
I chose the theatre as a place in which I am best equipped to
    fight for the world
I want.[44]

It is clear that Bryony Lavery has made a considerable contribution to theatre, particularly women's theatre, as actress, director and, above all, writer. I have chosen to give a more detailed analysis of one particular play because it was very popular when it was taken on tour, and it has a specifically lesbian theme.

Her Aching Heart, performed by The Women's Theatre Group (for whom she had already written *The Wild Bunch* in 1979 and *Witchcraze* in 1985), is a lesbian comedy which used a nineteenth-century melodramatic form intercut with scenes from contemporary life. It is also a love story, the historical romance reflecting the progress of a blossoming twentieth-century friendship. It deals with the pain of falling in love, the irresistible nature of sexual attraction. Molly and Harriet have met each other at a conference, where they were instantly drawn to one another. Since neither wanted to fall in love, the resistance is strong. Harriet's song, 'Uninvited', begins:

> After too many cigarettes
> after too much gin
> When I think 'I'll go to bed'
> That's when you come in
> You creep into my mind
> and say 'Hello'
> Babe ... you weren't invited
> Please will you go?[45]

By a remarkable coincidence, both Molly and Harriet choose the same bedtime reading to distract them, *Her Aching Heart*, a story of passionate romance between Lady Harriet Helstone and a simple (though very well-educated) peasant girl on her estate, Molly

Penhallow. They are fatally drawn to each other, experiencing lesbian desire for the first time in their lives. Both have rejected male suitors; indeed Lady Harriet almost kills one of hers in a duel, but neither had imagined sexual attraction to women, because no one had ever told them that such things were possible. Their differences, based on both class attitude and personality, are so strong that they begin with violent antagonism. Unable to hate each other as they would like they muddle through a series of misunderstandings until they find themselves at last in bed together. Instinct tells them they must kiss. The ending is not happy, however. Lady Harriet, bungling almost everything she undertakes, flees to France, only to find herself caught up in the French Revolution. Rescued by the Scarlet Pimpernel,[46] she returns to England to find that Molly made a vow to become a nun if Harriet was returned to her. So they never got it right. The modern Harriet and Molly are wiser; they admit their love, whatever the cost, before it is too late. Together they sing the final song, 'In love again'. Fiction may of necessity have had to end in tragedy, in a censoriously heterosexual world. Lesbians in real life can admit their love and stand a chance of happy fulfilment.

Notes

1. Interview with Nina Rapi, July 1995.
2. Nina Rapi, *Ithaka*, pre-publication script, p. 51.
3. *Ibid.*, p. 38.
4. Interview with Nina Rapi, July 1995.
5. Nina Rapi, *Dream House*, unpublished script, p. 12.
6. Nina Rapi, *Dance of Guns*, unpublished script, p. 1.
7. *Ibid.*, p. 31.
8. *Ibid.*, p. 65.
9. Interview with Nina Rapi, July 1995.
10. Interview with Phyllis Nagy, May 1995.
11. *Ibid.*
12. Phyllis Nagy, *Weldon Rising*, in Annie Castledine (selector), *Plays by Women: Ten* (London: Methuen, 1994), p. 144.
13. *Ibid.*
14. *Ibid.*
15. *Ibid.*, p. 136.
16. *Ibid.*, p. 128.
17. *Ibid.*, p. 134.
18. *Ibid.*, p. 136.
19. *Ibid.*, p. 140.
20. Interview with Phyllis Nagy, May 1995.
21. Phyllis Nagy, *Butterfly Kiss* (London: Nick Hern Books, 1994), p. 16.
22. *Ibid.*, p. 9.
23. *Ibid.*, pp. 12–13.
24. *Ibid.*, pp. 42–3.

25. *Ibid.*, p. 42.
26. Phyllis Nagy, *The Strip* (London: Nick Hern Books, 1995), cover blurb.
27. *Ibid.*, pp. 11–12.
28. *Ibid.*, p. 43.
29. *Ibid.*, p. 77.
30. Sarah Daniels, Introduction, *Daniel Plays: One* (London: Methuen, 1991), p. xii.
31. *Ibid.*, p. 13.
32. *Ibid.*, p. 16.
33. *Ibid.*
34. *Ibid.*, p. 48.
35. *Ibid.*, pp. 58–9.
36. Lizbeth Goodman, *Contemporary Feminist Theatres: To Each Her Own* (London: Routledge, 1993).
37. Sarah Daniels, *Neaptide*, in *Daniels Plays One*, p. 287.
38. *Ibid.*, pp. 295–6.
39. *Ibid.*, p. xii.
40. *Ibid.*, pp. 404–5.
41. *Ibid.*, p. 392.
42. Bryony Lavery, 'Calling the shots', in Susan Todd (ed.), *Women and Theatre* (London: Faber & Faber, 1984), p. 27.
43. *Ibid.*, p. 29.
44. *Ibid.*, p. 31.
45. Bryony Lavery, *Her Aching Heart*, unpublished script, p. 1. The play has been published with *Two Marias* and *Wicked* (London: Methuen, 1991).
46. The Scarlet Pimpernel is a character in a series of novels by Baroness Orczy. An apparently effete English aristocrat, Sir Percy Blakeney disguises himself in order to snatch noblemen and women from the jaws of the guillotine.

Chapter 10
Messages and Audiences

All those who were involved in the production of Jill Posener's *Any Woman Can* were amazed and delighted by the fact that wherever they performed they had large numbers of lesbians in the audience. It was reassuring to actors and spectators alike to realize that they were part of a larger community than they had imagined. There was an assumption that coming to see a play about lesbian concerns, written by a lesbian, performed by lesbians, was to make a statement of solidarity, which, in some instances, was tantamount to 'coming out'. The actors came out to the audience, the audience came out to the actors. Needless to say the nature of the performance is particular under such circumstances, when the performers have the confidence that spectators will recognize references to their own personal experience, will hear the characters making statements on their behalf, statements which they may not yet have dared to make. The consciousness-raising sessions were largely a call to stand up for the right to practise a sexuality which society had denied as valid. Liberation could not be achieved by remaining in the dark.

But what of heterosexuals in the audience, men or women? The performances were not separatist. They often took place in venues which attracted largely heterosexual audiences – arts centres and university theatres. We have already noted that the opening speech of the play addresses the heterosexual other, being a defiant elaboration of the numbers of 'invisible' lesbians in British society. The approach is provocative and confrontational:

GINNY: Just think, at this precise moment there are lesbian nurses touching up lovely women in hospitals, quite legally ... / adjusting their dressings round their / injured thighs. Washing, rubbing, massaging ... oh, stop it.[1]

However, the challenge is immediately followed by a reasonable argument, that in fact the real 'perverts' are the men who verbally assault the lesbian, the men who make dirty phone calls with obscene proposals. This is a call for sympathy, a moment of identification with the 'straight' members of the public who would naturally condemn such sexual harassment. Thus after the initial aggression there is a realization that everyone, straight or gay alike, will be 'on the side' of the actors. The performance space is assumed to be a safe space. Of course when a company is on tour they will find some spaces safer than others; however, a venue which is prepared to accept an unequivocally lesbian play is clearly lesbian friendly and the administration will try to make sure, through the right sort of publicity, that no threatening elements will intrude.

The political purpose of *Any Woman Can* was straightforward – by an open declaration on the part of the author and performers of their sexuality to persuade other lesbians to do the same. There were no broad statements about the condition of women in general; there were no criticisms of marriage, no suggestions of change in social structure. This was theatre about what it is like to be a lesbian, making statements that had not previously been heard on the British stage. The whole thrust of the Gay Liberation movement at this time was towards coming out as an essential first step to social change, and coming out was the performance of a gay identity to as large an audience as possible. The minority thus gains strength in the face of the heterosexual majority, not by making converts but by drawing practising homosexuals into the open. By the end of *Any Woman Can*, Ginny is no longer isolated.

It is debatable whether a commercial West End theatre or even a large subsidized theatre is the sort of safe space needed for coming out. It is not a question of large audiences being more homophobic than audiences in fringe-type venues; they come to the theatre with expectations which have been nurtured by their previous experience. A large theatre must feel like a safe space for thousands of spectators, which means in the end that 'normal' social conventions are upheld. Commercial managements are not in the business of being provocative; their main concern is with 'bums on seats' (a widely used expression in professional theatre circles), and in order to pull in the crowds the public must be given what it wants. What it wants (what it will pay for) is to 'have a good time', to feel better leaving the theatre than going in. Hence the large proportion of musicals and comedies in the West End. Since the function of much alternative theatre appears to be to disturb rather than reassure, it is assumed that it is not what most people want to see. It is considered to have been proved that theatre which makes a profit (the sole aim of commercial theatre) is that which faithfully reflects conservative bourgeois values. Should there be any proof to the contrary, if an apparently provocative play were to do well in an Off West End theatre such as the Royal Court or Hampstead, then it might be transferred. Whether it would have the same meaning for West End audiences is doubtful. All spectators interpret a performance in the light of their own prejudices. Any message which is diametrically opposed to what one believes will be either not heard or completely misinterpreted. We have already seen that the Stone Butch character in Joelle Taylor's *Whorror Stories* was seen as a man by at least one man in the audience, although the author thought she had made it abundantly clear that this character was a lesbian. And this was at the Oval House. In the same venue, a heterosexual (male) friend of mine, a sophisticated theatregoer and literary critic, watched a performance of my play about the Ladies of Llangollen with a certain amount of discomfort. Having always found very supportive comments to make about any of my plays, he remarked to me afterwards, 'I really loved that scene between the gardener and the maid', a scene between a straight man and woman enjoying a picnic lunch. When heterosexual critics complained about feeling they were in a 'ghetto' at the Oval, they were complaining about the audiences as well as the plays. Had they seen the same play in a different, more mixed venue, they would have understood it differently because the other spectators would have responded differently. The recognition of the collusion which existed between the lesbian authors, actors and audiences led to a perception of difference and a feeling of being threatened by virtue of being excluded.

Let us take three plays concerned with coming out, Jill Posener's *Any Woman Can*, Jackie Kay's *Twice Over*, and Sarah Daniels' *Neaptide*. The first two are Gay Sweatshop productions, performed in fringe venues, the third a Royal National Theatre production. There are no male characters in the first two; in the third there are eight men and four male children. The first does not in fact address the relationship between men and women, the second addresses it indirectly in the way the women talk about their husbands and boyfriends, the third addresses it directly and indirectly. The heroine of the first is presented as an individual, operating outside the circle of the family, refusing to be identified as daughter, wife or mother; the main character in the second is still confined by the family but begins to see alternative ways of being. She is too young to have made choices about motherhood or heterosexuality. Claire in *Neaptide* has functioned and continues to function in a heterosexual world where husbands and children are the norm. In spite of her managing to escape the court's judgment by fleeing to another country, hetero-patriarchy is shown to be all-powerful, since she loses both her job and her right to live with her daughter in her own country. The first two demonstrate that coming out will not ruin one's life, the third indicates that it will. Speaking to a wide, mixed, mainly heterosexual audience, *Neaptide* is a plea for tolerance and sympathy. Lesbians are good mothers like Claire; if they are conscientious citizens then surely they should be able to do what 'normal' mothers would be allowed to do, that is have custody of their children? Note that Claire is not even a practising lesbian, she has no lover; she shares a flat with an exem-plary heterosexual friend, also an excellent mother, who has an equally exemplary male lover. There are no nasty examples of sexu-ally deviant behaviour. In 1986, when there was no official theatre censorship in Britain, the climate of public opinion created by the media militated against an unequivocal defence of deviance in a national theatre in receipt of large sums of the taxpayer's money. Claire talks about the lesbian relationships she had, but we are given no indication as to whether she will continue to have women lovers. There are no scenes with a woman to whom she is sexually attracted. In both *Any Woman Can* and *Twice Over* there are scenes between lovers. Are we to conclude that in the 'mainstream', love between women may be suggested but not shown? And if so, is this because the 'average' member of the audience would be offended?

When she commissioned plays for the Oval House, Kate Crutchley asked for sexually explicit scenes to be included – women kissing, touching each other's breasts. In that safest of safe environments, in which the gaze was mainly lesbian, erotic exchanges between two women reflect and perhaps arouse *legitimate* desire, in that the desire of the characters is identical to the desire of the spectator, and this desire is validated in performance, thus providing reassurance through identification. I am well aware that identification is a problematic word, associated with the kind of psychological realism which may be judged to be unpolitical, but identification is as unstable as identity, and as fragmented. When a lesbian sees two lesbians kissing on stage, *at that moment* she identifies herself *as* lesbian, through identifying *with* the actors. Plays such as Debby Klein's *Coming Soon* and Jill Flemming's *The Rug of Identity*, which are high camp, totally 'unreal-istic', still allow audiences to recognize a source of community with the action. The references, the cultural signs used are taken from lesbian culture, which has appropriated heterosexual forms – soap opera, farce, melodrama.

Jill Dolan writes about the difficulty of mixing theatre written for the 'ghetto' into the mainstream, basing her argument on the American experience:

> When lesbian subjectivity became part of the feminist theoretical discourse, discussions about its construction were located staunchly in the alternative performance tradition. The post modernist, camp, collectivist performances of Split Britches and the WOW Café became the space of debate on the radical implications of lesbian desire's disruption of conventional paradigms of spectatorship. The lesbian work at WOW is very specific about the audience it addresses – an ad hoc lesbian community culled mostly from its East Village New York neighbourhood. The lesbian subcultural context and mode of production often make these performances illegible to the heterosexual reader/spectator.
>
> . . .
>
> As lesbian work is brought out of its marginalized context and traded as currency in heterosexual and academic theatre venues, the question of the performance's readability becomes complicated.[2]

Jill Dolan wonders if the creation of lesbian performance for 'mixed' audiences will prompt a return to more conventional forms and their meanings. Certainly if we go back to the example of *Neaptide*, the narrative form is more conventional than that used by Daniels in most of her other plays, there is a stronger realist element although the story is not told in an entirely linear way. There are no monologues addressed directly to the audience, which would break the naturalistic illusion. Claire's mother has a long speech which, instead of being told to the public, is told to Claire, who is presumed to be listening elsewhere.

It would seem reasonable to conclude that theatre which is specifically created for lesbians cannot be played in venues which have a predominantly heterosexual audience, whose 'reading' would be so different from that of a lesbian audience that the sense of the play would entirely change. The will to interpret, to comprehend on the part of every spectator, will lead to an assimilation into the dominant culture.

> Lesbians disappear under the liberal humanist insistence that they are just like everyone else. Difference is effectively elided by readability.[3]

This assimilation is most likely to occur when the author makes concessions to realism in an effort to make her situations clear to the heterosexual spectator, who will then equate lesbian experience with straight experience and claim to have 'understood'.

So far we have used the terms 'lesbian' and 'heterosexual' as though they were mutually exclusive – if one is a lesbian one cannot be heterosexual and vice versa. We have also referred to audiences as homogeneous entities. However, in the 1990s gender is regarded as unstable, the 'queer' movement has put a question mark over separation, bisexuality is no longer totally rejected as politically unsound. The lesbian feminist will be concerned to preserve her 'difference' from heteropatriarchal society, but for other sorts of lesbians 'difference' is too complicated to be simply political. I have already demonstrated in Chapter 1 that the definition of 'lesbian' is problematic and we have subsequently seen that for this very reason performers such as Penny Casdagli hesitate now to identify with a label that they may happily have worn in the past. So perhaps the distinction between 'lesbian' and heterosexual audiences may after all be less important than we think, as spectators themselves become less sure of their gender-orientation. What we call heteropatriarchy could be changing, so the reception of lesbian and gay informed drama might be quite different from that of audiences in the 1970s.

The dream of every playwright is to mould a disparate bunch of people into a whole by leading them together on a theatrical journey: they will leave the theatre slightly changed, having all heard and received the author's message. Every performed playwright knows this is impossible. Another personal anecdote. Some years ago I wrote a play about Constance Markiewicz (1868–1927), one of the leaders of the 1916 Easter Rising in Dublin, called *Constance and Casi*. I chose to base it on the early part of her life, to show how she moved away from her aristocratic Protestant Anglo-Irish family through her period in London and Paris as an art student and her subsequent marriage to a bohemian Polish count, also an artist and writer. The painting and unconventional marriage were her first steps towards the rebellion which finally took her away from her husband into Irish nationalist politics. My aim was to tell the story of a courageous woman who was able to stand by her own ideals even when they brought her into direct confrontation with her family. After one performance an Indian friend of mine told me that she recognized the situation so well, because an Indian friend of hers had been in exactly the same position. I was delighted. The 'message' had got through. In another venue, a stranger clearly not of my political persuasion said, 'I enjoyed it so much. You've got it just right. It just shows that if a woman goes into politics she neglects her family and it leads to divorce.' It was true that the play could be read in precisely that way, something I had not even considered, believing naïvely that every

171

woman in the audience would be sympathetic to Constance. No two people whatever their gender 'read' a performance in the same way. It is possible to unite spectators in their *emotional* response – to make them cry, to shock them, frighten them (making everyone *laugh* at the same thing is somewhat more difficult!); it is in fact quite easy to contrive a situation in which there is not a dry eye in the house, but this is not the project of the politically aware dramatist, as it does not lead to social change.

Nevertheless, if we work on the assumption that an audience is characterized by a 'majority gaze', that there exists the phenomenon of the 'male gaze', the 'lesbian gaze', how should we perform as lesbians for these distinct audiences? I have suggested that if you present the same performance to the lesbian gaze and to the heterosexual gaze, the reaction will be different. Do we assume therefore that theatre which comes from the ghetto will have to be performed differently? Can and should a lesbian present herself in one way to the lesbian gaze, in another to the heterosexual gaze? Should this representation be based on the audience's expectations of what a lesbian might look like, move like, talk like? Nina Rapi found that straight actresses would contradict her assertions about the characters: 'She can't be a lesbian because ...'.[4] The heterosexual actress has an image of the lesbian based on popular prejudices; she will feel more comfortable performing the stereotype, which she imagines will be acceptable to her heterosexual audience. The heterosexual performer always imagines a heterosexual audience, whereas the lesbian performer has to imagine both a heterosexual and homosexual one. To take a precise example: Joelle Taylor's *Whorror Stories* is a play which has themes of interest to any socialized human being, so that there should be moments of recognition or identification for everyone. So far it has been performed only at the Oval House, with its particular audience. Should it be transferred to the West End (let us fantasize for a moment!), would the portrayal of the Stone Butch need to be changed in order for her to be properly identified as what the author intends her to be? If a man in the Oval House audience thought she was a man, would not the same mistake be made by men who had not had the benefit of seeing the spectrum of gender representation that Oval audiences are used to? Does this mean that Billy has to have more 'feminine' characteristics which prevent her from being identified as a male? It is doubtful whether there is any infallible way to portray Stone Butch to a 'straight' audience; what is likely to come across is a disturbing androgyny.

Leaving aside the question of audience complexity, lesbian performers, as opposed to heterosexual performers of lesbian roles, are constantly faced with the decision of how to play lesbian. A lesbian signals her position outside the male–female dichotomy by her body language, her dress, in fact her whole demeanour. External fashions change: an actress playing Ginny in *Any Woman Can* in 1996 is unlikely to dress in the same way as those who played her in 1974. The choice of costume is much wider, the reasons for choosing to present a particular appearance will be the same, i.e., to signal to the observer 'I am not a "woman", I do not want to attract men sexually, I do not wish to be defined in relation to men.' The signal will be the same whether one believes lesbians are 'essentially' different, are born, or whether gender is perceived as a political choice. The straight actress's way of conveying this message is often to be extremely 'masculine' or childlike. The lesbian actress resorts to such stereotypes only in parody and farce.

To take the case of a particular play: my *Supporting Roles*, first performed at the Oval House on 18 March 1988, was written around five lesbian and one heterosexual character (see Chapter 8). Three of the actresses were lesbian, three straight. The director, Kate Crutchley, who also played a part, was lesbian; therefore it was, according to Penny Casdagli's definition,[5] lesbian theatre (see Chapter 6). The dynamics were predominantly lesbian, which set up a particular sexual tension in the action, tension communicated to the predominantly lesbian audience. An extra frisson was added by the presence of Sarah McNair, one of the 'stars' of lesbian theatre, in the central role of Jo, an older woman with a younger lover. One of the 'straight' actresses playing Kate Crutchley's partner of fourteen years had already appeared with Gay Sweatshop in *Any Woman Can*, so she was able to fit into her role comfortably. The other 'straight' actress required to play a lesbian character had more problems, in that such a role was completely new for her. In addition she was playing the most 'dykey' part, Rick, a seventy-year-old, old-fashioned butch. Her portrayal was in the end very convincing. Although the play was a farce, there was a strong 'realist' base which required the characters be, to a greater or lesser degree, 'believable'. The appeal for recognition from the audience was strong, in spite of the fact that most of the characters, and indeed the actors, were older than the average spectator. The setting was London in the 1980s, the performance venue in London in 1986.

In 1994, I saw a production of *Supporting Roles* in a small theatre in Boston, performed by a gay and lesbian theatre company. The director, also the artistic director of the company, Triangle Theatre, was lesbian, but all the actresses were heterosexual. They were also young, in their twenties, apart from the actress playing Rick. This meant that three of them were playing much older characters, menopausal lesbians. In addition they were playing foreigners, since, to my surprise, they did not transpose the setting to Boston. The perfection of their English accents resulted in a clarity of diction which is rarely heard these days on the English stage, except in the performance of a play by Noel Coward. The seduction of an older dyke by a younger one was more overtly sexual, more heavily demonstrative, but lacking the real dynamic of the London production between two actresses who had, in fact, been lovers. The elderly butch was played as a charming bohemian eccentric. I sat among an American audience, an audience which looked to me predominantly heterosexual, since it was composed largely of male/female couples, wondering what they made of all this. I still do not know. The reviews were good, longer and fuller than they had been in Britain, so I suppose that is some indication that whatever messages came across were well received. When I asked the director and cast why they had not set the play in the USA, they replied, 'It's an English play. It's written in English'. And so it is, an obvious point which had escaped me when I was writing it. I was so excited by this revelation that I offered to write a piece set in Boston with English and American characters, in which the American dialogue could be improvised upon by the cast. The script as I wrote it (*Blue Line to Wonderland*) has had a rehearsed reading, followed by discussion, the full production being scheduled for 1996, so at the time of writing I do not know what adaptations will be made. My instructions were that the English dialogue would be my affair, which I would rewrite where necessary, whereas the American speeches were wide open to change.

The performance of English plays in what are considered to be other English-speaking countries is something to which I had given very little thought. English plays are performed in Australia, Canada, USA, New Zealand by natives of these countries and vice versa. Occasionally, transposition does take place – Kate Crutchley transposed Jane Chambers' *Late Snow*, set in New England, to Scotland – but generally it does not. This means that actors are required to perform the stranger, whose otherness is embodied in the very words they have to speak. An English actress playing an American is working on pure imitation and imagination rather than drawing on the depths of personal experience. The Tennessee Williams Deep South portrayed by an English company is an invented construct which no southern US citizen would recognize. There is a particular kind of unintentioned artificiality. The same kind of artificiality is involved in heterosexuals playing homosexuals. (Homosexuals are better able to play heterosexuals because they have usually been required to play that role throughout much of their real life.)

In the USA in the 1980s Sande Zeig and Monique Wittig offered classes in 'Dynamics of Language and Semiotics of Gesture' at New York University. They aimed to deconstruct gender through gesture, by learning and imitating the gesture system of the other sex-class. Students were encouraged to discover their 'impersonator', i.e. themselves as the opposite sex. The task of the lesbian actor was, Sande Zeig wrote, 'to change the form of the actors' movement and gestures' [6] Zeig had herself toured Monique Wittig's play *The Constant Journey*, playing a female Don Quixote, using gestures that were such a subtle blend of masculine and feminine that they were outside the binary gender system. It is the work of Wittig and Zeig which has mainly influenced the workshops of Joelle Taylor and Spin/Stir in their search for the performance of deconstructed gender through movement, a truly revolutionary performance mode which contests the masculine–feminine, master–slave relationship.

To move from form to content, the playwrights I have interviewed affirm that even when their work seems to be about subjects which are not specifically lesbian, their treatment of any theme will reflect their lesbian point of view. What *is* a lesbian point of view? It is surely the view from outside 'normal' social structure based on marriage and the traditional nuclear family, husband, wife and children, living together in economic interdependence. A writer who identifies as lesbian will not describe the nuclear family as the ideal social unit. I use the terms 'husband' and 'wife' rather than 'father' and 'mother' since the first two are entirely based in social practice rather than genetic relationships. A lesbian may choose to be a mother, may decide to have an identifiable father for her child, without becoming a 'wife'. In Sarah Daniels' plays wives on the whole suffer loss of individual freedom leading to identity crises. *Ripen Our Darkness* (see Chapter 9) offers the most extreme examples – battered, ignored, and driven to suicide. Husbands are brutal, insensitive, vindictive, totally ego-centric. The married woman finds herself torn between her obligations as wife and mother, with no norms for a role as independent person.

However, most lesbian theatre is less concerned with woman as wife than with woman as mother. The link between mother and daughter is a sharing of body and blood, of ancient instinctive female knowledge.

Unfortunately fear of the unconventional may weaken this link. In Nina Rapi's plays we see that in trying to 'do her best for her daughter' a mother may come close to ruining that daughter's life. The heterosexual mother's experience is what she would expect her daughter to reproduce – the experience of cooking for a husband, getting married and having children. No other sort of life is considered possible. The mother in Phyllis Nagy's *Butterfly Kiss* can only invent a wealthy husband and stereotypical children as the ideal reality for her daughter. In Nagy's *The Strip*, the mother lives in a Happy Family fantasy world, which she imagines is where her daughter would wish her to be. Both these mothers care deeply for their daughters, are bonded to them in an almost uncanny way, which makes them incapable of conceiving of 'daughters' except as an extension of self. Similarly in Joelle Taylor's *Whorror Stories*, Billy's spider mother forces her violently into femininity, raping her in order to make her a woman. Thus we see that the priority of the definition of mother as the one who gives birth to a child becomes quickly contaminated by the role of mother within the family, spontaneity blocked by convention.

In both Daniels's and Taylor's work the father is such a powerful force that the mother is unable to protect the daughter should he attack her. In Joelle Taylor's *Naming*, specifically inspired by father/daughter rape, we see that the mother becomes the enemy, siding with the father or stepfather. The wife colludes with the husband, abdicating the role of mother altogether. When Claire's daughter, Catherine, carves into her wrists with a knife and smears the blood across her lips, Claire refuses to see the blood as blood, calling it lipstick, and threatening to report Catherine to her stepfather for wearing make-up. The stepfather abuses Catherine, treating her as his property. All fathers are suspect, especially the friendly Father Xmas. They disguise themselves as protectors in order to trap their helpless prey the more easily. They are the most powerful, dangerous, violent figures in a girl's life. Male sexual desire knows no taboos and fatherhood gives the right of possession. Uncles too abuse the intimacy of the family circle. In Nagy's *Butterfly Kiss*, the father sets up the circumstances of his daughter's first sexual encounter with an older man; in Taylor's *Whorror Stories* a farmer force-feeds his anorexic child like a prize cow. Although not all fathers in the plays we have looked at are as evil as this, some being simply insensitive or intolerant, not a single one is kind and loving.

The relationship between siblings is dealt with less extensively. Brothers occasionally appear or are mentioned in passing, with a suggestion of sibling rivalry; sisters crop up from time to time, sometimes presenting a problem, as in Debby Klein's *Coming Soon*, sometimes displaying the kind of solidarity we call 'sisterly', as in several of Daniels's works. Generally speaking the lesbian finds freedom by escaping from the family to live alone or with another lesbian. Eleanor Butler and Sarah Ponsonby became role-models by defying parents, guardians, brothers and setting up home in a foreign country where they had to create a totally new identity (see Chapter 8). At the end of the eighteenth century, when the concept of the lesbian had not yet been imagined, the example of their friendship and their withdrawal from society in the lonely hills was an inspiration to many women and praised by many men. They were certainly not censured for having cut off from their roots in order to devote themselves to each other. In any case, Sarah was an orphan, taken in by a kindly aunt and a lascivious uncle, and Eleanor had spent many years away from her native Ireland in a French convent. They were already lonely outsiders who gave each other the feeling of kinship they had never had elsewhere. Like so many lesbians since, they had nothing except love and instinct to guide them. Their reading of Jean-Jacques Rousseau's exhortations to return to nature and Eleanor's experience of intense, perhaps sexual, friendships in the convent, partly supported and inspired them, but most of the time they had to make it up. Although a rather nasty little article about them in a national newspaper suggested that Eleanor was the 'masculine' one and Sarah the 'feminine', that they were in imitation of the husband–wife couple, it was clear to all who came into contact with them that this was a partnership of another order. In both *Ladies of the Vale* and *The Ladies – The Musical*, power and control move backwards and forwards between the younger and older woman according to each particular situation, sometimes one taking charge, sometimes the other.

It is in depicting emotional/sexual bonding between women that lesbians may be said to have a special authority. This is the insider's not the outsider's point of view. The first representation of the clearly lesbian couple (the word was never mentioned because of censorship) on the English stage was in Frank Marcus's *The Killing of Sister George* in the West End in 1965. This was a heterosexual male view of a relationship in which one partner is completely, cruelly dominant, the other slavishly subservient. Jill Dolan comments:

> June/George expresses her masculinity through vicious sado-masochistic power plays. The binary operative alongside good and evil in Marcus' play is that of masculine and feminine behaviour as inserted over female

sexuality. George, the butch, is described as cruel, evil, and irredeemable because her masculinity is a perversion of heterosexual manhood and of femininity. Alice is allied with dominant cultural values – she gets up before dawn to queue up for ballet tickets – and is described as appropriately feminine. Her sexuality is ambivalent – George casts aspersions on Alice's ability to faithfully refrain from liaisons with men. The possibility of her return to heterosexuality threatens George's hegemony. ... The play's subcultural references and its levels of gendered characterisation could be read as referring ironically to constructions of both gender and sexuality in a heterosexual culture, but the vicious portrait of the butch/lesbian makes such a revisionist reading difficult.[7]

Played by lesbian actresses to a lesbian audience, the performance of *Sister George* could go against the apparent reading of the heterosexual text. However, the lesbian text would then be the performance text, not the one written down by Marcus. In the written text there are no positive feelings between this depressing pair. Did they ever love each other? Did they ever feel even desire for each other? Were they capable of giving each other sexual pleasure? The text does not answer these questions; the performance could if the text were played as a ritualistic game that both enjoyed equally. In the film of the play, when George forces Alice to eat her cigar, Alice feigns enjoyment to thwart George's sadistic intention of giving her pain. Neither party is therefore satisfied. There is only one moment of real playfulness, when June and Alice dress up as Laurel and Hardy to go to a fancy-dress party in a gay club.

The lesbian lovers in all the plays we have considered obviously desire each other and are capable of giving each other physical satisfaction. They experience the tensions that go along with sexual attraction, which means that they can be possessive, jealous, demanding as well as considerate, tender and supportive. The roles they play with each other are neither fixed nor pre-ordained. Conflict in the end is less important that what is shared. I quote a bantering conversation from Daniels's *Ripen Our Darkness*.

ANNA: Hang on, is this the same person who had to be physically removed from the pub last night, screaming 'Off with their rocks'?

JULIE: So? So?

ANNA: So? Half my colleagues were there.

JULIE: Do you want to live a lie?

ANNA: That's not fair. They know I'm gay.

JULIE: Gay? You're the most humourless, miserable fucker this side of the Blackwall tunnel.

...

ANNA: I'm honoured to have witnessed such a conversion in your personality. In the days when I first met you, you were a feminist with a few lesbian tendencies. Then you became a lesbian with a few feminist tendencies, to a radical revolutionary terrorist feminist, to a lesbian fuckwit.

JULIE: Am I still allowed to come to the school dance?

ANNA: Only if you can manage to keep from screeching out your obscenities. And this time keep your lecherous thoughts to yourself.

JULIE: Bleedin' cheek, I ain't a man. Women don't feel lust.

A few seconds later she kisses Anna on the ear:

JULIE: ... Oh Anna, stop this bloody boring knitting.

ANNA: We've only just got up! Women don't feel lust, my arse.[9]

Some reviewers of *Supporting Roles* read the long-term relationship between Suzie and Lyn as entirely comparable to that of a heterosexual couple. They had lived together for sixteen years, shared a mortgage, socialized with other couples, almost disappearing into the heterosexual majority. Many lesbians and gays set up their lives in this way and straight, liberal, married couples treat them as nearly as they can like husband and wife. However, there are problems in this attitude which tend to be glossed over. Who is the 'husband' and who is the 'wife'? We have seen that this is not a question of the outward characteristics of 'masculinity' or 'femininity'. Lesbian couples are much more obviously composed of two separate individuals negotiating every situation on terms of equality. I have written many scenes between husbands and wives; they are not like the following scene, which might be perceived as a typical marital quarrel.

LYN: There's only one question. A simple one. Not difficult to answer.

SUZIE: You're incredibly stubborn.

LYN: What about you?

SUZIE: That's one of the things I've always found difficult about you, your pig-headedness.

LYN: (*Incredulously*) My pigheadedness! My God! The number of times I've given way to you. Where we're going to go on holiday, what we're going to buy for the house, even what we're going to eat.

SUZIE: That's because you don't care, you can't be bothered to think of any of those things. If it were left to you to decide, we'd never go away and we'd live off take-aways.

LYN: You've always taken these decisions quite happily. You'd
        be very unhappy if I started putting my oar in.
SUZIE: I don't mind taking the responsibility.
LYN: You like it. You actually like it. You're a born organiser.
SUZIE: Maybe I don't like it any more. Anyway, that's not what
        I'm talking about. That's got nothing to do with
        stubbornness. I'm talking about (*she searches for a long
        time*) a quality of mind.
LYN: What?
SUZIE: (*More complacently*) A quality of mind. Refusing to listen.
        Never giving way to other people's opinions. Blinkered,
        being blinkered.
LYN: What about you?
SUZIE: You see!
LYN: What?
SUZIE: Exactly what I mean. I say something, try to get through
        to you and all you do is turn it back on me. You won't
        listen. You never listen.[9]

In this scene Suzie appears to be dominant, the stronger of the two,
whereas throughout the rest of the play she has been insecure, disori-
entated, almost at breakdown point. Lyn has been not only bullying
and interfering, but also panic-stricken. They have to work out
together how to deal with the crises of confidence, the depression and
fear of the future that often accompanies the menopause. However
they deal with the moment of change their reactions will be different
from those of husband and wife. Suzie comes back to Lyn not for the
sake of maintaining the conventional couple, but because they both
still love each other:

SUZIE: (*Motioning to her bag*) I've come back. (*Pause*) Is it all right?
(LYN *stares at her.*)
SUZIE: Is it? Can I stay? Can you forgive me for putting you
        through all this?
(LYN *stares at her, then gets up, holds out her hands.* SUZIE *puts
down her bag, moves over to her. They hug each other tightly.*)
SUZIE: I'm sorry. I'm so sorry.
LYN: Hush. I expect it was partly my fault.
SUZIE: It wasn't, it was ...
LYN: Don't say anything now. We'll try to talk about it later.
        Not now. I'll try to listen. Oh Suzie, Suzie, just don't do
        it to me again!
(*They remain entwined and the lights remain up on them.*)[10]

Finally, the following quote from Phyllis Nagy's *Weldon Rising* illustrates the complexity of role play in a lesbian couple. Tilly is described as 'not quite 30', pretty, curious and romantic.[11] Jaye is the same age, very fit and 'thoroughly gorgeous'.[12] She is not at all girlish but not butch either.

JAYE: Hold still and let me bite your neck.

TILLY: It's too fucking hot for that. Do we have any more beer? I drink too much beer.

JAYE: You don't drink enough. You're coherent when you're drunk.

TILLY: It's 120 degrees and if I don't have another beer I'm gonna , , ouch, stop that. You're hurting me.

JAYE: When you're drunk you let me bite your neck,

TILLY: You know he's really very skinny. But he has a nice ass. WOULD YOU PLEASE STOP MAULING ME.

JAYE: Sorry. No more beer. We're dry.

TILLY: Liar. You're hoarding it. Under the floorboards.

JAYE: Tough. No sex, no booze.

TILLY: I can't believe you're doing this to me. It's blackmail.

JAYE: Hey. These are the rules. I bite your neck and you get a beer. I rip off your clothes and you get another beer.

TILLY: Don't be such a boy.

JAYE: Listen to yourself. Since when did you decide to be celibate?

TILLY: Since it's gotten to be so hot, I can't think straight. Jesus I need a drink. Please.

JAYE: Bulldyke.

TILLY: Flattery just won't work any more, honey.[13]

Notes

1. Jill Posener, *Any Woman Can*, in Jill Davis (ed.), *Lesbian Plays* (London: Methuen, 1987), p. 15.
2. Jill Dolan, '"Lesbian" subjectivity in realism: dragging at the margins of structure and ideology', in Sue-Ellen Case (ed.), *Performing Feminisms: Feminist Critical Theory and Theatre* (Baltimore: Johns Hopkins University Press, 1990), pp. 40–1.
3. *Ibid.*, p. 44.
4. Interview with Nina Rapi, July 1995.
5. Penny Casdagli, 'The whole nine yards', in Susan Raitt (ed.), *Volcanoes and Pearl Divers* (London: Onlywomen Press, 1995), p. 265.
6. Sande Zeig.
7. Dolan, '"Lesbian" subjectivity in realism', pp. 47–8.
8. Sarah Daniels, *Ripen Our Darkness*, in *Daniels Plays: One* (London: Methuen, 1991), pp. 19–20.

9. Sandra Freeman, *Supporting Roles*, in Jill Davis (ed.), *Lesbian Plays: Two* (London: Methuen, 1989), pp. 84–5.

10. *Ibid.*, p. 89.

11. Phyllis Nagy, *Weldon Rising*, in Annie Castledine (selector), *Plays by Women: Ten* (London: Methuen, 1994), p. 116.

12. *Ibid.*, p. 116.

13. *Ibid.*, pp. 117–18.

Conclusion

It may well have occurred to the reader by now that I have said little or nothing about an important source of lesbian entertainment, namely cabaret. This is partly because cabaret is more ephemeral than any of the performances I have described, there being an element of spontaneity, of improvisation each time an 'act' is performed in a different venue for a different audience. Each act is aimed by a specific performer in the way that scripted plays are not. If there *is* a script, it cannot be handed to anyone else. The only meaningful script is the performance script, the communication through body and voice to those who are actually present. Some performers talk more easily than others about what they do on stage, but an articulate analysis is no substitute for the experience of being there, particularly if the performance itself is wordless, or using words completely differently from the way they are used in rational discourse. Cabaret acts often involve singing and dancing or music and movement, which are impossible to convey in words.

Having said all that, it has been clear throughout the book that cabaret performance and the presentation of longer, more sustained pieces of theatre have been closely connected. Many plays that I have seen used song, music and movement, and many of the actresses have also been cabaret in such groups as the Sadista Sisters and Parker and Klein. Stella Duffy not only wrote a play for Gay Sweatshop and performed with Character Ladies but also plays and sings in various pubs and other venues. Siren were The Bright Girls, a popular band, as well as a theatre collective. It is often through cabaret at events such as Lesbian and Gay Pride in London, which attracts thousands of straight as well as gay people from all over Britain, that performance concerned with lesbian issues has the widest exposure. For these reasons I would like to describe briefly the organization of Alice's Cabaret, a whole lesbian evening of stand-up comics and music.

In 1989 Maria Esposito and Fleur Howard, who met while working at the Nuffield Theatre, Southampton, decided to form a women's cabaret group. Fleur gives the following reasons:

> The idea evolved from a joint concern to raise the standards of perform-
> ance art for specifically lesbian audiences, and to improve standards of
> working conditions for cabaret artists. This issue had been raised at an
> Equity A.G.M., and the debate highlighted the appalling situation faced by
> performers in pubs and clubs, regarding both health and safety at work,
> and the way in which artists were treated by bookers. In addition to raising
> standards of women's cabaret performance, we were keen to create a
> leisure environment in which gay women could relax, have a drink and see
> a show which was relevant to themselves and from which they were not
> excluded in any way. It seemed to us that gay audiences were being short-
> changed. We wanted to create an ambience in which women could enjoy
> good quality entertainment; fine musicianship, pertinent lyrics and comedy
> which was *for* them.[1]

Maria Esposito was already establishing herself as a stand-up comic, having appeared in several assorted venues. Both she and Fleur Howard felt that there was an area of entertainment, a step away from the bar culture, which was completely disorganized and associated with clubs and pubs who negotiated one-off appearances with different individuals. Fleur notes:

> As far as we were aware we were the first cabaret of this kind, that is the
> first specifically organised gay women's cabaret show performing regularly
> in the same space.... One of our rules was to carefully vet any act we
> employed. The only risks we took were during the 'open spot' for new
> performers, which sometimes took place, but this was publicised as such.
> Our other consideration was cost to the audience. We knew that by and
> large gay women were not wealthy, so we introduced a number of conces-
> sions as well as a reasonable ticket price.[2]

They found their acts in talent contests and in pubs like the King's Head and Apples and Snakes, both in Islington, London. Their ideal was to have a women's centre with a stage, an auditorium, a coffee bar and a bookshop. They gave their audiences as much consideration as their performers, encouraging participation, arranging a wide variety of acts for each bill. They began at the Duke of Wellington pub in Hackney, London, already an established meeting-place for gay men and women. They put on performances once a month on Sunday evenings in the women's room attached to the main bar, and from their first performance they were hugely successful.

We crammed people in until it became almost illegal. Women queued down the road and many were turned away. The format was a mix of entertainment and thus continued over the years in other venues. On our first bill was Julia Brustick doing Egyptian Raqs Sharqui dancing! Other artists included performance poets, mime artists, comedians, singer/songwriters, musicians playing jazz, blues and so on. Maria included fire-eating and tap-dancing in her stand-up routines. We organised competitions with prizes, and a nucleus of very supportive friends acted as Box Office and get-in and get-out crews, with myself co-producing, mixing sound and designing lighting. Initially the box office take was split between the artists and at the 'Duke' four lanterns created several different moods, with the aid of coloured filters! The centre-piece of our set was the Alice's Cabaret board, flown in most venues, with lettering in reflective two-dimensional paper. It was our trade mark.[3]

Their run at the 'Duke' came to an end after eighteen months when the room was turned into a women's bar. They looked in vain for a more permanent venue, their search being hampered by the fact that they both had to work at other things to earn their living. So they moved from venue to venue, the shows becoming bigger and ultimately mixed gay and lesbian. Alice's Cabaret worked in conjunction with the London Borough of Newham to put on *Out 'n Proud* in the old Town Hall in Stratford, London E15, shows aimed at providing lesbian and gay equality in the borough. These included well-known names such as Lily Savage, Labi Siffre and Julie Felix. The last of these was in 1993, when Fleur had to begin to devote her time seriously to the full-time degree course in English she had registered for. *Out 'n Proud* had been mainly due to her own organization as Maria was no longer able to continue with the venture.

In 1996 Fleur Howard is company manager for a West End show. She is also completing a part-time MA, which means that she has had to forget Alice's Cabaret since 1993. However, she is thinking of reviving it and looking once again for a permanent venue in a club, as well as aiming at theatres. She remarks ruefully:

> During the period during which Alice's has not been producing, I am not aware of any similar producing structure being formed. Women's cabaret is still sadly lacking in base structure and continuity of policy.[4]

She hopes to scout for new acts as well as contacting people she already knows and to 'infiltrate' small theatres and larger women's centre spaces. She has a considerable directory of performers, some of whom she has seen mature since the late 1980s, polishing their performances, attracting a wider and wider public, gaining greater confidence through experience which the more limited possibilities of acting in a play would not give them. They are then able to bring the fruits of this experience back into their roles in plays.

In May 1996 I went to a performance in the Zap Club, Brighton, by Club Bent, a collection of British and Australian performers in a show compered by Lois Weaver which had come from a Gay Festival in Manchester and was going on to London. The emphasis was on the naked, or nearly naked, body as a means of communicating sexuality. In the publicity leaflet one of the performers, Jeremy Robins, was described thus:

> acrobat, gymnast and dancer [who] combines circus skills with queer iconography to perform a ritual of bath time balance in 'Slippery when wet'.

Another, Marisa Carr, was billed as starring in 'her dazzling deviant new club show, "Betty Page is a Bisexual and has a Hairy Chest", a fleshy carnival of song and striptease'. And a third, Azaria Universe, gave a performance which claimed to be 'feral drag in all its glory, as Universe gives her all, lip-synching the deeply emotional lyrics of the Bonnie Tyler "classic" (Total Eclipse of the Heart)'. These were indeed physical theatre, more performance art than song and dance.

If the lack of funding makes it increasingly difficult to put on plays, then lesbian theatre may survive through cabaret style events. But it may well not be able to be separated out from gay entertainment. Is the future queer? I shall end with a quote from Lois Weaver:

'I think our theatrical styles have changed.... What we are getting from the visual arts programmes, the performance studies, what's coming out will be the theatre of the future. That's not to say that we are going to lose realism or naturalism, because of the movies and the TV and that we'll always have it. But even in the TV, even in some films we start to see a break with that realism and a break with that tradition, and I think that is going to be much more the shape of it. I think that in a sense what I see, particularly in queer theatre, is another move, we've had several of these, is another move back to vaudeville and to the variety show. Like with Club Bent, where you get performers who come in and do their two, three, five-minute pieces and they tour on the basis of that. I think we'll see a lot more of that and a lot more of these visual, cross-art kinds of collaborations in the theatre. As Sue-Ellen Case says, naturalism works against us.... For lots of us it's not just a queer aesthetic it's a performance aesthetic. I also think the desire for the live person on stage, to see the actual person on stage, we have a greater and greater hunger for that, as a consuming audience. TV's given us so much and film's given us so much, and the Internet's given us so much, that we are going to want to see live people talking to us, giving us something about who they are, something that's personal. I think a lot of the performance that you get is very personal, sometimes simply story telling, sometimes a personal opinion, and I think people are hungry for that, they want to see the real thing.'[5]

Notes

1. Notes prepared by Fleur Howard prior to an interview, May 1996.
2. *Ibid.*
3. *Ibid.*
4. *Ibid.*

Appendix
List of Plays Mentioned in the Text

Aid Thy Neighbour Michelene Wandor

Any Marks or Deviations Charlie Hughes-D'Aeth

Any Woman Can Jill Posener

Awake Phyllis Nagy

The Beggar's Opera John Gay

The Beggar's Opry Sue Frumin

Belle Reprieve Split Britches and Blootips

Bohemian Rhapsody Sue Frumin

Bubbly Siren

Butterfly Kiss Phyllis Nagy

Byrthrite Sarah Daniels

Byte Susan Hayes

The Captive Edouard Bourdet

Care and Control Michelene Wandor

The Changeling Thomas Middleton and William Rowley

Chiaroscuro Jackie Kay

Chic to Chic Siren

The Children's Hour Lillian Hellman

Cloud Nine Caryl Churchill

Coming Soon Debby Klein

The Constant Journey Monique Wittig

Crossing Over see *Julie*

Curfew Siren

Dance of Guns Nina Rapi

Dangerous Roses Nina Rapi

Death on Lesbos Penny Gulliver

Desire by Design Red Rag

Disappeared Phyllis Nagy

Double Vision Women's Theatre Group

Drag Act Claire Dowie

Dream House Nina Rapi

Dress Suits to Hire Holly Hughes

Echo Susan Hayes

Entering Queens Phyllis Nagy

Fanny Whittington Sue Frumin

Female Trouble Bryony Lavery

Fires of Bride Red Rag

For Ever Karen Parker and Debby Klein

For She's a Jolly Good Fellow Jill Flemming

From the Divine Siren

*F***ing Martin* Malcolm Sutherland

Girl Bar Phyllis Nagy

The Great Wendy Sue Frumin and The Red Bucket

The Green Ginger Smuggler Maro Green

Hamlet William Shakespeare

The Hand Stella Duffy with Cherry Smyth and Caroline Forbes

Her Aching Heart Bryony Lavery

Home, Sweet Home Sue Frumin

Hotel Destiny Siren

The Housetrample Sue Frumin

The Human Voice Jean Cocteau

I Like Me Like This Sharon Wassaner and Angela Stewart Park

The Infamous Life and Times of Nell Undermine Red Rag

In Your Face Jan Maloney and Gay Sweatshop

Ithaka Nina Rapi

Jack David Greenman

Jigsaws Jennifer Rogers

Jingle Ball Gay Sweatshop

John Adele Saleem with Hard Corps

Johnny Is Dead Nina Rapi

Julie Catherine Kilcoyne

Kennedy's Children Robert Patrick

The Killing of Sister George Frank Marcus

Kitchen Matters Bryony Lavery

Ladies of the Vale Sandra Freeman

The Ladies – The Musical Sandra Freeman. Music by Carol Sloman

Lady or the Tiger Michael Richmond and Jeremy Paul. Music by Nola Yorke.

Late Snow Jane Chambers

Les Autres [That Lot] Sarah McNair with Hard Corps

Les Les Siren

Look Back in Anger John Osborne

Lovers and Other Enemies Jill Flemming

Lust and Comfort Split Britches with Gay Sweatshop

The Madness of Esme and Shaz Sarah Daniels

Madonna in Slag City Hard Corps and Sadista Sisters

Mama's Gone A-Hunting Siren

Masterpieces Sarah Daniels

The Meeting Place, see *Chiaroscuro*

Memorial Gardens Maro Green and Caroline Griffin

More Maro Green and Caroline Griffin

Mortal Maro Green and Caroline Griffin

The Mousetrap Agatha Christie

Mr X Drew Griffiths

Naming Joelle Taylor

Neaptide Sarah Daniels

Now Wash Your Hands Please Siren

Oh! Calcutta! Kenneth Tynan

Oh, What a Lovely War! Joan Littlewood

Oleana David Mamet

Ooh Missus Red Rag

Ophelia Melissa Murray

Oresteia Aeschylus

Out 'n Proud Alice's Cabaret

Pack of Women Robin Archer

Pardon Mr Punch Maro Green

Patience and Sarah Joyce Halliday

Plaza Dolores Phyllis Nagy

Pulp Siren

Rabbit in a Trap Sue Frumin

Raising the Wreck Sue Frumin

Ripen Our Darkness Sarah Daniels

The Rug of Identity Jill Flemming

Running Out of Time, see *For She's a Jolly Good Fellow*

Sappho and Aphrodite Karen Malpede

The Scarlet Letter Phyllis Nagy

Serious Money Caryl Churchill

Seven Sins for Seven Sisters Red Rag

Sexual Orienteering Red Rag

Sharing Sandra Freeman

The Sisters Mysteries Penny Gulliver

Son of a Gun Helen Darmohy, Kate Phelps and Tash Fairbanks

Split Britches Peggy Shaw and Lois Weaver

Stockings and Shares Red Rag

A Streetcar Named Desire Tennessee Williams

The Strip Phyllis Nagy

Strumpets Red Rag

Stupid Cupid Phil Wilmot

Supporting Roles Sandra Freeman

Swamp Siren

The Threepenny Opera Bertolt Brecht

Trevor John Bowen

Trip's Cinch Phyllis Nagy

True Love Jennifer Rogers

Twice Over Jackie Kay

Two Marias Bryony Lavery

Vinegar Tom Caryl Churchill

Weldon Arising Phyllis Nagy

What the Hell Is She Doing Here? Gay Sweatshop

Whorror Stories Joelle Taylor

Wicked Bryony Lavery

The Wild Bunch Bryony Lavery

Witchcraze Bryony Lavery

Select Bibliography

The lesbian

Most of these books have extensive bibliographies which will indicate further reading.

Butler, Judith, *Gender Trouble, Feminism and the Subversion of Identity* (London: Routledge, 1990)

Faderman, Lillian, *Surpassing the Love of Men: Romantic Friendship and Love between Women from the Renaissance to the Present* (London: Women's Press, 1985)

Faderman, Lillian, *Odd Girls and Twilight Lovers: A History of Lesbian Life in Twentieth Century America* (New York: Columbia University Press, 1991)

Fuss, Diana, *Essentially Speaking* (London: Routledge, 1989)

Fuss, Diana (ed.), *Inside Out: Lesbian Theories, Gay Theories* (London: Routledge, 1991)

Jeffreys, Sheila, *The Lesbian Heresy: A Feminist Perspective on the Lesbian Sexual Revolution* (London: Women's Press, 1994)

Kitzinger, Sheila, *The Social Construction of Lesbianism* (London: Sage, 1987)

Lesbian History Group, *Not a Passing Phase: Reclaiming Lesbian History 1840–1985* (London: Women's Press, 1989)

National Lesbian and Gay Survey, *What a Lesbian Looks Like: Writings by Lesbians on Their Lives and Lifestyles* (London: Routledge, 1992)

Suzanne Neild and Rosalind Pearson, *Women Like Us* (London: Women's Press, 1992)

Wittig, Monique, *The Straight Mind and Other Essays* (Hemel Hempstead: Harvester Wheatsheaf, 1992)

Critical books on theatre

Aston, Elaine, *An Introduction to Feminism and Theatre* (London: Routledge, 1995)

Austin, Gayle, *Feminist Theories for Dramatic Criticism* (Ann Arbor, MI: University of Michigan Press, 1990)

Bentley, Eric (ed.), *The Theory of the Modern Stage* (Harmondsworth: Penguin, 1976)

Case, Sue-Ellen, *Feminism and Theatre* (London: Macmillan, 1988)

Case, Sue-Ellen (ed.), *Performing Feminisms: Feminist Critical Theory and Theatres* (Baltimore: Johns Hopkins University Press, 1990)

Craig, Sandy (ed.), *Dreams and Deconstructions: Alternative Theatre in Britain* (Ambergate, Derbyshire: Amber Lane Press, 1980)

Davies, Andrew, *Other Theatres: The Development of Alternative and Experimental Theatre in Britain* (London: Macmillan Education, 1987)

Goodman, Lizbeth, *Contemporary Feminist Theatres: To Each Her Own* (London: Routledge, 1993)

Griffiths, Trevor R. and Llewellyn-Jones, Margaret (eds), *British and Irish Women Dramatists since 1958. A Critical Handbook* (Buckingham: Open University Press, 1993)

Hart, Lynda and Phelan, Peggy (eds), *Acting Out: Feminist Performances* (Ann Arbor, MI: University of Michigan, 1993)

Holderness, Graham (ed.), *The Politics of Theatre and Drama* (London: Macmillan, 1992)

Itzin, Catherine, *Stages in the Revolution* (London: Eyre Methuen, 1980)

Keyssar Helene, *Feminist Theatre: An Introduction to the Plays of Contemporary British and American Women* (London: Macmillan, 1984)

McGrath, John, *A Good Night Out: Popular Theatre, Audience, Class and Form* (London: Eyre Methuen, 1981)

Willett, John (ed. and trans.), *Brecht on Theatre: The Development of an Aesthetic* (London: Methuen, 1982)

Published plays

Daniels, Sarah, *Ripen Our Darkness*, *The Devil's Gateway*, *Masterpieces*, *Neaptide*, *Byrthrite*, in *Daniels Plays: One* (London: Methuen, 1991)

Daniels, Sarah, *The Gut Girls*, *Beside Herself*, *Head-rot Holiday*, *The Madness of Esme and Shaz*, in *Daniels Plays: Two* (London: Methuen, 1994)

Flemming, Jill, *The Rug of Identity*, in Jill Davis (ed.), *Lesbian Plays* (London: Methuen, 1987)

Freeman, Sandra, *Supporting Roles*, in Jill Davis (ed.), *Lesbian Plays: Two* (London: Methuen, 1989)

Frumin, Sue, *The Housetrample,* in Jill Davis (ed.), *Lesbian Plays: Two* (London: Methuen, 1989)

Green, Maro and Griffin, Caroline, *More*, in Mary Remnant (ed.), *Plays by Women: Six* (London: Methuen, 1987)

Kay, Jackie, *Chiaroscuro*, in Jill Davis (ed.), *Lesbian Plays* (London: Methuen, 1987)

Kay, Jackie, *Twice Over*, in Philip Osment (ed.), *Gay Sweatshop: Four Plays and a Company* (London: Methuen, 1989)

Kilcoyne, Catherine, *Julie*, in Jill Davis (ed.), *Lesbian Plays: Two* (London: Methuen, 1989)

Klein, Debby, *Coming Soon*, in Jill Davis (ed.), *Lesbian Plays: Two* (London: Methuen, 1989)

Lavery, Bryony, *Her Aching Heart* with *Two Marias* and *Wicked* (London: Methuen, 1991)

Nagy, Phyllis, *Weldon Rising*, in Annie Castledine (selector), *Plays by Women: Ten* (London: Methuen, 1994)

Nagy, Phyllis, *Butterfly Kiss* (London: Nick Hern Books, 1994)

Nagy, Phyllis, *The Strip* (London: Nick Hern Books, 1995)

Posener, Jill, *Any Woman Can*, in Jill Davis (ed.), *Lesbian Plays* (London: Methuen, 1989)

Rapi, Nina, *Ithaka*, in Cheryl Robson (ed.), *Female Voices, Fighting Lives: Seven Plays by Women* (Aurora Metro, 1991)

Split Britches, *Lust and Comfort*, in Sue-Ellen Case (ed.), *Lesbian Practice/Feminist Performance* (London: Routledge, 1996)

Wandor, Michelene, *Care and Control*, in Michelene Wandor (ed.), *Strike While the Iron Is Hot* (London: Journeyman Press, 1980)

Women's Theatre Group, *Double Vision*, in Jill Davis (ed.), *Lesbian Plays* (London: Methuen, 1989)

Unpublished plays consulted

Duffy, Stella (with Cherry Smyth and Caroline Forbes), *The Hand*

Freeman, Sandra, *Ladies of the Vale*; *The Ladies – The Musical*

Frumin, Sue, *Bohemian Rhapsody*; *Rabbit in a Trap*; *Home, Sweet Home*; *Raising the Wreck*; *Fanny Whittington*; *The Beggar's Opry*

Hayes, Susan, *Echo*

Hughes-D'Aeth, Charlie, *Any Marks or Deviations*

Lavery, Bryony, *Kitchen Matters*

Red Rag, *Fires of Bride*

Rapi, Nina, *Dream House*; *Dance of Guns*

Siren, *From the Divine*; *Now Wash Your Hands Please*; *Pulp*

Taylor, Joelle, *Naming*; *Whorror Stories*

Articles

Casdagli, Penny, 'The whole nine yards', in Susan Raitt (ed.), *Volcanoes and Pearl Divers* (London: Onlywomen Press, 1995)

Freeman, Sandra, 'Fluid lines', in Susan Raitt (ed.), *Volcanoes and Pearl Divers* (London: Onlywomen Press, 1995)

Lavery, Bryony, 'Calling the shots', in Susan Todd (ed.), *Women and Theatre* (London: Faber & Faber, 1984)

Mohin, Lilian, Interview with members of Coventry Lesbian Theatre Group, *Gossip 4* (London: Daily Women Press, 1987)

Rapi, Nina, 'Lesbian theatre', *Rouge 1990–1991*

Rimsk, Tara, 'Moving away from self-censorship', *GLINT*, vol. 2, no. 1, winter 1994

Taped interviews

Jane Boston: February 1995

Penny Casdagli: May 1995

Kate Crutchley: October 1994

Sue Frumin: February 1996

Fleur Howard: May 1996

Charlie Hughes-D'Aeth: July 1995

Sarah McNair: December 1994

Phyllis Nagy: May 1995

Julie Parker: July 1995

Nina Rapi: July 1995

Red Rag (Lois Charlton, Jackie Clune, Winnie Elliott): November 1994

Joelle Taylor: July 1995

Lois Weaver: May 1996

Index